INTRODUCTION

Beyond the Flames by Darlene Mindrup
For Amy Lattimer, growing up with an abusive father has been a way of life, so when four people enter her world with a message of love and acceptance, she struggles to understand a Father who is so completely unlike her own. Having been told all her life that no man would want her, she is skeptical when a young and handsome policeman begins to show her marked attention. Is Evan's interest really in her or the mysterious arson fires that seem to involve her family?

Web of Deceit by Carol Cox
Jennie Montgomery's elation over her job at the *Golden Gate Gazette* dissolves when she finds herself relegated to writing household hints instead of hard-hitting news stories. When an emergency forces her editor to send Jennie to cover a funeral, an altercation at the cemetery piques Jennie's curiosity and sends her on an investigation that has her butting heads with veteran reporter Nick Edwards and scrambling to make sure the next funeral isn't her own.

Misprint by Kathleen Y'Barbo
Bookkeeper Helen Morgan is horrified when her inept attempt at helping her friend Penney with typesetting results in a misprint that causes an innocent man to be pursued by criminals. Has the mistake that caused mayoral candidate Henry Hill's name to be linked in error with a murder investigation also cost Helen and Henry a chance at love?

Missing Pages by DiAnn Mills
When Russell Madison assigned Penney Brice the task of writing obituaries, she was determined to do her best. Russell has a problem, though. He's thoroughly smitten with Penney, and the thought of losing his heart angers and frightens him. What would a beautiful and spirited young woman ever see in a silver-haired man who declares his preference of a good cigar to a woman's company? Russell is safe with his secret until he senses potential danger for Penney in a whirlwind of romance and intrigue.

GOLDEN GATE GAZETTE

Love and Suspense Make Headlines in Historic San Francisco

CAROL COX

DIANN MILLS

DARLENE MINDRUP

KATHLEEN Y'BARBO

BARBOUR
PUBLISHING

© 2005 *Beyond the Flames* by Darlene Mindrup
© 2005 *Web of Deceit* by Carol Cox
© 2005 *Misprint* by Kathleen Y'Barbo
© 2005 *Missing Pages* by DiAnn Mills

ISBN 1-59310-274-7

Cover image © PhotoDisc

Illustrations by Mari Goering

All scripture quotations are taken from the King James Version of the Bible.

Published by Barbour Publishing, Inc., P.O. Box 719, Uhrichsville, Ohio 44683, www.barbourbooks.com

Our mission is to publish and distribute inspirational products offering exceptional value and biblical encouragement to the masses.

 Member of the
Evangelical Christian
Publishers Association

Printed in the United States of America.
5 4 3 2 1

GOLDEN GATE GAZETTE

Beyond the Flames

by Darlene Mindrup

Dedication

To Matthew Wouters,
Grandma's special angel.
I love you.

Chapter 1

San Francisco, October 1859

The blazing fire lit up the midnight sky as San Francisco's fire department and a hastily improvised bucket brigade worked furiously to keep the savage flames from reaching the surrounding buildings. Often portions of this teeming city would be set on fire, sometimes by recklessness, sometimes by arson. Whatever the reason, entire sections of the city burned to the ground before the fire department could get the inferno under control. Even with thousands of tons of water in the nearby ocean, it was not enough, for there was no way to get that water to the burning buildings.

The horses pulling the fire wagons shied as portions of the timber structure quickly caught fire and collapsed in upon itself. The firemen using the hand pumpers were fighting exhaustion, but they kept pumping wildly.

Amy Lattimer stood staring at the shimmering inferno, her notebook hanging by her side from lifeless fingers. How many years had it been since she had witnessed such a spectacle? Nine years? Ten? She shivered at the long-suppressed terrifying memories trying to push forward through the forced barrier of her mind. Only by sheer willpower was she able to send those suddenly awakened recollections back to the dark abyss from whence they had stirred.

Though the October temperatures were well beyond freezing, the heat from the fire warmed the air around her considerably. Everywhere, men from San Francisco's volunteer fire department rushed around trying to get the blaze under control before it could do like so many times before and raze half the city.

A timber from the frame structure crashed to the ground, and several people in the crowd screamed, quickly moving away from the conflagration. Policemen and firemen both were trying to hold back members of the crowd who were trying to surge forward for a better look. Amy stood immobile, silent and morose, unable to take her eyes from the bright orange and yellow flames. She coughed as the smoke thickened around her.

"Miss?"

She jerked when a warm hand touched her own chilled arm. Dully, she lifted her gaze to confront a pair of worried brown eyes in a handsome though soot-streaked face. Although the man released her arm at once, his mesmerizing look held her firmly in place.

"Ma'am, you need to move away from the fire."

The scathing glance that raked over her told her more clearly than words that he believed her to be one of the gawking spectators hovering on the edges of the fire line. The badge on his chest added to the authority of his deep voice.

She blinked up at him for several seconds, trying to focus on what he was saying. Shaking her head slightly to clear her thoughts, she gave him a tight half smile. "It's not what you think, Officer. I'm here covering this story for the *Golden Gate Gazette*."

She had known from the beginning that it was a bad idea for Mr. Madison, the editor, to send her out on this assignment. Her normal duties were as society columnist with the paper, covering various fetes and functions around San Francisco. Her impulsive offer to cover the fire was foolish. She just didn't have it in her to be a reporter of this caliber. But with the newspaper strike practically crippling the newspaper industry in the city, Russell Madison had had to depend on those who were willing to cross angry picket lines. There hadn't been many.

The man's eyes darkened, his face seemingly etched in stone. Amy noted with fascination the tick working in his cheek and realized that he was exceedingly angry. The way he studied her made her feel as though she were some vile insect that had just crawled out from under a rock. She pushed suddenly nervous hands down the length of her blue wool hoopskirt wishing that she were anywhere but here.

"I see," he responded, the two little words somehow imbued with a wealth of meaning. He noted the paper still clutched in her hand before his gaze came back to challenge hers.

He reached out to grip her arm in a gentle but uncompromising hold and pulled her farther from the burning building. "You still need to move," he told her, his voice hard. "You're much too close."

Amy noticed movement off to her side and saw three

disheveled women moving through the crowd toward them. Their looks barely skimmed over Amy before they surrounded the young officer.

One woman placed her hand on the man's sleeve. Huge, gold-brown eyes stared out from a white face, the paleness intensifying the freckles sprinkled across her nose. Her dark, coffee-colored hair was falling from its bun, and she brushed it away from her face impatiently.

"What are we going to do, Evan?" she asked of the man. "Everything we owned was in that apartment house."

Evan's face softened as he stared down at the petite brunette. He brushed a hand lightly across her cheek, pushing the straggling hair behind her ear. Evan wrapped his arms about the young woman, tugging her close. In the next instant he reached out with both arms and gathered the other girls close in a group embrace.

"It's okay, Penney," she heard him whisper. "There wasn't anything in that apartment that can't be replaced, unlike the three of you. God was good enough to spare all of you; I have no doubt He will continue to take care of you."

All three women smiled up at him, and one by one, he wiped the tears from their grimy faces.

"The most important thing is to find you girls a place to stay for the night."

The smallest of the three women lifted tear-drenched eyes to stare grimly at the crumbling building. Showers of sparks shot high into the cold night air, the ash raining down around them like tiny snowflakes. She shuddered, throwing her blond hair over her shoulders. "Even our purses were in there," she told Evan. "We haven't any money for a hotel."

Evan looked slightly discomfited, but he shrugged good-naturedly, trying to look more composed than Amy suspected he actually felt. She knew she was eavesdropping, but for some reason she couldn't help herself. The little group held an inexorable fascination for her.

"That's okay, Jennie," Evan told the girl. "I think I have enough."

A loud voice called to Evan from the other side of the thickening crowd. Evan nodded his head at the caller before squeezing Penney's hand.

"Wait here," he said. "I have to see what O'Hannon wants."

Penney touched his face with gentle fingers, smiling wryly. "You go ahead, big brother. You have a job to do. We'll be fine."

The other two nodded their heads in agreement. Evan hesitated but, after gently patting Penney's cheek, he hurried off. All four women watched him as he moved away with obvious reluctance. Amy decided it was time to make her presence known.

"Excuse me," she called softly.

The one called Jennie stared at her curiously. "Yes?"

Amy felt the color warm her face more thoroughly than the fire had just moments earlier. She moved closer to the huddling group. "I couldn't help overhearing. This was your apartment house?"

They all nodded, their looks ranging from suspicious to openly friendly on the part of Evan's sister. She held out her hand. "My name is Penney Brice. I saw you talking to my brother. Do you two know each other?"

Amy grew even more embarrassed, though she had to admit to a sense of relief at knowing the young woman standing before her was the officer's sister and not his wife. Why she should feel that way when she barely knew the two was a mystery she would try to solve at some other time. "Actually, no. He was just warning me to get away from the fire."

The third girl, who had yet to speak, lifted a dark supercilious brow. "You like watching fires in the middle of the night and in the freezing cold?"

"Helen!" Penney rebuked quietly.

Irritated at Helen's obvious reference, Amy still couldn't blame the young woman. It must seem odd to see a woman alone on the streets of San Francisco, especially in the middle of the night. Not far away was the notorious Sydney Town, and many women had been known to disappear from the streets in that area without so much as a trace. If her father ever found out, he would probably lock her in her room and throw away the key.

Suddenly realizing Penney was patiently continuing to offer her hand in greeting, Amy hurriedly gripped it. "My name is Amy Lattimer. I work for the *Golden Gate Gazette*."

"A reporter?"

Amy smiled at Penney's enthusiasm. "Not really. I'm normally the society columnist."

The one called Jennie frowned and stepped forward. "How come you're here then?"

Amy stared into the woman's china blue eyes and read the suspicion lurking there. She wondered what had happened in

14

the girl's life to make her so suspicious of others.

"There's a newspaper strike," she answered quietly. "Everyone else in the office was busy, so my editor sent me."

Amy noticed Penney shivering against the biting cold. "What I wanted to say was that I know of a place where you can stay the night. It's not far from here, and I know the proprietor. I'm sure he'll be glad to take you in."

Jennie looked at her in relief. Before she could say anything, Evan joined them once again. His narrowed gaze focused on Amy then on the notebook still clutched in her hand.

Penney took her brother's arm. "Evan, this is Amy. She knows of a place where we can stay the night."

"Really?" he asked, the softness of his voice belied by the hardness of his eyes. "And where might that be?"

Amy thought that in those few short seconds Evan's looming presence grew even larger. His vastness seemed to increase right before her nervous eyes, his look intimidating in the extreme. Obviously he took his big-brother role very seriously. She had to swallow twice before she could answer him. She pointed down the street without taking her eyes from his.

"The. . .the Hamilton. It's a small hotel, not very fancy but clean and respectable."

Penney looked at Evan. "It sounds perfect, Evan. After all, beggars can't be choosers. If the Lord was kind enough to send us help just when we needed it, then far be it from me to turn Him down."

Evan's grim visage relaxed. "I know the Hamilton. It *is* a nice hotel."

Amy withstood his intense scrutiny with an outward composure she was far from feeling. What did the man think she was going to do anyway? Shanghai his sisters?

Those dark brown eyes were causing funny little butterflies to flitter around inside her stomach, and she wasn't certain if the feeling being generated was fear—or something else entirely. She had never been affected by a man this way, and it was unsettling to say the least. He finally turned his gaze and focused once again on his sister.

"The fire is pretty much under control. O'Hannon says that I can leave now and take care of getting you girls settled."

His look went once more to Amy. "Since you obviously have work to do here, I'll see my sister and her friends to the Hamilton."

Amy met his gaze unflinchingly. "Actually, I was finished. I'll be glad to go with you and introduce the ladies to Mr. Jenson, the proprietor. Sometimes he can be rather particular about whom he allows to stay in the hotel."

One dark eyebrow flew upward. "You know him that well then?"

For a moment Amy was at a loss for words. She wondered how to explain without giving away too much information about herself. She smiled slightly.

"I've lived in this city most of my life, Mr. Brice. I happen to know a lot of people."

She could tell that her explanation hadn't entirely satisfied him. The suspicion seemed to intensify in his dark eyes.

Penney tugged on his arm. "Come on, Evan. We can't stand around here all night, or we're going to freeze to death."

Finally taking his sister by the arm and giving a slight nod to Amy, he told her, "Lead the way then, Miss Lattimer."

Amy led the way down the deserted street, thankful for the oil lights along the way that at least gave some vestige of light. When they reached the hotel, she preceded the others inside. If not for her presence, she knew Mr. Jenson would take one look at the ragtag group and tell them there was nothing available. Instead, his eyes met Amy's, his eyebrows lifted in question.

"Mr. Jenson," Amy told him, "these are friends of mine. Their apartment house just burned in a fire, and they need somewhere to stay."

Mr. Jenson's face settled into a look of congeniality. "I see." He smiled at the group. "I wondered what all the commotion was outside earlier. Of course we can put you up. The Hamilton is always willing to lend a helping hand. How many rooms will you be needing?"

Evan stepped forward. "Two will do, thank you."

The proprietor eyed him shrewdly before glancing Amy's way. She nodded imperceptibly.

"Two it is," Mr. Jenson replied, reaching behind him for the keys.

Evan laid some money on the counter, but the proprietor motioned him away. "We always settle up at the end of the stay." He rang the bell on the counter, and a young boy hurried up.

"Show these ladies and the gentleman to their rooms," Mr. Jenson told him, handing the boy the keys.

Amy noticed that Evan didn't bother to deny that he would be taking one of the rooms. She wondered again at his relationship with this small group.

Before they reached the stairs, Amy pulled Penney to a stop. "If you come by the *Golden Gate Gazette* in the morning, I think I might be able to help you find a job."

Evan's resounding no startled them both.

Chapter 2

Evan listened to his sister's tirade for a full five minutes before he finally stepped forward and placed a hand over her mouth.

"All right, I admit I was a little testy."

"A little!" His sister's eyes, a replica of his own, flashed fire at him. Before she could start in on her harangue again, he held up a hand.

"If you'll just calm down, I'll go and find the woman and apologize."

That seemed to appease her somewhat. "I'd appreciate that. She was only trying to help. What's gotten into you, anyway? I've never seen you treat anyone that way and especially not a woman."

How could he answer that one? From the moment he had laid eyes on the woman, something seemed to have jumped into life inside of him. Never having experienced it before, he found it rather disquieting, if not downright alarming. Something about the woman set warning bells ringing in his mind.

"I said I was sorry, all right? Now let me get out of here and find the woman before she gets too far away."

He kissed his sister's cheek, smiling into her pouting face. "I'll explain later."

He hurried out of the building. Taking the time to listen to his sister's diatribe had given the woman a head start, and he would have to move quickly to catch up with her.

He stood on the deserted street, looking all around, but Amy had seemingly disappeared. Lambasting himself for his own foolishness, he picked a direction, sending up a swift prayer that it would be the right one.

The answer to the prayer came quickly, for Evan hadn't gone far before he came upon Amy surrounded by several drunken miners. He didn't think he had ever seen a living person with a face so white. She was huddled amid the group, her terror-filled eyes going from one man to the other. Although it was possible that they were harmless enough, merely wanting some female companionship after such a long time away from such society, Evan wasn't about to take chances. He strode forward with determination.

The miners noticed his police uniform and began to back away, but Amy looked to him with relief mingled, he felt certain, with guilt. He had told the woman to wait for him and he would see her home. By now he was certain she was feeling just a little foolish for her show of independence.

"I think you fellas need to move along now, don't you?" he asked, taking Amy by the arm and glaring from one man to another.

"Aw, we was just having some fun," one man insisted. "Why else would a lady be out on the streets at night?"

The very question he was asking himself.

"The lady was going home," Amy told them, her voice cold enough to match the surrounding temperature. With Evan's presence, some of her bravado seemed to be returning, though the color had yet to return to her face.

Mumbling their complaints, the three men reluctantly departed, throwing longing glances over their shoulders as they went.

Evan turned to Amy, intent on rebuking her for her foolishness, but he never got the chance. If her small, shivering form hadn't stopped him, the tears trickling down her cheeks were enough to dry up the words before Evan had a chance to utter them.

"Come along," he told her gruffly. "I'll see you home now." He gave her a slight smile. "If you'll be good enough to show me the way."

He thought she was about to refuse his offer, but after several seconds' pause, she finally heaved a sigh and turned to him. "I live on Rincon Hill."

He couldn't have been more surprised if she had told him she was from Sydney Town. Frankly, that was more the type of address he had been expecting to hear. Instead, here she was telling him that she was from San Francisco's upper-crust society. At least that's what he *thought* she was saying.

"You mean you work there?"

She gave him a look that would have shriveled a worm. "No, my name is Amy Lattimer, and my father is Cyril Lattimer."

Evan stared at her in openmouthed amazement. He wasn't quite sure what to say. The woman was the daughter of one of the richest, most notorious men in San Francisco. Noticing the look on his face, she turned and began walking away.

He quickly caught up with her. "Does your father know that you are out roaming the streets at night?" He couldn't quite suppress the anger in his voice.

She continued walking without even glancing his way. Smoke from the fire many blocks away hung heavy in the air even at such distance, giving an eerie, ghostly feel to the atmosphere.

"My father is out of town on business. He won't be back for some time."

That certainly explained a lot. He remembered the stories he had heard about Lattimer and his tight control over his little empire. Evan found it hard to believe that that control would be any less over his own daughter.

He took her by the arm and pulled her to a stop. "Well, you certainly can't walk all the way to Rincon Hill tonight. Let's go to the Plaza, and I'll rent a hack to take us there."

She peeled his fingers from her arm. "Mr. Brice, I'm perfectly capable of getting myself home on my own steam."

Her slang reference to the steamboats that went from San Francisco to Sacramento brought a slight smile to his face. Remembering the drunken miners, the smile disappeared.

"Like you handled the situation earlier?"

When her face colored brightly, he lifted one eyebrow, tilting his head slightly. Although her cheeks were fiery from embarrassment, it was still good to finally see some color in them.

"Is there a particular reason you are being so stubborn," he asked her, "or is it just in your nature?"

She stopped in her tracks, her eyes sparking with anger. "Is that how you deal with your sisters to get your own way?"

"Sister."

"What?" Her brows wrinkled with confusion.

"Penney is my sister. Helen and Jennie are friends."

She seemed to be digesting that bit of information before once more lifting huge purple-colored eyes to meet his gaze. There was a curious mixture of hurt and resignation in those telling orbs.

"Regardless, I saw the way you looked at me just now when I mentioned my father."

Evan slid his hands into his pants pockets, studying her belligerent face. "I won't deny that your father has quite a reputation."

If anything, her eyes grew colder. "My father's reputation has nothing to do with me."

Evan decided it was about time to change the subject. The woman was about as prickly as a frightened hedgehog.

"Why do you work for the *Gazette*? Surely you don't *need* to work."

She drew herself up to her unusually tall five feet six inches, which left her still short of his equally unusual height of six feet. It was nice not to have to bend low to look into a woman's face, though he doubted whether Miss Lattimer appreciated her amazon size.

"Mr. Brice, are you *deliberately* trying to provoke me?"

He pulled his hands from his pockets, slapping them against his thighs and rolling his eyes heavenward.

"Confound it, woman, I was merely trying to start a conversation. Do you have to take everything I say so personally?"

He wasn't certain if the twitching of her lips was from amusement or trying to keep a tight rein on her anger.

"Do you have any idea how late it is, Mr. Brice? I hardly think now is the time to begin a conversation."

That something that had jumped into life inside of him flamed even brighter. Something about this woman both exasperated and intrigued him. He wasn't certain what it was, but he thought he just might like to find out.

Taking a deep breath, he reached out and wrapped his hand around her upper arm, and with a none-too-gentle tug, he pulled her along at his side. Instead of her being angry, he noticed the slow smile on her face. It was then that he realized that she had successfully diverted him from asking more about her father. His eyes narrowed, but he said nothing.

When he reached the Plaza, he hired a hack and helped her into it. Except for giving the driver directions, the silence between them was broken only by the clopping of the horse's hooves on the board roadway.

Evan settled back against the carriage, leaning his arm along the back of the seat. He could feel Amy tense against where his fingers barely touched her shoulder. She pulled herself farther into the corner of the seat.

"You never did tell me why you are working for a newspaper," he told her.

The look she gave him made him grit his teeth. "All right, let me put it another way. Would you *mind* telling me how one of the wealthiest women in the city comes to be working in a newspaper office?"

She turned away from his probing look and stared ahead to

the rising hill in the distance. As they climbed farther away from the downtown area, the air around them cleared. The tangy sent of the salt air blew inland on a stiff sea breeze. He saw her shiver and, reaching across to the other seat, lifted the blanket set there for just such a purpose. He wrapped it around Amy, tucking her in securely. Perhaps it was an unconventional thing to do, but this had hardly been a conventional night.

He lifted his gaze to her face, his own face mere inches from hers. Her mouth parted in surprise, and Evan noticed that her breathing had quickened. Was she afraid of him? The thought was disturbing. He retreated to his own corner of the coach.

Amy sucked in a deep breath and turned away from him. "My—my father knows the editor. Since I wanted to work and he wasn't having any luck getting me to attend the social soirees where he hoped to marry me off, he thought this might be a fitting compromise." She glanced back at him, smiling wryly. "As the society columnist, it's my job to attend these functions and write about them."

"Convenient. But if I may ask, why do you want to work if you don't have to?"

A shutter seemed to come down over her face, masking her thoughts and feelings. She chewed her lip nervously. "I have my reasons."

The look on her face kept him from asking any more such personal questions, though he would have given a hefty sum to know the answers. She cocked her head slightly, studying him with an intensity that suddenly unnerved him.

"And you? Why are you so adamantly opposed to your sister and her friends working on the paper?"

He met her look unflinchingly. "I don't want my sister roaming the streets of San Francisco alone at night, and quite frankly, she's truly capable of doing something as impetuous as that."

Amy smiled. "I liked your sister."

Evan snorted. "I've spent most of my life keeping her out of trouble. When I told her about San Francisco, I had no idea she would pack up and follow me the fifty miles here. I thought I had left her safely at home in Plattsville."

The smile on Amy's face broadened. "She's not so easily controlled, I take it."

"You take it correctly. Heaven help the man she marries."

The hack stopped, and Evan looked up to see that they were in front of one of the most palatial mansions on Rincon Hill. Before he had a chance to get out, Amy had already alighted, shutting the door behind her. She leaned forward, her face now unsmiling.

"At least she has the choice of whom she will marry."

With that, she hurried up the stairs and disappeared from his view.

Chapter 3

Amy knocked on the door of room 232 early the next morning. She felt a twinge of anxiety knowing how Evan felt about his sister working in a newspaper office, especially when there was a strike going on. Still, she knew that the girls were desperate for a job—and she knew where they could probably find one.

The door opened, and Penney peeked her head out. Tired lines were etched against her normally smiling mouth.

"I take it you didn't get much sleep last night," Amy sympathized.

Penney opened the door wider. "You take it correctly. Come on in."

The room was shrouded in semidarkness, the curtains still drawn against the morning light. Jennie sat at a table reading a Bible with the help of the room's small oil lamp. Helen still lay snuggled under the covers, sound asleep.

Amy turned surprised eyes from the sleeping figure and raised a brow in question. Penney shrugged her shoulders, the first smile of the morning tugging at her mouth.

"Don't ask me how," she said.

Jennie closed the Bible and came to join them. Amy smiled from one to the other.

"I know it's early, but I thought we could talk to Mr. Madison after he gets his second cup of morning coffee."

The two girls grinned in response.

"Are you telling us he's not a morning person?" Jennie asked.

Amy hesitated. "Let's just say he's a little more human as the day wears on."

She noticed the spark of curiosity in Penney's eyes. "He sounds interesting," Penney told them, going to the bed and shaking Helen awake. "I look forward to meeting him."

Amy wasn't as certain. Mr. Madison was rather gruff and at most times extremely outspoken. She wasn't sure how this meeting was going to go, but she decided they had nothing to lose and everything to gain.

Since the fire had destroyed most of their belongings, it didn't take Helen long to make herself presentable. In a very short time, they were out on the streets of San Francisco walking along in the chilling fog that was rolling in from the ocean. Like wraiths, other people appeared and disappeared in the souplike atmosphere.

Helen glanced around apprehensively. "A person could get lost in this fog."

When they reached the building where the *Golden Gate Gazette* was housed, Amy paused.

"You'd better let me go in first," she suggested.

Taking a deep breath, she made her way through the building to Russell Madison's corner office. The rest of the building was eerily quiet for this time of morning. The only sound she could hear was Mr. Madison's gruff voice coming from his office. She was reluctant to intrude upon his meeting, so she hesitantly peeked her head around his office door to identify the person to whom he was speaking. No one else was in the room.

"Mr. Madison?"

He glanced up from his desk, brushing agitated hands through his gray hair and causing it to stand on end. She often thought he would look much younger without the beard he sported.

"Amy," he stated, impatience threading his voice. "Did you get me the story from last night?"

"Well. . .I. . ." His lifted brows hurried her on. "Well, you see, something came up."

He sighed heavily pushing his eyes into his palms. "No story."

Amy had never seen him like this. He looked up at her, his face suddenly full of weary lines. "I'm not sure what we are going to do. Three more men have refused to show up for work."

That explained the silence in the other room. Those who were moving about were doing so almost silently, their voices emanating in sepulchral whispers.

Now was her chance. "Mr. Madison, I have brought you some help. They aren't experienced in newspaper work, but they are willing to learn and work."

For the first time since she had entered the room, his eyes lighted with hope. He grinned at her. "Well, bring them in. What are you waiting for?"

He was standing ready to greet them when Amy returned with the three women. The smile slowly slid from his face. He turned hard eyes to Amy.

"What is this? I thought you were bringing me some *men*."

"Now, Mr. Madison," Amy cajoled, "you know there's not a man in this city who is willing to cross a picket line."

He glared at each woman in turn. "And you think it's any safer for women?"

"We'll take our chances," Penney told him.

"Well, I won't!"

He returned to his chair behind his desk, nodding his head in dismissal. The trouble was, the three women refused to be dismissed.

Jennie folded her arms across her chest, her blue eyes challenging. "From the lack of movement in the other room, I'd say that you must be getting ready to close your paper, then."

Mr. Madison blinked heavy-lidded eyes at her. Amy could see the desperation written on his features.

Before he could speak, a commotion in the outside room caught their attention. A man entered the room, his large size dwarfing the other occupants. His eyes blazed angrily. "I knew I would find you here!"

"Evan!" Penney exclaimed. She straightened her shoulders, obviously ready to do battle.

One look from those fierce eyes, and Amy couldn't have spoken if she wanted to. He blamed her for this.

He glared at Russell Madison. "Forget it. They aren't working for you."

Madison rose to his feet, his heavy brows forming into a

frown. "Now look here—"

Penney stepped between the two men. "Now you listen to me, Evan Brice," she declared hotly. "You have taken this big-brother bit a little too seriously, lately. I am quite able to look after myself!"

Evan placed his hands firmly on his hips, and Amy suddenly realized that he wasn't in uniform. A fisherman's knit sweater molded against his broad shoulders like a glove on a hand. He was also wearing a pair of miner's jeans that had seen better days. It occurred to Amy that he had probably come prepared to help his sister find a place to move. The look he threw her way was anything but friendly.

"I'm not arguing with you!" he told Penney, but Amy knew that he was including the other two as well.

Jennie bristled at his domineering tone. "Right. You're not arguing, because there is nothing to argue about. Mr. Madison has already decided to close his paper since he can't get the help he needs."

"Now, just a doggone minute!" Russell Madison came from behind his desk, his smoking cigar switching from one side of his mouth to the other. He glared at each person in the room, but it was to Evan that he spoke. "I already decided to give these girls a try," he told Evan, surprising them all.

"Really?" Jennie squeaked.

"Really?" Helen echoed.

Penney just stared at the man openmouthed.

Knowing Mr. Madison like she did, Amy thought he probably decided to give the women a job just to spite Evan. Russell Madison hated to be told what to do. Besides, he really had no other option, and she was sure that he knew it. She held her breath, waiting for the explosion she knew was to come. She wasn't disappointed.

"Over my dead body." The steel in Evan's voice sent shivers down Amy's back.

Jennie stepped forward until she stood toe to toe with Evan, although he had to look a long way down to meet her flashing eyes. Penney stood reluctantly nearby, obviously loathe to create a scene with her brother.

"Since we live in a republic, I suggest we vote on it," Jennie told him.

Amy was surprised the young woman didn't just tell Evan to mind his own business. She grew even more curious about the relationship between these four people. Perhaps Jennie and Evan were romantically involved. That would certainly explain her reluctance to defy him.

Seeing the look on Evan's face, Mr. Madison hastily intervened. Like Amy, he must have decided that Evan was a force to be reckoned with.

"Mr. . . . ?"

Without taking his eyes from Jennie's, Evan answered him. "Brice."

"Well, Mr. Brice," Mr. Madison said, "perhaps you would like to state your objections to having the women work in my office."

A tick worked in Evan's cheek, and Amy knew that he was holding his temper tightly in check. She would hate to be the recipient of that temper. Even Jennie seemed to lose a little of her bluster.

"I won't have my sister working in a newspaper office. It's not a job for ladies."

Russell Madison cut his eyes toward Amy, and she could have cheerfully crawled beneath his desk.

"Are you suggesting, sir, that Miss Lattimer is not a lady?"

"If the shoe fits."

"Evan!"

Penney's horrified voice brought his eyes swinging to her. Some of his anger seemed to leave him, his tense shoulders relaxing somewhat.

"I'm sorry. I didn't mean it like that at all."

Amy thought his apology lacked substance. Still, she had known what his opinion was from the night before. She couldn't say she was surprised, but she did consider him a bit narrow-minded in his views.

He continued, "I just don't want my sister or Jennie or Helen wandering around the streets in the middle of the night like Miss Lattimer was last night." His steely-eyed glare fixed on Russell Madison. "Did you know that she was accosted by a couple of drunks?"

The three girls stared at her horrified. Mr. Madison paled. "Miss Lattimer?"

Amy met Evan's glare with one of her own. "It was nothing, sir."

Russell turned to Evan. "Thank you for telling me. I will see that that doesn't happen again. However, the jobs I would allow the women to fill would be here in the office."

Although Helen seemed satisfied, both Jennie and Penney were not. Amy almost laughed at the mutinous looks that crossed their features, but she doubted they would argue. They really needed the jobs.

"What kind of jobs?" Evan asked warily.

"I need a bookkeeper, some print setters, information collectors, things like that."

Evan took his time considering. Penney placed a hand on his arm.

"You don't have a problem with that, do you? How is keeping books in a newspaper office any different from keeping books in a store?"

Evan finally sighed, relaxing his rigid stance. There was a softening in his eyes.

"I suppose there isn't."

"Then. . . ?"

He sighed, his lips tilted into a lopsided smile. "Okay. You might as well go ahead with it."

Three huge grins met his statement. Rolling his eyes and shaking his head, he turned to Amy.

"May I speak with you a moment?"

Amy was certain her heart had just stopped beating, but no, just as suddenly it was about to jump from her chest. Her time of reckoning was at hand. She nodded, and Evan followed her from the room. The other three remained behind to speak with Mr. Madison.

Evan pulled her to a corner of the room away from the few other workers going about their jobs.

"I owe you an apology," he told her peremptorily.

Her eyes widened in surprise. "For what?"

"I didn't mean to suggest that you weren't a lady. I shouldn't have said that. I was angry."

The softness of his voice spoke clearly of his sincerity.

She studied him seriously. "You *do* have a temper, don't you?" she said, her smile softening the sting of the words. His returning smile left her slightly breathless.

"I wonder," he said thoughtfully, cocking his head slightly to study her. "Do you?"

Amy went cold all over. If she had a temper, she had long ago buried it deep within. Her father would have taken care of it if she so much as *thought* about letting her temper show.

Helen, Jennie, and Penney came from Russell Madison's office, looking anything but confident. Helen glanced back over her shoulder nervously.

"Is he *always* like that?" she whispered.

Amy knew what she meant. Having grown used to the man, she just smiled. "Always."

Penney breathed out softly from between compressed lips. "Heaven help us all."

The three girls agreed to meet Evan for lunch to discuss places to live. Amy hoped that they would agree to stay at the hotel until they absolutely wanted to leave. She was intrigued by the closeness of the three women, and for the first time in her life, she realized just how nice it would be to have a friend.

Since her mother's death, she had lived secluded and apart from the rest of the world. She had not known any other way until now. Her shyness was the major contributing factor, but then, there was also her father. She refused to even think about what might happen if he should find out what she was up to.

What made these girls so happy in the face of adversity?

Where did they get their courage, their stamina? She felt like a coward in comparison.

If they were working together, maybe she would be able to find out.

~

Evan watched Jennie and Helen cross the hotel dining room and disappear through the exit. His lips twitched slightly.

"Jennie wanted to tell me to go to blazes," he told his sister.

Penney sat back in her chair, her arms folded across her chest. Her eyes sparkled dangerously. Evan knew that look from times past.

"She wasn't the only one."

His twitching lips turned into a full-fledged grin. "Now, Penney, I could never see Helen doing such a thing. She's too sweet."

The look she gave him could have dried up a river in a monsoon. "I wasn't referring to Helen, and you know it." She leaned forward, picking up her teacup. "Honestly, Evan, what have you got against newspapers anyway?"

Evan reached across the table and took one of her hands into his. "Promise me, Penney, that you won't even think about going out at night, nor to any places that might be dangerous."

She met his gaze squarely. "You heard what Mr. Madison said. I will be learning to set type for the articles that his few remaining *men* are willing to write. Did you know that he is still receiving articles, even though they won't cross a picket line? It's done in secret, and Mr. Madison puts his name on the byline."

"How do you know that?"

"Amy told us."

Even the mention of the woman's name sent a charge of electricity coursing through his veins. He studied his sister seriously for a moment before deciding to confide in her.

"Be careful of Amy Lattimer, Penney. She might not be all she seems."

The sudden darkening of her eyes told him he had hit a sensitive issue.

"She's lonely, Evan. I can see it in her eyes."

He nodded agreement and opened his mouth to reply, but Penney interrupted him.

"She needs what we have, Evan. She needs the love of a Savior."

What could he say to that comment? He sighed heavily. "I agree, but Penney, there are things about her father you should know."

Penney pulled her hand from his and nervously began making circles on the tablecloth with her finger. She wouldn't look him in the eye. "Is what you are about to tell me *fact* or hearsay?"

Surprised, Evan hesitated. "Well. . ."

"You know how I feel about gossip, Evan."

He retreated into silence. She was right. Until he had proof, he should give Amy and her father the benefit of the doubt. Penney stared at him unyieldingly, and he sighed. "You've made your point. I haven't forgotten how the gossip back home almost destroyed our family."

"Should I tell her about *our* father? That he abandoned us

when we were young? That our mother died with a broken heart? Should I tell her that, too?"

Evan felt like crawling into a hole somewhere. How was it that his sister could somehow always manage to turn the tables on him? He met her look and saw her eyes dancing with mischief. He knew he was cornered, and so did she.

"Just be careful," he advised.

Her look turned solemn. "I will, but I intend to invite her to prayer meeting tonight."

Evan grabbed the check on the table and, rising, gave her a halfhearted smile. "Well, for your sake, I hope she accepts."

"For *her* sake I hope she does. You don't mind that we decided to stay here?" she asked before he could leave.

He glanced around, frowning. "It's a nice place, I'll grant you that. But it must be expensive."

She shook her head. Picking up her new reticule, she rose from her seat to stand beside him. Together they left the dining room, Penney's arm coupled with Evan's.

"Actually, it's not. I was really surprised at how reasonable it was. The manager said that since we were willing to share one room, he could give us a discount rate." She smiled brilliantly. "Wasn't that nice?"

Evan didn't know if it was nice or not. He hadn't missed the look that passed between the desk clerk and Amy Lattimer. Something was going on here that he would have to check out before he could make a decision one way or another.

Penney stared up at him waiting for his answer.

"Yes," he agreed. "That was very nice indeed."

Chapter 4

It was late. Darkness had settled across the land hours ago. Amy stood at the door of the church, waiting for her friends to join her. The other members of the congregation had left long ago, but Jennie, Helen, and Penney had stayed behind to help put the place in order.

Evan joined her, taking her by the arm. That curious sensation she felt whenever she was in his presence filled her once again.

"Come on," he told her, leading her out the door. "I'll take you home. The girls are going to be awhile."

She tugged against his hold. "I should stay and help them."

His smile didn't quite reach his eyes. "They will be some time. Mr. Carlton, the minister, has asked them to help him plan for the picnic next Sunday after morning services."

"Picnic?"

He continued leading her along, his mind obviously on other things. "Every month the church sponsors a picnic for the children's home on Market Street."

Intrigued, Amy stopped. "That sounds wonderful. Maybe I can help."

The hand that latched onto her arm was firm. "Maybe another time."

She opened her mouth to protest when it occurred to her that Evan had something on his mind, and from the look on his face, it had to do with her. She retreated into silence, following along and allowing him to help her into the rented hack he had acquired.

They traveled some time before either one spoke. Amy broke the long silence between them. "Is there something you wanted to talk to me about, Mr. Brice?"

An indefinable look darkened his face. "Are you aware, Miss Lattimer, that the apartment house that burned belonged to your father?"

The shock of his words was like a fist to the stomach. She couldn't breathe. Memories she had tried so hard to repress for so many years forced themselves on her once again. Memories of her mother standing at the upstairs window of another apartment building, her small figure surrounded by flames. Her terrified screams had filled the night only to end in abrupt silence. Amy shuddered, the stars in the night sky suddenly wheeling around her.

"Amy, are you all right?"

Evan's concerned voice reached her from a distance, but she couldn't respond. He suddenly forced her head between her knees and in a moment, the world steadied and became firm once again. Taking a deep breath, she weakly pushed out of his hold.

"I'm sorry," he told her, his voice filled with contriteness. The hand rubbing across her back slowed and then stilled.

She had unnerved him, she could see that, but he had no idea just exactly how much his words had affected her. The niggling fear that had lived with her since that night surfaced again. Had her father been involved? She hadn't wanted to believe it the first time, nor the second, but three times was no coincidence, she felt certain. Why had Evan asked her the question? And then she knew.

She turned to him, her eyes blazing. "Are you suggesting that I had something to do with the fire?"

He hesitated, and she had her answer. Her throat went tight. What kind of woman did he think she was? Once again, her father's reputation fell heavily upon her shoulders. Her anger faded to a slow sense of despair. She sighed in defeat, turning away from Evan and watching the surrounding scenery.

"I didn't really think that you had anything to do with the fire, but I was hoping maybe you had some information concerning it that might be helpful in our investigation." His voice was soft, apologetic. She felt his fingers on her chin, and then he firmly turned her to face him. The confusion in his brown eyes mirrored that which she was feeling.

"I don't know anything," she told him firmly. "And since you so obviously mistrust me, perhaps it would be just as well if I stayed away from your sister and her friends."

And you. The words hung unsaid in the air between them. "Amy. . ." He paused, brushing his hair in agitation.

"You can't get past the fact that my father is Cyril Lattimer, can you?" she asked, annoyed with herself for caring what he thought. "Well, I'm *not* my father!"

They had arrived at her house, and she jumped from the carriage unassisted, her hoopskirts swishing about her. When he moved to get out, she firmly shut the door to the coach.

"Don't trouble yourself," she stated unequivocally. Turning, she hurried up the stairs and into the house without bothering to look back.

Once inside, she unfastened her cloak and, crossing the marble floor, dropped it onto the settee in the entryway. She stared into space, her thoughts miles away.

"Where have you been?"

The quiet voice startled her. She whirled around and found her father standing in the doorway of the parlor. Even late at night, his appearance was immaculate. His brown hair was barely touched with gray, his mustache and beard clipped short. At the age of forty, he was still an extremely handsome man.

"Father," she said, her surprise evident. Her heart began to pound with trepidation. "I wasn't expecting you until Saturday."

"Obviously," he snapped. "Do you have any idea what time it is?"

Her look flew to the ancient grandfather clock standing majestically beside the stairs. The hands showed that it was about to chime out the hour of ten o'clock. She swallowed hard, bracing herself for her father's wrath. To her surprise, he merely moved aside and motioned her into the parlor.

"Come inside. I want you to meet someone."

Amy was tired and in no mood to socialize, but she knew

better than to disobey her father. She went past him, recognizing the dark look in his eyes. Retribution would come when they were alone.

A young man rose from the chaise lounges that sat before the great fireplace. His look flicked over Amy briefly. The expression in his eyes was hardly flattering. She stiffened, her opinion of him set by the look on his face. In that instant, she decided she didn't trust him.

He was handsome, in a courtly sort of way. His dark hair was parted in the middle and slicked back on both sides. His pencil-thin mustache did nothing to make him look older, but it did give him a decidedly worldly air. Surely he couldn't be much older than she was herself, yet he had an air of confidence that made him appear much more experienced.

"David, this is my daughter, Amy. Amy, David Andrews."

Both men stood courteously, waiting for Amy to take her seat. She nodded at David, sliding gracefully onto the chair across from him.

"Mr. Andrews."

"David will be staying with us for a time," her father told her, exchanging a look with David. The message that passed between them was lost to Amy, but it unsettled her nevertheless.

"How. . .nice," she answered inadequately.

"I was hoping that you would show me something of the city," David said, his smile never reaching his cold blue eyes.

Amy glanced at her father. She knew what was expected of her, but she felt a sudden urge to rebel.

"I'm sorry, Mr. Andrews. But I *am* employed."

Her father flashed her a look, his voice so quiet it caused

her to shudder. "That can be changed."

David rose to his feet. He must have read something on her face that gave him pause, for he suddenly bowed. "Perhaps after work then," he suggested placatingly.

Feeling trapped, Amy nodded. She knew if she didn't agree her father would ask Mr. Madison to fire her, and she didn't want that to happen. Until she was twenty-one, a trustee controlled the inheritance she had received from her mother. She still had several months to wait, and until then, her job was her only means of independence, the only way she had to support her projects.

"That would be fine, Mr. Andrews."

David smiled at her father. "Well, Mr. Lattimer, if it's all the same to you, I'm extremely tired. I think I would like to retire for the night."

Cyril rang the servant's bell. When the butler appeared, he motioned to David. "Take Mr. Andrews to his room." He returned David's smile. "We will see you in the morning then."

They watched the young man leave the room, the butler closing the door behind him after a quick look at her father.

"Now you will tell me where you have been," he hissed, turning and facing her, his gray eyes blazing.

Amy took a deep breath. She was tempted to lie, but her father would only find out the truth, and the consequences didn't bear thinking about.

"I was at church," she stated quietly.

For one moment, he merely stared at her in astonishment. When he finally overcame his surprise, he threw back his head and laughed, yet somehow Amy didn't think that he found it the least amusing. Something dark and sinister flickered through his eyes briefly.

"I hope you're not thinking of following in your mother's footsteps," he pronounced quietly.

Amy didn't answer him. If her father knew the things she had been doing, she had no doubt her freedom would be greatly limited in the future.

"I only went to church," she told him, somehow managing to keep out of her voice the quaver that usually existed when speaking with her father. He glanced at her suspiciously.

"See that you keep it that way."

He lifted a decanter of brandy and poured himself a glass. She could tell it wasn't his first.

"I think I'll go to bed now, too," she told him. He merely nodded his head. She could feel his attention focused on her as she exited. For the first time in many years, she found herself uttering a prayer.

Evan called himself all kinds of a fool. He, of all people, should understand what it meant to be judged because of a parent. It was the reason he had left home in the first place.

Still, he certainly hadn't expected the reaction he had received when he told Amy about the apartment belonging to her father. If she had been acting, she was in the wrong business. She should be on the stage. No, her response had been genuine, he was certain of it. In fact, it had frightened him half out of his wits. He should have been more sensitive about her feelings, but this confounded reaction he had to the woman was impeding his normally sharp senses.

He was now convinced that she was not involved, but he still had the feeling she knew more than what she was saying.

He had checked the records and had found that this was not the first piece of property belonging to Cyril Lattimer that had burned to the ground. The money he had collected on insurance had made him a wealthy man.

There was something strange about the insurance company's willingness to insure Lattimer, even after two other arson attacks. It would be interesting to see if he still managed to be insured after a third.

Evan hadn't had the opportunity to tell Amy that the fire was arson, but she would find out sooner or later. Mr. Madison had been made aware of it by one of his secret reporters. No doubt it would be front page in tomorrow's news. He suddenly felt very sorry for Amy Lattimer. Then again, *he* had done nothing to make things any better.

He would have to try harder in the future to get over his mistrust of her. He still wasn't certain if his suspicions of the girl were because of who she was or because of what she managed to do to him. He found himself at times thinking about what it would be like to court her, yet adversely, he wanted to keep her at arm's distance. She was hardly his type. Still, he hadn't been able to get the woman off his mind since he had first set eyes on her.

He returned the hack to the stable, his emotions swaying like the signpost above him. The wind had picked up, the breeze from the Pacific chilling in its intensity. He regretted not bringing a warmer jacket.

As he was about to leave, the proprietor called to him.

"Hey, mister," he puffed, his squat legs working furiously to complete the distance Evan's long strides had already taken him. "This belong to you?"

Amy's parasol. He took it from the man, giving him a smile. "Thanks."

"No problem."

Evan watched the man walk back to the stable then turned his gaze in the direction of Rincon Hill. Now he had an excuse to see her again and apologize. He only hoped she would hear him out before whacking him across the head with the dainty article.

~~~

Amy pushed aside the green velvet curtains of her bedroom and stared at the dark ocean in the distance. Fog was forming over the waters and would soon roll inland.

She opened the door that led to the balcony and went outside. A chilling wind hit her. She tugged her robe closer about her but refused to retreat inside. Moving forward, she leaned her palms against the iron banister that surrounded her private porch.

Words the minister had spoken that night now came back to haunt her. He had spoken of a love beyond anything the human mind could comprehend. She had long ago given up on a God who would let such a wonderful woman as her mother die and in such a horrible way. Such a thing did not speak of love to her.

Her mother had been a devout Christian. Even now Amy could remember her mother's beautiful voice lifted in song to the Creator. The same voice that had screamed until silenced by ravaging flames.

Mr. Carlton had spoken of serving a loving God. Well, her mother had done just that and died in the process. Her mother had found joy in helping others less fortunate than herself.

Father had despised Mother for it, but that hadn't stopped her. She had a fortune of her own that her father hadn't been able to touch until after her death. What had surprised Amy's father was that her mother had left most of that fortune intact bequeathed to her daughter.

Amy had known from a young age that her parents had no love for each other. Theirs had been an arranged marriage, a marriage that combined fortune with property. Father had hoped for a son, but instead he was saddled with a rather plain daughter who had done nothing to improve her social skills. Due to complications after Amy's birth, there had been no other children.

After her mother's death, Amy had retreated into a world of her own.

It was only when her lawyer had made known to her that she had various properties as well as other sources of wealth that she had struggled her way out of her grief and begun to take an interest in life once again.

Now she had taken up where her mother had left off. She utilized her properties to bring in money that she used to help those less fortunate. She wondered what her father would say if he knew that she managed a safe house for girls wanting to flee prostitution. Not to mention the money she handed out to help others in the lower sections of the city.

She smiled without mirth, the smile slowly fading as she thought once again about the words the minister had used. Was it true that God loved her? Mr. Carlton had sounded so sincere. So convincing. His words had sparked a yearning inside her to be loved like that. The only example she had of a father was nothing like the one Penney and the others spoke of. Perhaps that had been what had impeded her for such a long time. It was hard to see past her own pain to believe in a father like that.

Without thinking, she lifted her face to the night sky. Her silent prayer was more a plea, a plea she was unaware of uttering.

Chapter 5

Evan caught Amy before she had time to enter the *Gazette* building. Her look was hardly encouraging.

"I wanted to give you this," he told her, "and to apologize to you."

She took the parasol from him and twirled it in her fingers. The look she gave him spoke volumes.

"I know you probably want to hit me over the head with it, and frankly I don't blame you, but I'm hoping that you will have dinner with me instead."

Her surprise rendered her speechless, giving Evan hope since she hadn't turned him down outright. He could see her mentally processing his request. When it finally came, her smile lacked vitality.

"I can't."

"Can't. . .or won't?" He was surprised at the intense disappointment he felt. In truth, he had asked her to dinner to nullify his own guilt over causing her such hurt, but now he realized just how much he had been looking forward to it.

"You needn't pay penance, Mr. Brice. I forgive you."

Was there just a touch of hurt in her voice? He stared hard at her trying to fathom her feelings.

When she turned to leave, he took her by the arm to restrain her. "I'm not doing penance, Miss Lattimer," he told her softly. "I really would like to take you to dinner. I would like to get to know you better."

He could see her struggling to respond. Had the woman never been asked out before? But then, knowing her father for the kind of man that he was, he thought he understood better.

"If not dinner, how about going to the picnic after church with me?" When she hesitated, he smiled with a charm that had served him well before. "The girls will be with us, if that makes you feel any safer."

"I. . .want to," she told him, her voice faltering, "but my father has arrived in town and has made plans for me. I'll need to ask him first."

Evan nodded with understanding. "Do you plan to come to church, then?"

A fire of determination lit her purple eyes. "Yes, I plan to come to church."

Realizing that he was still holding on to her arm, he released her. Stepping back, he gave her a slight bow. "I'll see you then."

He watched her enter the building, a timid woman with a suddenly stiff backbone. He shook his head slowly. What had ever possessed him?

~⁓

David was waiting in a buggy when Amy came from the *Gazette* building several days later. Had she not doubted his motives, his attention might have been flattering, but his phony smile put her teeth on edge. Here was a problem she would have to deal with. She knew that in all likelihood her father had arranged a marriage for her since he had been speaking of it for some time. The thought didn't surprise her, but she could only wonder what Mr. Andrews brought to the relationship.

Although she had lived in fear of her father for many years, she had no intention of falling in with his plans. Soon she would be twenty-one and free to do as she pleased.

David climbed down from the buggy and reached out a hand to help Amy in. She wanted to ignore the outstretched hand, but she couldn't bring herself to be so rude.

When they were seated and on their way, David turned a smiling face to her. She shivered at the look from his cold eyes.

"I'm afraid that I'm going to have to postpone our date to see the city," he told her. He searched her face, frowning at her lack of response. "Your father and I have been called back to Sacramento on business. We'll need to leave this afternoon."

Amy felt a little thrill run through her. She had been praying all day that something would happen to allow her to go to church on Sunday, yet she hadn't really held out much conviction that it would. Now she realized that, even without her having faith, God had truly answered her prayers.

"Miss Lattimer?"

Amy jerked her attention back to David. "I'm sorry. What did you say?"

He studied her curiously. "I said that we will have to get to know each other better when I next return."

"And when might that be?"

A slow smile spread across his face, and Amy realized that he had misunderstood her eagerness. He reached out and took her hand, giving it a slight squeeze.

"Don't worry. It won't be long."

Amy remained silent. If her prayers continued to be answered, she might never have to see David Andrews again.

For the remainder of the evening, Amy was careful to be at her most congenial. David and her father swapped satisfied smiles, certain that Amy would do what they intended. She could return their smiles with complete confidence. After all, hadn't God answered her prayers once? She suddenly had a little more faith that He would do so again.

Sunday dawned bright and beautiful, a rarity in the last few weeks. The day grew progressively warmer, and hopes for the picnic were finally realized.

Evan settled himself on the quilt next to Amy, turning his gaze in the direction she was staring. He smiled with her at the rambunctious children cavorting across the sand in the gusting winds. Several were jumping up and down, pointing to the seals sunning themselves on the rocks far out in the water.

Amy held down her bonnet with one hand and the quilt with the other. Despite the heavy breeze, they had chosen this site so that the children could run along the beach and have some fun collecting shells.

Penney, Helen, and Jennie were chasing the children, their adult laughter mingling with that of the joyous children.

"How's your ankle?"

Amy had twisted her ankle on a buried rock when descending from the coach that they had hired. Evan reached to check the injured appendage, but Amy quickly pulled her leg under her. She flinched with the sudden movement.

"My ankle is as well as can be expected," she told him. "I'm afraid the same can't be said of my attitude."

She gave him a halfhearted smile, and he had to sympathize with her plight.

"Well," he rejoined, "someone needs to look after the food." She wrinkled her nose at his obvious attempt to cheer her up. He reached out and brushed a hand lightly down her cheek. "I know," he said softly. "You think you're missing all the fun, but there will be other times."

She turned away, her attention once more on the scene before her. "I hope so," she answered just as softly.

Pulling her bonnet from her head, she grimaced ruefully. "I might as well give up on trying to keep this thing in place."

In seconds, the wind was tearing at her hair, loosening some of the pins and causing little tendrils to curl across her cheeks and neck. Evan found himself wishing he could finish the job the wind had started. He suddenly found himself wrangling with a wayward imagination.

"Evan?"

He was surprised at her use of his given name when she had always taken pains to keep him at a distance with the more formal Mr. Brice. He found he liked the sound of it, her voice soft and melodious.

"Hmmm?" He allowed his gaze to roam over her features and realized that his emotions were slowly being entangled.

When she turned those large, pansy-colored eyes on him, he found himself slightly rattled. He had been feeling strange ever since he had seated himself beside her in church. Having known the girl for such a short time, he still couldn't deny that she made him feel things he never had before.

She tucked her bottom lip behind her teeth in uncertainty. "If I wanted to find out more about God the Father, how would I go about it?"

He was so surprised, he didn't know what to say. "Don't you have a Bible?"

She turned away from him, pulling her coat more tightly against her to protect from the chilling wind. She hesitated before answering him.

"Well, of course I do."

Evan was confused. He decided to tread carefully, not wanting to chance rupturing their slowly growing friendship. "Do you mean, where in the Bible can you find more information on God the Father?"

She turned to him in astonishment. He could read the dawning comprehension on her face.

"Yes, that's what I meant."

He had the decided feeling that that wasn't what she had meant at all. "Well, the four Gospels are probably the best place to get a true picture of God since they tell us of His Son who was God made flesh."

"I. . .see."

No, she didn't see at all, he could tell. Growing more curious, he was about to question her further when Jennie came running up.

"Hey, you two. We're ready to eat."

Evan laughed. "After all that running around, I'm not surprised."

Penney joined them, smiling down at Amy. "How's the ankle?"

"I think it's just bruised."

Penney pointed an admonishing finger at her. "Well, let's not take any chances. You stay put, and we'll continue to see to things."

Amy frowned up at her. "But I wanted to help, too."

Helen came up and plopped down next to her on the quilt. "You always want to help," she said wryly. "You can help next time. Right now, let's just eat!"

They called the children and passed out the food. Silence settled around them save for the cries of the gulls and the barking of the seals in the distance. Convention was ignored, and all of them ate with their fingers, giggling over spilled food and wet chins.

After their meal, the girls allowed the children to remove their socks and shoes and paddle through the very edge of the water. They were delighted with tempting the waves, howling with pleasure when the water rushed forward and surrounded their legs.

When it was time to leave, Evan reached down and lifted Amy into his arms. The action so startled her that she quickly wrapped her arms around his neck, staring into his eyes in amazement. Evan couldn't begin to describe the feeling that washed over him at that moment, yet he knew with certainty that something had just transpired between them that would forever change him.

How long they stood thus, he was uncertain. A slight cough behind him turned their attention to the three girls standing just off to the side. He recognized that knowing look on Penney's face.

Helen and Jennie exchanged grins. Rolling his eyes, he made his way to the omnibus coach the group had rented for the journey.

The silence between Amy and himself grew until Evan felt very uncomfortable. Eventually the children's laughter and excitement relieved the strained atmosphere somewhat as Amy finally joined in the camaraderie.

On the return journey, Evan took pains to make himself congenial, pointing out landmarks along the way. He wasn't certain what had made Amy so uneasy, even fearful, but he did his best to reverse the effects.

The horses' hooves *clopped* along the macadam highway, discernible now that the children had been rendered silent by fatigue. Although they tried hard to prevent it, it wasn't long before all the children were sound asleep.

The opening to the bay, the Golden Gate, could be seen in the distance. The sound of the waves breaking on the shore could still be faintly heard. Miles of ocean spread out into the distance. The sight and sound never failed to awe Evan. It soothed him, made him feel closer to his Creator than anything else ever had.

They soon passed the San Francisco Industrial School for depraved juveniles. Amy glanced at the sleeping children, her gaze thoughtfully resting on the school.

"Thank goodness Mr. Carlton started a mission home."

"It's not because of his goodness," Evan disputed, "but rather because of his heart for God."

"Is there a difference?"

Evan smiled. "There are many good people, Amy. That doesn't make them godly. Even that school was started because of someone's goodness, but it's God who changes people's lives."

She quietly continued to study the building until they had passed. Eventually the view gave rise to lush green hills dotted with pretty little houses.

Traffic was heavy since Sunday was a favorite time for sightseeing. They passed many coaches with laughing tourists, along with the dray carts that brought water, milk, meat, and bread into the city. Single-horse carts and double-horse carts lined the roadway. An omnibus stopped to allow visitors to view the sights.

Wending their way between numerous pedestrians and vehicles, they finally made their way to Third Street where they returned the coach. Mr. Carlton was waiting to take the children and return them to the home.

Evan rented another carriage to take all the girls home. This time when he lifted Amy into it, she didn't demur. He ignored his sister's speculative stare as he helped the others into the carriage.

After dropping the other three girls off at the hotel, Evan slowed his pace to give him more time to be with Amy. He suddenly felt reluctant to let her go.

"Will I see you at church on Wednesday?" he asked.

Roused from her preoccupation, she gave him a bright smile. "I'll be there."

"I could pick you up."

A weighty silence descended between them. When he looked at her, her found her twisting the ribbon on her bonnet until he thought for certain she would shred it to bits.

"I would like that," she answered quietly, and Evan felt his heart give a great thump.

When they reached her house, Evan lifted Amy from the cart and ascended the steps that led to the Lattimer mansion. Held securely in his arms, Amy rang the bell beside the door.

The servant who answered made a humorous picture, his mouth open in amazement. Huge eyes stared out of a black face.

"Miss Lattimer has injured her ankle. Perhaps you could send someone for the doctor and show me where to place her."

The servant hurriedly motioned Evan inside, his worried gaze fixed on Amy.

"Miss Amy, what you done to yo'self now?"

She gave him a halfhearted smile. "It's nothing, Sam. I merely twisted my ankle."

Evan followed the man as he led them up the oak stairs to Amy's bedroom. Everywhere he looked, Evan could see ostentatious displays of wealth. It suddenly brought home to him the huge difference in his and Amy's backgrounds.

While Evan settled Amy on the settee in front of her window, Sam pulled the bell beside the fireplace. He studied Evan suspiciously.

Ignoring him, Evan knelt in front of Amy, resting his hands beside her on the settee. He examined her tired face.

"Are you in much pain?"

She hesitated before answering him. He lifted her chin until he could look her in the eye. One dark brow lifted in question.

She sighed. "It *does* throb a bit."

"You probably need to put some ice on it."

She smiled. "Thank you very much for your concern." Her voice softened. "And for today."

He returned her smile, slowly getting to his feet and allowing his fingers to graze her chin. "Take care of yourself. I'll come by tomorrow to see how you are. You might need to skip work for a few days."

Panic flared in her eyes. "I don't think that will be necessary."

"We'll see," he challenged, and saw the panic change to fiery determination. When she opened her mouth to argue, he bent forward and pressed his lips against hers. Surprised, she didn't resist him, and he allowed the kiss to slowly deepen until she at last responded to it.

"Ahem."

Evan pulled back reluctantly and turned to find Sam glaring at him. One of these days, he promised himself, he was going to get Amy on her own and find out just how far these feelings went. When he glanced back at her, her fiery cheeks spoke of her embarrassment, but the glitter in her eyes told him more plainly than words that she had not been unmoved by his kiss.

"Tomorrow," he told her huskily and quickly left the room.

Chapter 6

Amy frantically searched the entire mansion, trying to find a copy of the Bible. Why hadn't it occurred to her to do so before? How foolish. Evan must surely think that she was some kind of simpleton. But since her mother's death, there hadn't been a reverent word spoken in this house. Her father hated any shows of piety.

Frustrated, she finally called for Emma, the cook who had been with her family since long before her mother had died. The old woman entered the parlor, wiping her hands on the towel wrapped around her waist. Her kerchief kept her springy hair held tightly in place. Despite the somber atmosphere that so often permeated this house, laugh lines wrinkled her dark face.

"What is it, Miss Amy?"

"Emma, do you know where a Bible is? Do we have one anywhere in this house?"

The old servant surveyed her suspiciously. "What you want with a Bible? You knows yo' daddy don't hold with such notions."

"I want to read it," Amy told her impatiently. "What else

would a person do with it?"

Emma folded her arms across her ample bosom, her dark eyes serious. She shook her head slowly. "Mmm, mmm, mmm. I recognize that look. You gots the fire in yo' eyes all right."

Amy frowned. "What fire? What in the name of heaven are you talking about?"

"Yo' mama had that same look. You done found the Lord."

Sinking slowly to the sofa, Amy stared up at the old woman. So many things were running through her mind. Is that what had made her mother so special, so loving? But then, hadn't Evan said that it was God who changed people's lives?

She knew now what made the difference between her mother and the other women of the ladies aid society. Yes, that had to be it. Even when she was spurned by those she was trying to help, her mother had a positive, loving attitude. The other ladies would shrug their shoulders and walk away, but not her mother. She continued to serve with a humble heart. The ache for her mother's company that had dimmed over the past few years rushed back upon her in force.

She glanced back at Emma. "Where's my mother's Bible, Emma?" she whispered. "I believe you must know."

"Yo' daddy wouldn't like it, Miss Amy. You best forget this business."

They both knew what would happen to the old woman if her father ever found out that she had disclosed the location of something he strictly forbade.

"Emma, please."

Sighing heavily, Emma unfolded her arms. "In the attic," she finally said. "They's a trunk with yo' mama's things in it.

I put it there after she died, thinking you might like to some-day have some of her things. Yo' daddy doesn't know."

Amy felt a frisson of ice run along her spine. The thought of what her father might do if he found out about her mother's pre-cious trunk brought her to her feet. Why had she not thought to ask before? Probably because she believed her father had destroyed every item that had been a memory of the woman he considered had failed him so miserably.

Heading for the door, she stopped beside Emma and placed a hand reassuringly on her shoulder.

"Don't worry, Emma. He'll never know that it was you who told me; I'll make sure of that."

Emma called to her, and Amy paused on the stairs.

"Child, don't let yo' daddy know that you have no Bible."

Amy hesitated before answering. Although she wouldn't lie, neither was she about to volunteer the information. "I don't intend to."

She hurried up to the attic, her heart pounding with antic-ipation. What would she find in that trunk Emma spoke of? She searched frantically, finally finding a large trunk buried behind stacks of useless items. Her gratitude grew for the old woman who had thought so much of Amy that she would risk her master's wrath.

Opening the lid, Amy sank to the dusty floor and began slowly lifting out item after item. Each piece was carefully inspected and placed lovingly to the side. At the very bottom of the trunk, well hidden by masses of clothing, was the pre-cious item she sought.

She took the leather-bound book into her hands, gently

stroking her fingers over the words on the cover. *Holy Bible.*

Opening to the first page, she found a lineage chart. Her mother had carefully recorded the date of her marriage and the date of Amy's birth. After that, the columns were empty. How sad. How tragic to have a life cut down at such a young age.

Continuing to flip through the pages, she found the contents page. Yes, it was coming back to her now. Her mother had taught her a song to memorize the books of the Bible. Frowning, she tried to recall more, but her mind seemed to be closed to other memories.

The introduction spoke of the books Matthew, Mark, Luke, and John being the four Gospels that Evan had spoken of. According to him, this was the place where she would find the Father she was seeking. Growing excited, she closed the book and hurriedly limped from the attic.

She went to her room and shut the door, hastening to the settee in front of the window. She sat down, found the book of Matthew, and started reading. The words settled into her heart like a healing balm. All along the pages, her mother's beautiful cursive handwriting spoke of thoughts and feelings shared only with her Maker. To Amy, this most precious book became even more treasured than before.

She continued reading for hours. A knock on the door interrupted her. Placing a finger in the book to mark her spot, she called impatiently, "Come in."

Sam entered carrying the lantern and stick he used to light the oil lamps. Amy stared at him in surprise.

"What are you doing lighting the lamps so early, Sam?"

He tutted at her. "Miss Amy, in case you haven't noticed,

it be getting dark outside."

Amy turned to look out the window, astonished that the sun was, indeed, descending to the horizon.

She waited until the servant had left, then resumed her reading. She had come to a part in the second book of Timothy where her mother's handwriting had stopped her. She read the verses and frowned. It spoke of women submitting to their husbands. In her mother's careful handwriting, the note said, *I must obey God rather than man. Acts 5:29.*

Amy quickly turned to the passage cited and read the whole chapter. A firm resolve settled into her own heart. Yes, from now on, she would obey God. That her father was bound to object chilled her, but she pushed the feeling aside.

Evan had stopped by as he had promised and had been able to talk Amy into taking a few days off. The fact that her father was gone from home probably accounted for her sudden willingness to comply.

Each day he had continued to check in on her, until he found himself counting the hours until he could do so again. Amy had decided that she would return to work today, so he hurried his steps a little faster so he wouldn't miss her.

He found her being helped into a buggy by the old servant, Sam. The old man grinned at Evan, his teeth showing whitely against his dark skin.

"How do, Mr. Brice?" he greeted. "Maybe now that you here, you can drive Miss Amy to work."

Evan met Amy's eyes, intrigued to find a light of joy shining from them. Surely that couldn't be on his account, as much as he would like to think so. He smiled.

"I can do that, Sam," he agreed, relieved that the old man had decided to accept him. The servant's fondness for Amy was evident.

"I don't want to bother you," Amy argued, but Evan sensed that it was a less than wholehearted response. The look in her eyes contradicted her words.

Evan climbed into the buggy and turned to Amy. "Are you comfortable?"

She nodded, and Evan snapped the reins to start the horses moving. He briefly allowed his gaze to pass over the finely matched pair of chestnuts, impressed despite himself.

"I appreciate this, Evan, but am I not keeping you from work?"

She glanced at his uniform before meeting his eyes.

"I'm just on my way. I can find my way from the *Gazette*; it's no problem."

She settled back to enjoy the ride, the day still bright although there were clouds forming on the horizon. It would storm before evening. Something occurred to Evan.

"If I'm taking you to work, who will return your buggy to the house?"

"I will."

Evan blinked at her. "Excuse me?"

She gave him an amused smile. "I'm quite capable of handling a buggy, Mr. Brice."

He ignored the first part, focusing instead on the second part. "Mr. Brice? What happened to Evan?"

Her cheeks would have rivaled the ripest apple. She seemed at a loss for words.

"I tell you what," Evan continued as he pulled up to the *Gazette* building, relieving her of the need to speak. "I'll come by and drive you home later. What time would you like me to do so?"

If anything, her cheeks darkened farther. "That's not necessary."

"It would be my pleasure," he told her, his voice slightly husky.

Her eyes met his, and she held his look for quite some time. Evan wanted nothing more right now than to repeat the kiss he had given her a few days ago. His attraction to her was spreading like a wildfire with no chance of control. Did she feel the same? Her chest rose and fell more rapidly than usual, and he realized that she was just as affected as he.

What might have happened, he wasn't certain, but just then Penney, Helen, and Jennie rounded the corner. They spotted Amy and rushed to her side.

"We missed you."

"How are you?"

"Are you sure you should be out?"

Their words tumbled over each other, and Amy grinned at them. Evan noticed the softening of her eyes as she stared at the three girls.

"I'm fine, just a little tender. It wasn't a sprain after all, just a strain."

Evan climbed down from the buggy, crossed to Amy's side, and lifted her to the ground. Their eyes met again briefly before Amy quickly pushed out of his hold and was soon surrounded by the three girls.

"I'll return for you at three o'clock, all right? Until then I'll have someone from one of the stables come and look after the horses."

Amy nodded, hobbling inside after Helen and Jennie. Penney turned back at the door and threw him a cheeky grin. He frowned fiercely at her, which only succeeded in bringing forth a giggle. Blowing him a kiss, she disappeared inside.

Evan sighed. It was too soon to be thinking of love. Still, he knew with certainty that he had found the woman he wanted to marry. The problem was, he doubted her father would ever agree.

Amy's world was perfect. She had a heavenly Father who loved her and friends who did as well. Just what classification she could place Evan into she hadn't quite decided. After years of being told that her looks would never get her a man, she was having a hard time taking Evan's little approaches as anything more than friendship, regardless of that one kiss that refused to be dislodged from her mind. She had firmly convinced herself that he was just feeling sorry for her.

She entered the mansion, and her perfect world suddenly collapsed. Her father was waiting for her in the hallway.

"Where have you been? It's after five o'clock."

She stood frozen into place. It had been more than three weeks since he left and somehow, Amy had convinced herself that he would be gone indefinitely. It hadn't been deliberate, just a thought simmering below the surface.

"I—I was with some friends."

His dark brows drew down ominously. "What friends?"

"Some girls who work with me at the paper."

"Madison has hired more women?" he asked in astonishment. "He must be out of his mind."

Amy brushed nervous hands down the sides of her hoopskirt. Her father's eyes followed the movement, their color darkening.

"And where did you get that rag?" he demanded.

Amy had dressed in one of her older dresses since she had been helping the girls at the mission home. She bit her lip nervously, not sure how to answer.

"Emma!" he bellowed, and the old woman hurried from the kitchen. She glanced from one to the other, anxiety radiating from her dark eyes.

"Take Miss Amy upstairs and help her change." The two women glanced at each other apprehensively. Amy started to follow the servant. "And see that that rag is burned."

Amy whirled on her parent to argue, but the look in his eyes stopped her. Something was wrong. His anger went beyond the fact that she was wearing an old dress. That look had always preceded some form of assault on those around him. Sucking in a breath, Amy quickly withdrew from the vicinity and followed Emma up the stairs.

"What's dat you muttering about?" Emma asked peevishly.

"I was praying," Amy answered her and continued her prayer.

Chapter 7

Amy's father was preoccupied. She didn't know what was going on in his little world that had him so on edge, but she was thankful to be spared from his watchfulness. It allowed her the freedom to continue her life much the way she did when he was absent for such long periods.

He had stayed in San Francisco much longer than usual, but she rarely saw him. He disappeared from the house at all hours of the day and night, which left her free to attend church services without fear of rebuke.

Although she loved being at church and being able to worship a God she had come to love, she had to admit, if only to herself, that having Evan's company made the experience much more enjoyable. She eagerly anticipated Sunday afternoons when he would walk home with her, both of them enjoying going over the sermon they had just heard. It was growing increasingly hard for her to get Evan off her mind and to keep from him the extent of her feelings.

She saw the way he treated Helen, Jennie, and Penney, and she could see no difference in his attention to herself. At times she thought there might be some greater emotion on his part, but she hadn't the confidence to pursue it. What if she was wrong?

She arrived home one afternoon to find her father in an agitated state. The servants were scurrying around the house doing his bidding as he commanded them from the hallway.

"You there," he called to one of the maids who was pulling down tapestries from the wall. "Forget that and pack the silver."

Amy looked around at all the activity in surprise. "Father, what's going on?"

He whirled around. The look on his face made her take a hasty step in retreat. "Where the devil have you been? Get upstairs and get your things packed."

Amy stood blinking at him in confusion. "Packed? Whatever for?"

He crossed the hall, taking her by the arm in a none-too-gentle manner, and propelled her toward the stairs. "Because I said so, that's why. Now move!"

Still she hesitated. "But where are we going and for how long? I can't just leave my job."

"I've already taken care of that. I told Madison that you wouldn't be returning."

"Father!" Amy stared at him, appalled.

He pulled his pocket watch from his jacket. "I haven't time to discuss it with you. There's a clipper ship waiting for us."

All the confusing ideas swirling around in her head finally settled into one thought. Cold chills raced through her.

"You're not coming back, are you?"

His dark eyes rested on her enigmatically. "*We're* not coming back."

"I don't want to go. I would rather stay here."

His smile was icy. "You have no say so in the matter. This house has been sold."

Amy couldn't breathe. Everything was happening too fast. She couldn't think straight. She looked at her father and saw only a man who had provided her with a house to live in. There had never been any love to make it into a home. If not for the servants, she would have had no one in her life to share with her any kind of feeling whatsoever.

Mouth settling into a firm line, she told him, "I'm not going with you. I'm staying here."

His set look was forbidding. "And just where will you stay?" He shook his head. "No, my dear. I have plans for you and David Andrews. You'll go, or else I'll—"

"You'll what, Father?" she interrupted. "Kill me like you killed Mother?"

His face paled. He glanced furtively around and noticed that the servants had stopped their moving about to listen. With a snarl, he grabbed Amy by the arm and dragged her into the parlor, firmly closing the door behind them.

"Are you out of your mind?" he hissed. "How dare you say a thing like that to me, and in front of the servants. I didn't kill your mother."

Amy felt strangely calm. This was the storm she had been preparing for for years, and now that it had come, she found that she was ready to do battle.

"You might not have lit the match, Father, but you ordered it done. You are just as much to blame for her death as whoever you hired to set that fire."

He glared at her, his hands forming into fists at his side. "Who told you such a pack of lies?"

"I figured it out by myself," she told him softly. "I investigated David Andrews and found that his father owns the company that insures your property. Between the two of you, you have become very wealthy men."

His breathing intensified. He looked at her as though seeing her for the first time. "You're smarter than I gave you credit for."

Calm purple eyes met glacial gray. "Why not? I *am* your daughter after all."

Amy saw her father's shoulders relax, and paradoxically her own tension increased. Her father was more dangerous when he was calm than when he was ranting.

"That's true," he told her ominously, "and until you are twenty-one, you are under *my* authority. I have the right to make you go with me, whether you like it or not."

Her legs began to shake. Not wanting her father to suspect her weakness, Amy sank gracefully to the chair behind her.

"And what would that accomplish?"

The look he fixed on her reminded her of a snake preparing to strike. "I owe Oscar Andrews a considerable debt, and I haven't the money to repay him."

"But you are an extremely wealthy man," Amy disagreed in confusion. "How much can you possibly owe him?"

Her father crossed to the liquor cabinet and poured himself a glass of brandy. He swirled the amber liquid, watching its circular movement in the glass.

"I've made some rather bad investments lately," he told her quietly. "I'm flat broke until I get the money from the last apartment fire, and I can't get that money until Oscar gets what I owe him."

The atmosphere in the room thickened with tension. Amy knew that this was a battle she *had* to win. She stared at her father, trying to fathom the reason he would be so determined to take her with him when he so obviously despised her. Comprehension dawned.

"You need my money!"

The look on his face confirmed her fears. He nonchalantly seated himself across from her, his casual pose belied by the anger she saw burning in his eyes.

"And that's where David comes in," he told her calmly.

She finally understood. Coming to her feet, she swept by her father and angrily headed for the door. She turned back to him, one hand on the doorknob. "You think you can sell me off? Well, let me tell you something, Father. I'm not some strumpet from Sydney Town."

She wasn't certain of the look she saw on his face, but it terrified her nonetheless.

"I'm going to pack," she told him, "but I will not be going with you. I will move my things into the Hamilton for the time being."

He lifted the brandy and took a long swallow, his dark gaze focused on her face, but he said nothing.

Amy hurried from the room, not certain if she had won the battle or not.

Evan felt the tension coiling within him. "I can't do it, sir."

The chief of police studied Evan from behind his desk. He leaned back in his chair, giving Evan a look that made him feel like a coward. Evan suddenly bristled.

"She's a friend of mine," he firmly rebutted. "I don't want to use her that way."

"You think she's not involved?"

"I'm certain of it, sir."

The chief steepled his fingers together. "Then where's the problem?"

Evan straightened. "You're asking me to question her like some common criminal."

Placing his palms against the desk, the chief lifted himself slightly from the chair, leaning forward until he could look directly into Evan's eyes.

"We have O'Halloran's confession of starting the fires. We know he was hired by Lattimer; now all we need is proof."

"I'm telling you that Amy won't know anything about it!"

The chief straightened at this impassioned declaration. His beetling brows drew together in a frown. "You're in love with the girl!"

Evan didn't deny it. He sighed heavily. He knew that if he didn't comply, the chief would in all probability pull Amy into the station for questioning.

"All right," he conceded. "I'll talk to her." He fixed his chief with a steely glare. "But I'll do it in my own way."

Chief Quincy nodded in understanding. "So be it."

Amy hurried down the stairs to the dining room of the

Hamilton. Evan had asked her to dinner here, and she was running late. Excitement at seeing him again was tempered by this morning's debacle. She was afraid to face him but equally afraid not to. She needed advice badly, and she thought Evan might be the one to help since he knew the law.

He saw her crossing the room and rose to his feet. How handsome he was. Amy's pulse increased, and her breathing quickened. It was so every time she saw him.

The expression on Evan's face was one of relief. He pulled out her chair, and she slid into it, smiling up at him as she did so. "Thank you."

He seated himself across from her. "I was afraid you weren't coming."

The waiter came to take their order, and they both waited until he had departed before speaking again.

"Actually," she told him, her lips twisting wryly, "I live here now."

She registered his surprise, but he waited for her to continue.

"My—my father and I had a disagreement."

"And he let you leave?"

She bit her lip. "That's what I wanted to talk to you about. Can I *legally* do so without his permission?"

Evan shook his head regretfully. "Not if he chooses to pursue the issue."

Amy felt the color drain from her face. "I *can't* go with him."

She saw the quickening of interest in Evan's eyes. He leaned forward, impaling her with a glance. "He's going somewhere?"

She sensed that this information was more important to

him than it was to her. She nodded. "He says that a clipper ship is waiting in the harbor to take us somewhere. He didn't say where."

Amy was reluctant to share with Evan the extent of her father's duplicity. After all was said and done, he was still her father. And she had no proof, although her father hadn't denied anything she had said except that he had killed her mother.

"From what you've told me, there's no love lost between you and your father. Why is he so adamant about taking you with him? Does he know about this place?" he asked, motioning around the room.

She dropped her gaze to the table, twisting her water glass nervously. "He knows that I am here, but he doesn't know that I own it."

"I thought that might be the case."

She glanced up at him quickly, surprised that he had guessed. Evan smiled wryly.

"Anyway," she continued, "he wants me to marry David Andrews."

Seeing the expression on his face, instinctively Amy sat back in her seat. She had never seen him look that way before. He appeared ready to kill.

"Are you going to?" he asked, the quietness of his voice negated by the look in his eyes.

How could he even ask such a thing? Perhaps she hadn't been quite clear in expressing her feelings for Evan, but surely he could tell that she was in love with *him*.

"Of course not," she denied hotly. "I could never marry

someone I didn't love. Why do you think I'm here now?"

He leaned forward, his expression intent. "Amy, the man who started the apartment fire has confessed to it. We have him in custody."

At the look on her face, he reached out and enfolded her hand within his own. The warmth and strength of it implied a security she was far from feeling.

"Amy," he asked quietly, "was your father involved?"

So he knew. Hot color flooded her face. She jerked her hand from his, embarrassed. What must he think of her, to be related to such a man? She lifted her eyes to meet his potent gaze. Did he believe she had something to do with these fires? He had seemed to before.

As though reading her thoughts, he shook his head.

"No, Amy. I don't believe you had anything to do with it."

She sighed heavily. "Evan, I confronted my father about it, but although he didn't deny it, neither did he admit to it. He only said that he owed Oscar Andrews money that he couldn't repay until he had the insurance money from the fire."

"Who is Oscar Andrews?"

"He owns the insurance company that insures my father's properties."

Evan tensed. "This could be the connection we are looking for."

The waiter brought their meal, interrupting their conversation. Amy could hardly eat it. Her insides were churning like the ocean in a storm. She pushed the food around on her plate.

Evan took the fork from her fingers, his look one of understanding. Amy turned away. She couldn't bear it if he pitied her.

After dinner, Evan asked her to walk with him in the gardens at the back of the hotel. They ambled along the seashell paths together, each intent with their own thoughts. Evan reached out and took her hand, cupping it within the crook of his arm.

"Amy, there's something I need to tell you."

What now? She had had so many revelations this day, she wasn't certain if she could handle anymore. "I'm listening."

He stopped suddenly and turned her to look at him. The emotions chasing themselves across his face frightened her with their strength.

"Amy, I'm in love with you," he blurted out, stunning her with his declaration.

"But. . ."

He placed his fingers against her lips. "Let me finish. I don't know how any of this is going to turn out, but please trust in me."

The words caused her to panic. "What do you mean?"

His look softened, and he pulled her close, his brown eyes roving restlessly over her face. "I can't explain right now. Do you trust me?"

"Evan, I—"

He gave her a gentle shake. "Do you trust me?"

She placed her palms against his chest and felt his heart thundering beneath them. She finally met his look. "I not only trust you, but I love you, too."

He smiled widely, his brown eyes taking on a strange glitter. He answered her words with a kiss that lingered in her mind long after their lips had parted.

"There's something I have to do," he told her anxiously. "I'll come back later this evening and explain."

He released her and turned to leave. She placed a restraining hand upon his arm.

"Evan, it's not. . .you won't be in any danger, will you?"

He took her back into his arms and kissed her again. His voice was like soft velvet when he spoke.

"Darling, I'll be back, I promise you." He grinned suddenly. "We need to finish this very interesting conversation."

She stared into his love-filled eyes, and all her doubts seemed to vanish into thin air. "I'll be waiting," she told him softly, feeling as though she were walking in a dream.

He kissed her again, briefly, and left her standing there, prey to all kinds of terrible thoughts. She was too restless to return indoors, so she sat on a nearby bench. The garden was bare of ornamentation, the cold having frosted the trees and bushes long ago. Still, the night was beautiful, made more so by Evan's declaration of love. She hugged the knowledge to herself, the wonder of it almost too much to bear.

The stars were bright in the dark winter sky. She marveled at their beauty and the thought that the God who had placed them there was her own heavenly Father. Oh, how she had grown to love Him in such a short time.

In the next instant, those stars were obliterated as someone threw a sack over her head. Her screams went unheard as she was bodily lifted and carried away.

Chapter 8

Evan hurried along the pier, white-hot rage racing through his blood. He had returned to find Amy missing. A thorough search had failed to find any sign of her. He had no doubt where he would find her. If she had been hurt, he wasn't certain he could control the feelings raging within him.

He found the ship he was searching for. Moving into the concealment of a stack of crates waiting for loading, he searched for signs of activity.

There appeared to be only one man pacing along the deck of the ship. Evan weighed his options. He could merely walk up and show the man his badge and insist on searching the ship. However, since Lattimer did most of his business in the gambling halls and bordellos of Sydney Town, Evan somehow doubted his office would be respected. More likely he would find himself at the bottom of the harbor.

The other option was to sneak on board, search until he found Amy, and hope that they could leave undetected. He opted for the latter.

Staying in the shadows, he stealthily crossed the dock until he was at the front of the ship. Ignoring the gangplank, he grasped the rope that tied the ship to the dock and, wrapping his legs around the rope, began to pull himself up.

His muscles strained against the activity, and he chastised himself for becoming so weak. Working in a lumber mill in Plattsville had helped him develop a strong body, but walking the streets of San Francisco had certainly softened muscles that only a short time before would have made light of the climb.

He heaved himself over the side of the ship, landing silently on his feet. When the guard moved to the other end of the ship, he quickly made his way down the steps to the compartments below.

Several doors lined the hallway, and he stood uncertainly, trying to decide his best move. The decision was made for him when he heard a slight pounding on the door to his right, and a muffled voice called out.

"Let me out of here!"

"Amy?"

His call was met by silence then a furious pounding. "Evan! I'm in here!"

He searched but could find no sign of a key. Worry lines furrowed his brow. In a moment, the guard would return.

"Amy," he called, "move away from the door."

He heard shuffling inside and knew that she had heard him. Quickly, he kicked at the door and heard a satisfying crack. Another kick, and the door slammed inward.

He hastened inside to find Amy huddled against the farther wall. With a cry, she rushed across the room and threw herself into his arms.

"Oh, Evan! I knew you would come. I prayed and prayed, and I knew you would come."

He held her close, trying to quiet her tears. The rage that had given him strength now gave way to concern.

"Hush, darling," he soothed. "Are you all right?"

She nodded, sniffling into his chest.

"We need to get you out of here." He glanced at the door, once again weighing his options. There was no way Amy could shimmy down that rope. It was far too dangerous to even contemplate. His jaw set firmly, he pulled back from Amy, studying her face. With his thumbs, he wiped the tears from her cheeks and gave her a quick kiss on the lips. She met his look calmly, and he was relieved to see no signs of hysteria. His Amy was a lot stronger than he had given her credit for.

"Stay here," he commanded quietly. "I'll be right back."

Panic flared in her eyes for a moment. He met her look patiently. "Honey, trust me."

Taking a deep breath, she nodded acquiescence. He quickly left the cabin and quietly dispatched the guard. In less than five minutes, he returned.

Amy once again moved into his arms. "This is like a nightmare," she whispered.

"It'll soon be over," he promised, uncertain whether he could hold to it. "Are you ready?"

She looked up at him with complete confidence. He felt humbled by her trust.

"I'm ready."

"Follow me, and be as quiet as you can." He stopped, turning to face her. He pulled her forward by her forearms, staring intently into her eyes. "If I tell you to run, run. All right? Don't stop, and don't look back."

The fear returned to her eyes. "Evan, I couldn't just leave you."

His lips tightened into a grim line. "I can take care of myself. I need to know that you are out of danger. Promise me."

She bit her lip in indecision, and his grip tightened. "Promise me, Amy!"

"All right," she assented reluctantly. "I promise."

As they hurried down the corridor, they could hear loud laughter coming from below. Evan had no doubt about what was keeping the crew's attention. Gambling was a leading problem among the riff-raff of the city. He was just thankful that they were engrossed elsewhere.

They were able to slip from the wharf and return to the hotel without being accosted. Amy breathed a sigh of relief when they reached her room.

Evan pushed Amy into a chair and knelt before her. He took her cold, trembling hands between his warmer ones and gently began to massage them, trying to reassure her.

She looked him in the eye, and he read the sadness lurking in the dark depths of her own eyes. "I never thought he would do such a thing," she whispered. She shuddered, and he stood, taking her with him. He held her close, his own heart racing like a flame rushing toward a stick of dynamite. The simile seemed appropriate. Just under the surface of his calm demeanor was a bomb waiting to explode.

"What do I do now?" she asked him. "If he would resort

to such an action as kidnapping to get his way, there's no telling what he might do when he finds his plans have been thwarted."

She pulled back and searched his face, the color suddenly leaving hers. "Evan, he might hurt you if he finds out that you helped me."

He brushed a stray tendril of hair back from her face, tucking it gently behind her ear. "Darling, let me worry about that."

He waited for a smile, but none was forthcoming.

"Evan, I can't let him harm you."

His finger traced her lips, his intent look meeting her more serious one. "To have and to hold, in sickness and in health, 'til death us do part," he quoted softly. "That's what I want for us, Amy."

Her mouth parted in surprise. "Are you asking me to marry you?"

A smile touched his lips. "I told you we would have to finish our conversation. Now seems as good a time as any. What do you say? Will you marry me?"

"I think not."

The deep voice startled them both. So intent had they been on each other, they had failed to hear the opening of the door. They turned to find Cyril Lattimer standing just inside the doorway flanked by two burly men.

"Father."

"I'm afraid I have to interrupt this tender scene," he told them sarcastically. "You see, Mr. . . ."

"Brice," Evan supplied, pushing Amy behind him. He faced her father while studying the other two men at his side.

"Well, Mr. Brice," Cyril continued, "Amy is already betrothed."

Amy stepped to Evan's side. "No! That's not true. I don't know why this is so important to you, Father, but you aren't having things your way this time."

Cyril motioned to the two men, and they moved closer. Evan tensed, and he saw Amy's eyes widen.

"If it's the money, Father, then take it. I give it to you."

Her father stared at her in surprise, something undefined flickering through his eyes. He shook his head regretfully.

"That's not possible. You see, your mother left her money in trust to you until you turned twenty-one or were married."

"Well, in two weeks I will be able to give it to you, then."

He shook his head again. "No, that won't work. I owe some people money, and I have two days to get it to them, or I will wind up dead."

Evan kept a vigil on the other two men, glancing briefly at Cyril. "What about all your insurance money? What happened to it?" he asked.

Cyril's eyes narrowed. "I don't know what you're talking about."

Evan fixed his look on the older man. "I think you do. You see, we have O'Halloran in custody, and he's already confessed to starting the fires. It's only a matter of time before he gives over to us who paid him. Oscar Andrews should be heading for jail in the next few hours."

He could see the fear enter Cyril's eyes. "All the more reason that I need my daughter's money," he stated dangerously.

Folding his arms across his chest, Evan tried to appear

relaxed. "Gambling," he suggested softly and had the satisfaction of seeing the other man pale considerably. Evan glanced at the other two men. "Let me guess. Sydney Ducks."

The other two men smiled slyly. One nodded agreement. "And we're here to see that Cyril pays what he owes our boss."

Evan knew there was no way that he could overpower the three men together. He offered up a plea for help, concerned for Amy's safety.

"Enough of this," Cyril snapped. "Get the girl, and let's get out of here."

As the other two men moved forward, Evan felt the boards move under his feet. Thinking it was the vibration of the two men's feet, he readied himself for a fight. But the vibration intensified, and the whole room began to shake. Fixtures on the table started sliding toward the edge. The two men stopped, glancing fearfully around them.

"Earthquake!" one shouted.

Evan grabbed for Amy, shoving her toward the door. "Run, Amy!"

Plaster began cracking from the walls and tumbling to the floor. Evan knew this was going to be a substantial earthquake. So apparently did the others. They instinctively headed for the door and the safety of the outside.

So consumed were they with their own safety, no one tried to stop Amy as she hurried out the door. Evan was only a step behind her. He could hear the others trying to shove their way out the door together.

The rumbling intensified, and the structure began to disintegrate around them. Pandemonium reigned as others in the hotel tried to get outside.

Evan and Amy made it to the street but not to safety. Buildings were collapsing all around them. Amy screamed as glass shattered around her. Pulling her across the street, Evan shoved them into the entry of one of the few brick buildings on the street. He wrapped his arms around her, pushing her face against his chest.

What seemed an eternity were mere moments in time. Before long the earth stopped shuddering and settled back to normal. Evan slowly released Amy, and together, they peered out at the damage around them.

The hotel still stood, a testimony to Amy's mother's foresight in having an engineer design it. The damage to it had been minimal. Several other buildings had collapsed in upon themselves, their rubble spilling over into the street. People were coming out from the safety of their positions to stare around them as the dust slowly settled.

Evan told Amy to stay where she was and then went to check for anyone who might be injured. He recognized the lifeless arm peeking out from under the roof section of the building next to the hotel. He felt movement beside him and turned to find Amy peering past him. Her horrified eyes rose to his.

He knelt and felt for a pulse but found none.

Her voice trembled. "Is he dead?"

Taking a deep breath, he looked up at her. "I'm afraid so."

She sank to her knees beside Evan, and he placed a comforting arm around her. Tears formed in her eyes.

"I should have tried harder to tell him about the Lord."

Taking her by the chin, Evan turned her to face him. "It's not your fault, sweetheart. He made his choices, just as you made yours."

"I know, but I can't help but wonder—"

"Gambling is an obsession, Amy. If you let it, it will eventually rule your life just as it did your father's." He got to his feet and held out his hand to her. "Come on. Let me take you home. I'll come back and see to things here."

~

Amy sank to the sofa in her room. Although the earthquake had been severe, the damage to the city had been restricted to a few localities. Even now the fire department was working furiously to put out the fires that had been started.

She buried her face in her hands. She was dirty and disheveled, but she simply didn't care. In a matter of a few days, her life had been torn apart.

Thank God for Evan.

"Miss Amy?"

She turned to stare blankly at the servant. "What is it, Emma?"

"That nice Mr. Brice is here."

Amy rushed from the room and hurried downstairs. Evan was waiting for her in the parlor, and he rose to greet her. She stopped short of reaching him and hesitated. His smile was strained, but he opened his arms to her, and she gladly walked into his embrace. He held her tightly, his voice muffled against her neck.

"I want to marry you now. Tonight."

Amy shivered, and he pulled her even closer.

"I want that, too," she whispered back, "but I can't. Not. . .yet."

He pulled back to look into her face, his own unsmiling. She was weary beyond description, probably more from nerves than anything else. Still, so much had happened in such a short time, she needed time to adjust to it. Would he understand if she told him so?

He touched her lips briefly with his own. "I know." His smile was halfhearted. "I'm afraid I'm not a very patient man once I have decided on something."

Amy touched his cheek with gentle fingers. "I want to be married in our church with your sister and her friends as my bridesmaids. I want to say my vows before God and let everyone know just how blessed I am." She wrapped her arms around his neck. "I love you so much, Evan."

Always before Evan had held himself in reserve as had she, but this time, his kiss started a spark within her that burst into flame and threatened to scorch her with its intensity. Their attraction had been fierce from the first time they had met, yet Amy knew that beyond the flames of their passion would be a lifetime of love.

A lifetime of forever.

DARLENE MINDRUP

Darlene Mindrup lives with her husband in Goodyear, Arizona. She has raised two children, daughter Dena and son Devon. Having served in the Air Force herself, Darlene is proud of her two children, one who has married a Marine, the other who is now proudly serving in the Air Force. After nineteen books with Barbour, Darlene still finds her most rewarding heroines to be those who are unconventionally lacking in beauty. As she has always said, "Romance is not just for the young and beautiful." Nowadays, Darlene spends a good portion of her time being the church secretary for the West Olive Church of Christ.

Web of Deceit

by Carol Cox

Chapter 1

May 1860

The pain resulting from a hornet sting may be relieved by plunging the affected part into cold water as long as may be tolerated. If stung numerous times all at once, a dose of salts is recommended.

Jennie Montgomery read the lines she had just penned and curled her lip. If someone had been stung by hornets, would they take time to look up a remedy in the *Gazette*? And could any information possibly be more boring for readers not so afflicted?

She laid down her pen then remembered the letter her employer had given her earlier. She sifted through the notes on her desk and fixed the elegant stationery with a baleful glare. The copperplate handwriting flowed gracefully across the page:

To remove spots of grease from a tablecloth, apply a hot iron to brown paper placed over the stain. You will find this a most efficacious remedy.

A brief line followed: "From the pen of Mrs. Sherman Widdesly."

Mrs. Widdesly had made it quite clear to Russell Madison, editor of the *Golden Gate Gazette*, that she expected full credit for her brilliant idea. And Mr. Madison had made it quite clear to Jennie that she would comply with Mrs. Widdesly's request.

Jennie harrumphed. "As if the woman ever lifted a finger to do a spot of cleaning in her life."

"Talking to yourself?" Amy Lattimer teased from her desk across the room.

Jennie felt herself flush. "I'm just aggravated. Mrs. Widdesly demands full credit for this idea, and I know full well she must have gotten it from her housekeeper. Mrs. Widdesly wouldn't know how to heat an iron, much less use one."

Amy chuckled. "You'd better not let Mr. Madison hear you talk like that about the wife of one of the *Gazette*'s biggest advertisers."

"I know, I know." Jennie copied the spot removal tip under the hornet solution, dutifully adding Mrs. Widdesly's name. She blotted the paper then shoved it to one side of her desk. At least that unpleasant task was finished.

"Try not to look so gloomy," Amy admonished. "I know you hate doing the 'Miss Minerva's Helpful Hints' column, but it could be worse. At least Mr. Madison didn't foist the obituaries off on you."

"Amy's right," Helen Morgan chimed in. "You could be spending your days trying to sum up someone's life in a paragraph or two."

Jennie nodded and rested her arms on the desktop. "Did

you ever stop to think how short life is?"

Penney Brice looked up from the typesetter. "Whatever brought on that dreary thought?"

"Talking about obituaries, I suppose. We read a person's name, their age, a bit about their life. Do you suppose any of them knew they would never see another summer, never celebrate another Christmas? Did they realize all their life goals?"

"And were they prepared for the life to come?" Helen added soberly.

"Exactly." Jennie pushed back from her desk and paced the office floor. "None of us knows when our days will end." She threw her arms wide. "How many years do I have ahead of me? And what am I going to do to make them count? My great-aunt Hattie lived to be ninety-two. If I hold out that long, that gives me another seventy years or so."

"Look outside," Penney countered. "It's a glorious spring day. Concentrate on the joys of life instead of letting your mind dwell on such morbid thoughts."

"I suppose you're right." Jennie resumed her seat and sorted through her notes. Her thoughts *had* been gloomy lately, filled with a vague feeling that life was slipping past at a breakneck pace. It would be hard to explain it to the other girls—even more difficult for them to understand the need she felt to make up for the lost years of her youth and for her family's transgressions.

When Amy talked Mr. Madison into hiring Jennie, Helen, and Penney, the idea of working for the *Gazette* had thrilled her. She imagined herself doing something productive and fulfilling her sense of adventure at the same time. Instead, she found herself rooted at a desk, penning the dullest pieces imaginable. Hornet sting remedies, of all things! She wanted to do more. So much more.

She sighed and skimmed her notes for material to put into the next day's installment of Miss Minerva's column. On the other hand, look how far she had come. A year ago, who would have imagined Jennie Montgomery sitting behind a respectable desk at a respectable newspaper in a respectable city?

A smile tugged one corner of her mouth. Not everyone would call the idea of a woman working a desk job an honorable one. Many people looked on members of the press—male or female—as even lower than those in the acting profession. And San Francisco's level of respectability. . .well, that depended on which part of the city a person might be talking about.

Even so, it was honest work, a far cry from a youth spent bilking the public and staying one step ahead of the law. Hopelessly boring, perhaps, but honest.

The outer door crashed open, and Gabe Neilson, one of the newsboys who hawked the *Gazette* on street corners throughout the city, came roaring down the center aisle. "Hey, everybody, have you heard? There's been an explosion in a warehouse down at one of the wharfs! Three killed, maybe more!" His feet pounded along the wood floor until he reached Mr. Madison's office. He burst through the door and banged it shut behind him.

Silence held the office in its grip for an instant; then the sound of chairs screeching across the floor filled the room as everyone converged on the windows.

"Can you see it from here?"

"Nah, too far away to see the wharfs."

"Look at the smoke. It's over in that area, all right."

Jennie stood on tiptoe and strained to see over the shoulders that blocked the window in front of her. Her heart pumped when she spotted the pillar of smoke, imagining what the scene must be like. Now *that* was a story! If only. . .

She shook her head. *Don't get your hopes up. That isn't likely to happen.* Sighing, she returned to her desk and resumed her perusal of her notes.

A shadow fell across the corner of Jennie's desk. She looked up to see Russell Madison standing over her, his ever-present cigar puffing like a chimney. Strands of silver hair stood on end like a porcupine's quills, making his agitation over the warehouse explosion evident.

"Miss Montgomery, you've hounded me for weeks telling me your talent is being wasted on household hints. Are you ready to get out and cover a story?"

At last! Jennie sprang to her feet.

"I'm on my way, sir." She settled her hat on her head and jammed the hatpin in place. "Do you know which warehouse the explosion was in? Never mind, I can follow the smoke and the crowds."

She flashed a triumphant smile at her friends and tried not to wince at Penney's wistful expression. She knew her friend longed to cover news stories every bit as much as she did.

Try not to be too disappointed, Penney. If I do a good job on this, there will be assignments aplenty for both of us.

Jennie gathered her parasol and a notebook and snatched up a handful of pencils. She could see it now: a story with her byline on the front page, above the fold.

Through the flurry of thoughts that vied for attention in her mind, she became aware that Mr. Madison was speaking.

Shouting, to be accurate. "Where do you think you're going?"

Jennie turned to face him. "Excuse me?" She looked at Mr. Madison with concern. His face had gone the color of a ripe tomato. The combination of red cheeks against his silver hair and beard brought a fleeting recollection of Clement Moore's St. Nicholas. Jennie took a closer look and shook her head, dispelling the fancy. This was no benevolent Santa Claus.

Russell Madison's teeth clamped his cigar in a viselike grip. Bits of ash flew from the tip and scattered around the room. He ripped the stogie from between his lips with his left hand and jabbed it in her direction.

"I asked you where you think you are going," he bellowed.

Jennie blinked. "To cover the explosion at the warehouse, of course."

Russell Madison snorted. A stream of smoke curled up from his noxious cigar, filling the air with a gray haze. "On a story of *that* magnitude? Hardly. I need someone who knows what he's doing to handle that one. I've sent word to Nick Edwards. He's on his way."

Mr. Madison shook the cigar like a schoolmarm waving her pointer at a dull student. "I want you to cover Vincent Collier's funeral. I'd scheduled Nick to follow that, but I have to pull him off, now that we have a real story to cover."

"But don't you think—"

"I think you can handle the funeral just fine." He assumed a kindly expression Jennie found more infuriating than his shouting. "Take some notes on the eulogy, who's attending, what the ladies are wearing, that kind of thing. Have my driver take you. You can just make it to the cemetery if you leave now."

He turned on his heel and headed back toward his office then slowed and called over his shoulder, "About four paragraphs ought to do it. Just enough to cover the basics."

Chapter 2

I need someone who knows what he's doing.' Ha!" Jennie's angry mutter melded with the clatter of carriage wheels. " 'I pulled Nick off because we have a real story to cover.' Honestly!" As if Mr. Madison's favorite reporter didn't already have a lengthy list of stories to his credit. " 'I think you can handle the funeral,'" she mimicked. Just as well she rode alone in the carriage. Here, she could vent her ire without fear of being considered insubordinate.

"Yes, I think I can just about manage that. Seeing as how the star of the show won't be likely to jump up and run away." She folded her arms and huffed. "I hope you aren't expecting a quote from the deceased, Mr. Madison."

The carriage slowed, and Jennie took note of her surroundings again. The driver maneuvered the conveyance into a place among the vehicles that had already arrived and jumped down to help Jennie to the ground.

She joined the stream of mourners and followed them across the broad expanse of grass. Up ahead, six pallbearers slid the casket from the hearse and struggled under its weight while they carried it to the graveside.

Jennie stopped a respectful distance away and focused her attention on the minister preparing to address the solemn group. After reading the twenty-third Psalm, the clergyman looked over the assembly with mournful eyes.

"San Francisco has lost one of its finest citizens," he began. "Vincent Collier spent his life in service to our fair city. His untimely demise will be mourned by many, and he will be sorely missed."

Jennie's pencil flew over the notebook pages, scribbling down the salient points of the eulogy. From the minister's account, Mr. Collier had been one of San Francisco's leading lights, both in business and social standing. With interests in shipping, freight, and real estate, and as part owner of Pacific Mutual Investments, the man had put his fingers in a lot of pies.

"A regular Little Jack Horner," Jennie murmured.

A gentleman standing nearby looked down at her with a disapproving air. Jennie felt her cheeks sting, and she pressed her lips together to hold back any further outburst.

She scanned the crowd, seeking faces she could name in her article. Henry F. Teschemacher, mayor of San Francisco, stood at the front of the mourners, as befitted his status. Beside him, Jennie recognized two city supervisors. She scribbled furiously, composing the headline in her mind.

"City turns out to mourn local businessman." Yes, that had a nice ring to it. Now she needed more names—social equals who would reflect the deceased's standing in the community. She searched the crowd, wishing she had positioned herself so she could see their faces better.

The minister called for prayer, and Jennie bowed her head. After the "amen," she seized the opportunity to walk among the clusters of mourners. Other than the mayor and city supervisors, she didn't recognize any of the others by name. Hardly surprising, since girls of Jennie's background didn't associate with the upper classes. Still, she needed names for her article. Mr. Madison might want only four paragraphs on the interment of the late, lamented Mr. Collier, but Jennie was determined to make it the four best paragraphs to ever land on Mr. Grouchy Madison's desk.

Sidling through the crowd, she dipped her head to the groups she passed. And all the while, she listened, adding names and snatches of phrases about the deceased to the mental store she would draw from when writing her article.

Twenty yards ahead, a figure stepped out from behind a grave marker. Jennie slowed and gave the man a closer look. His rough dress and general air of shabbiness hardly fit in with the well-dressed attendees.

Jennie watched, noting the way he kept a distance between himself and the edge of the crowd. He skirted the perimeter, bouncing on his toes from time to time and craning his neck as though looking for someone.

What is someone like that doing here? Her curiosity piqued, Jennie came to a halt and followed him with her gaze. *Could he be someone Vincent Collier befriended as an act of charity?* That might explain his presence here, as well as his reticence about approaching the polished group. The gathering began to disperse, with people leaving in twos and threes. A few, upon spotting the shabby man, made a point of stepping out of his path. Jennie winced. She knew all too well the feeling of being snubbed by those who considered her their social inferior.

She glanced at her notebook, seeing plenty of material there to cover everything Mr. Madison asked for. With a sense of satisfaction, she snapped it shut and started toward the carriage.

On second thought. . .

Jennie let her gaze drift past the crowd until she spotted the shabby man again. He still seemed to be seeking someone. If he did turn out to be someone Mr. Collier had helped, there might be a story in that, a human interest angle that might entice Mr. Madison to run a longer piece.

Jennie made her way through the departing mourners, formulating the questions she should ask. She would show Mr. Madison who had a nose for news! A flutter of nervousness tickled her insides. Would the shabby man mind talking to her? Surely not, she reasoned. The fellow might be as excited as Mrs. Widdesly at the prospect of seeing his name in print.

The seedy-looking man continued to circle the crowd, swiveling his head from side to side. Jennie wondered if he hoped for a glimpse of the casket, and a warm feeling of sympathy spread through her.

Threading her way through the throng, Jennie narrowed the distance between them and prepared to close in on her quarry. Up ahead, she saw Shabby, as she dubbed him in her mind, come to an abrupt halt. He stood staring at the group still standing at the graveside. His body tensed, like that of a hunting dog on point, then he beckoned with a quick wave of his hand.

Jennie swung her head to the left, wondering who Shabby might possibly know in that moneyed crowd. Near the waiting grave, a cluster of people surrounded the widow. All focused their attention on the grieving woman. . .with the exception of a tall, slender man. One of the pallbearers, Jennie remembered. The pallor of his face stood out in marked contrast to his black frock coat. He looked down his aquiline nose in Shabby's direction and gave his head an almost imperceptible shake.

Jennie swiveled her head to the right and stared at Shabby. He beckoned again, his gesture insistent. Back to the left. The pallbearer shook his head again, more decisively this time.

What is going on here? Jennie's gaze darted back to Shabby. He thrust his jaw forward and strode toward the group with a pugnacious swagger.

Fascinated, Jennie followed at a distance. The pallbearer left the graveside and walked stiffly toward a tall monument depicting the angel Gabriel with his trumpet.

Shabby sauntered over to him, a smug expression on his features. He joined the pallbearer, and the two stepped behind the statue.

Taking a cue from their furtive actions, Jennie slipped over to a large family marker. She took shelter behind the block of granite, taking care that it concealed her wide skirt. From her vantage point, she peered around the edge of the stone and found she had a clear view of the unlikely duo, deep in conversation.

The pallbearer's expression could have been chiseled from marble, so pale were his features. He leaned over the shorter man as though making some demand. Shabby slashed the air with his arm in an abrupt, negative gesture.

Forgetting her original reason for coming to the cemetery, Jennie leaned forward, mesmerized by the sight of the two angry men. With all her heart, she wished she could move close enough to hear what was being said, but their tense features and emphatic gestures convinced her she should remain unseen.

Her hands clenched in excitement. Paper crackled under her fingers. The notebook! Hurriedly, she flipped the pages to an empty sheet and made a quick sketch of Shabby, eyebrows drawn together and lips pulled back in a snarl. Yes, she thought, giving the drawing a quick glance. Anyone who knew him would be able to recognize the likeness. She turned to the next page and sketched the pallbearer, fist clenched and arm upraised, his face suffused with anger.

By the time she drew in the final strokes, the two men stood nose to nose. The pallbearer spoke, and Shabby answered with a few words of his own. Then he punched his grimy finger into the taller man's chest as if driving his point home, pivoted on his heel, and walked away without a backward glance. The pall-bearer stood frozen for a moment, his face pale and stern, then returned to the group attending the widow.

Jennie stood riveted to her spot behind the monument. Shabby had disappeared from view. The pallbearer now bent over the woman in widow's weeds. To all appearances, every-thing was as it had been before. Jennie knew better. Every instinct told her she had just witnessed something significant. But what?

She glanced around to find most of the mourners had already dispersed while she watched the altercation. It didn't matter. She had more than enough material to fill Mr. Madison's four paragraphs, plus an additional tidbit to chew over. A very interesting tidbit indeed.

"Here is my story." Jennie laid a page containing four neatly penned paragraphs on the editor's desk and clasped her hands at her waist.

Russell Madison grunted acknowledgment and slid the sheet to one side, never raising his gaze from the copy he was editing.

Jennie waited a moment longer, then cleared her throat.

Mr. Madison glanced up. "Is there anything else, Miss Montgomery?"

Jennie gathered her courage and tried to keep her voice steady. "The description of the graveside service is only the beginning. I'm convinced there is far more to this than what appears on the surface." Seeing she had her boss's attention at last, she went on to describe the argument at the cemetery. "I would like your permission to follow up on the story."

Her employer's right eyebrow lifted a fraction of an inch. "What story? You saw two men having a heated discussion."

"You didn't see their expressions," Jennie protested. "I've seldom seen men look so angry."

"Which proves nothing." Madison blew out a swirl of cigar smoke. "One of them just helped carry his friend to his final resting place. Emotions run high at a time like that. You can hardly blame him for being irritated by such an audacious interruption."

"It was far more than irritation," Jennie began.

Russell Madison waved his hand as though shooing a pesky fly. "More than likely, that seedy fellow was nothing more than a panhandler. They're known to hit people up when their resistance is low. He probably figured the pallbearer would be an easy mark."

Jennie stifled an unladylike snort. Mr. Madison was a fine one to be talking about spotting an easy mark. Jennie knew more about reading people than he could imagine. But she couldn't very well explain that to him. Instead, she opened her mouth to argue further.

Her employer cut her off with an upheld hand and gave her a patient smile that set her teeth on edge. "You've done your job, and I appreciate your willingness to help. Don't make more of this than there really is. Better get back to working on tomorrow's Miss Minerva column. We can't afford to get behind in the newspaper business."

Jennie marched back to her desk. Images of the two furious men flashed through her mind. She knew she was right. But it seemed there would be no convincing Mr. Madison.

Chapter 3

"What's bothering you, Jennie? You've hardly said a word all evening." Helen looked across their regular table in the dining room of the Hamilton Hotel. Concern crinkled her forehead.

Jennie crumbled her roll and piled the bits in a neat mound on her plate. Briefly she reviewed what she had seen and Russell Madison's dismissive reaction. "There's a story there," she concluded. "I'm sure of it. But how do I make Mr. Madison listen?"

"Don't ask me." Helen sipped water from her tumbler. "I'm the bookkeeper, remember? My strength is in dealing with numbers, not people."

Penney offered a sympathetic smile. "If I knew how to get anything across to that man, both of us would be covering stories on a regular basis." She squeezed Jennie's hand. "Why does he need to rely on male reporters who have to slip their stories to him undercover because of the strike when he has us around?"

"My point precisely." Jennie pressed down on the pile of crumbs with her fork, smashing them into a gummy mass. She pushed her plate away and stood. "We could have written any of the stories the *Gazette* published this week. . .if he would only give us a chance."

Helen patted her lips with her napkin and folded it neatly beside her plate. "But he isn't likely to do that, is he?" She scooted her chair back. "I know how much the two of you want to make your mark as reporters, but sometimes we just need to face facts."

Jennie exchanged a glance with Penney and saw her own frustration mirrored in her friend's eyes. It would serve no purpose to start an argument with Helen, but neither one of them had any intention of giving up their dreams just because a certain bullheaded editor didn't recognize their capability. Yet.

Penney pressed her hand over her mouth to conceal a yawn. "Let's go up to our room and talk. We can think of ways to persuade Mr. Madison while we get ready for bed."

Jennie bit back a sharp reply. Mere talk wouldn't solve a thing. Tired as she felt after the tumult of the day, the last thing she wanted was to sit tamely discussing their options. . .or the lack of them.

"I believe I'll take a short stroll," she told her friends. "I need some fresh air."

Penney gasped. "By yourself? That isn't safe, Jennie. You don't know what kind of unsavory characters you might meet out there." Her mouth stretched wide in another yawn. "We'll go with you, won't we, Helen?"

"No." Jennie forced a smile to soften her abrupt response. "You're both exhausted. Go on up to the room and rest. I won't be long. When I get back, we'll finish our conversation. I'm simply too wound up to sit still right now."

Penny wavered, obviously torn. "You should be all right, as long as you don't wander far." She glanced at Helen for confirmation.

The older girl nodded doubtfully. "I suppose so. Just be sure you come back before it gets dark."

"I promise." Jennie shooed her friends toward the staircase, where they hovered at the bottom step like anxious mother hens. "Go upstairs and relax. I'll be up as soon as I've worked off some of this steam."

Outside, Jennie breathed deeply of the salt breeze. Gulls wheeled overhead, splitting the quiet with high, keening cries. The tangy air lightened her spirits in spite of the mist that hung over the city like a gauzy curtain. She walked on, enjoying the feeling of being on her own. Much as she loved her friends, she needed this time to herself.

She skirted a puddle that lay in her path and thought back to Penney and Helen's concern about the unsavory denizens of San Francisco. A wry smile twisted her lips. They saw the city and its perils from the perspective of law-abiding citizens, nervous at the thought of danger and the places where it lurked.

Jennie, on the other hand, had more experience with the seamy side of life than her friends would ever guess. *What would they think if they knew I was once one of the people they try to avoid?*

The thought brought a pang of envy. Penney, Helen, and Amy all shared the confidence that came from spending their lives on the side of the angels, knowing they could summon a policeman if ever they needed help. Jennie knew the prickle of fear at having the breath of the law hot on the back of her neck.

Memories stirred, more wraithlike than wisps of San Francisco fog: her father, wearing a confident smile while he extolled the virtues of Professor Mountjoy's Elixir of Health to the crowd gathered around the back of the garishly painted medicine wagon; his far grimmer expression when the local citizenry discovered the professor's elixir proved no more helpful at curing their ills than any other patent nostrum, and less so than most. Jennie remembered all too well clinging to the inside of the wagon as her father whipped the horses to a faster pace to escape the latest angry mob.

She shook her head and heaved a wistful sigh. They had been little better than gypsies, she and her family, moving from one town to the next just one step ahead of the law. She had grown up wandering the streets alone and in neighborhoods that would make Penney and Helen blanch. One positive thing about it, though. Her brothers took her in hand early on to show her some defensive maneuvers for self-protection. Small of stature or not, she knew how to take care of herself.

The mist thickened. Jennie tightened her grip on her furled parasol, a faithful friend that had gotten her out of more than one close call. Applied strategically, the point of its ferrule worked wonders in persuading would-be mashers that their presence was required elsewhere. And if that failed to convince, she could always resort to the small knife she carried in her boot top.

The fog lifted again, admitting spangles of sunlight that

played over the wood fronts of the buildings along the street. Jennie walked on. She let her thoughts run freely, her tried-and-true remedy when she felt hard-pressed by some issue.

On just such an evening as this, she had been out on another solitary walk, hoping for a way to escape the life she had been born into and fearing there was none.

"Get out there, Jennie girl, and work the crowd. I see hard faces out there tonight that need some sweetening up." Her father's voice rang in her ears as clearly as it had on that San Francisco night only months before.

"Let Tom or Jack do it." She remembered how trapped she felt. Was there no way out? "Why does it always have to be me?"

"Because Jack and I don't have blond hair, blue eyes, and a disarming dimple." Her brother Tom's voice dripped with scorn. He stared down at her, brown eyes glaring from under the thatch of shaggy dark hair both brothers inherited from their father. "Can't you just see what would happen if I batted my eyes at the nice policeman? 'Truly, Officer, this sea air has a most fortuitous effect on a man's physique,' " he added in a high falsetto. " 'I've never seen shoulders as brawny as yours.' " Both brothers erupted in raucous laughter.

Their father looked on, unamused. "We're wasting time. God blessed you with the looks of an angel and the skill of a mountebank, my girl. Now get out there and use them."

"No!" Her explosive response jolted her family into silence. "God has nothing to do with this. I'm sick of trying to dupe people, sick of always having to run away. I won't do it. . .this time, or ever again."

"Jennie. It's going to rain soon. Let's give them a show and let them spend their money before it starts to pour."

She recognized the cajoling note in her father's voice, the same one he used to persuade his current marks to part with their hard-earned cash. It worked with everyone from housewives to farmers. But it wouldn't work with her. Not anymore. She spun around and darted away. Her father's voice changed from pleading to outright anger.

But still she ran.

Jennie stepped into a puddle, and mud splashed the hem of her pale blue dress. Pulled back to the present, she blinked and pressed her hand to her bosom. The mist must be thickening again. Its damp fingers had left trails of moisture along her cheeks. Or could those be tears?

She pulled a handkerchief from her reticule and blotted the wetness away without bothering to determine its source. Let those ugly memories remain where they belonged—in the past.

Remember the good part, she told herself. If she hadn't stormed off like that, she wouldn't have been navigating those rain-slicked streets that night, wouldn't have noticed the placards announcing a tent meeting. And if she hadn't ducked under the canvas of the huge tent seeking shelter from the wet, she wouldn't have heard that fiery preaching or the words that changed her life forever.

But she had seen the sign, she recalled, with a spurt of joy. She may have gone into the tent with no other thought than to escape the rain, but some note in the preacher's voice caught at her and drew her like a magnet. And in that unlikely setting, she found Jesus. . .and forgiveness. It had been so simple.

Far more difficult had been the task of trying to convey

that sense of freedom to her father and brothers the next day.

"Don't tell us you've come under the spell of some circuit-riding Bible thumper," Tom thundered.

Her father wore a look of keen disappointment. "If anyone knows about working a crowd, it's you, Jennie. How could you be taken in like that?" He spoke while he shoved the tailgate of the wagon into place and lashed the canvas down with a practiced speed Jennie recognized from long experience.

"Leaving town?" she asked.

"As a matter of fact, yes. We ran into a bit of unpleasantness. It seems the dear lady who purchased a case of the elixir is married to a physician, and the good doctor objects to sharing his territory with us. We'll overlook last night's foolishness, Jennie. Hop up in the wagon, and we'll be on our way."

She refused. They argued. The wagon left. She stayed.

The murmur of voices drifted toward her. Jennie peered through the fog, looking for their source. A prickle of unease ran up the back of her neck, and her heart beat faster.

Up ahead she could make out the forms of two men. Jennie slowed. Something didn't seem right. Their voices held a furtive, watchful quality.

A shaft of sunlight broke through the mist and settled on the men, glinting on the silvery hair of the one on the right. *Mr. Madison!* Jennie's heart resumed a more normal pace, then quickened again when a bold idea entered her mind. Maybe here, away from the office, he would be in a more amiable frame of mind, more inclined to listen to her make her case.

With a return of her earlier determination, she closed the distance between them with brisk strides.

Chapter 4

Mr. Madison!"

The two men sprang apart as though stung by one of Miss Minerva's hornets. Russell Madison swung around as if facing an attacker, while his companion stepped away and shielded his face. When Madison recognized her, she saw the tension drain out of his expression, to be replaced by an irritated scowl.

"Are you in the habit of prowling the streets alone, Miss Montgomery?"

"I am out for a stroll, hardly prowling. But since we met like this, I would like to talk to you about my story."

"There is no story."

"But you weren't at the cemetery. You didn't see the anger in those men's faces or hear what they said."

"You didn't hear them either." Russell Madison pulled a cigar from his coat pocket and rolled it between his fingers. "You're letting your imagination run away with you, seeing conspiracy where there is none. All marks of the novice reporter."

"But Mr. Madison—"

The editor beckoned to his companion. "I don't believe you two have met. Miss Montgomery, allow me to present Nick Edwards. One of our *seasoned* reporters."

The two men shared a smug look that made Jennie want to kick them both in the shins. Nick Edwards bowed. "I'm pleased to meet such a charming lady. Russell has told me of your work at the *Gazette*."

For a moment, Jennie found herself at a loss for words, able only to stare at the dark-haired man before her. Nick Edwards, her role model and, at the same time, the bane of her existence.

With a strike in progress, Jennie and her friends had the perfect opportunity to let their talents shine without being overshadowed by male competitors. And how far did it get them? Setting type and writing Miss Minerva's despised hints. All because of men like Nick Edwards. While they virtuously refused to cross the strike lines, they would slip their stories to the editor whenever they got the chance.

Voices echoed nearby. Russell Madison glanced over his shoulder, reminding Jennie of the secretive behavior she witnessed earlier. "I need to be going," he said. "We mustn't be seen together."

Jennie's eyes widened. "So this is how the two of you discuss stories without anyone knowing?"

"Not usually." Russell Madison tipped his hat low over his forehead, and Nick Edwards followed suit. "We happened to meet on the street and took advantage of the opportunity. Now I really must—"

Jennie planted herself squarely in his path. "Mr. Madison, in case it has escaped your notice, Penney Brice and I show up at the office each and every day. It would be far easier for you to assign stories to us there, rather than having to skulk around like one of the Sydney Ducks."

Her employer crooked his elbow. "Come along, Miss Montgomery. I'll be happy to escort you back to your hotel, but we must leave now."

Jennie drew back. "I am quite capable of making my way home alone, thank you. Besides, I have not yet finished—"

"I'll see her back safely, Russell." Nick Edwards nodded his head in the direction of the approaching voices. "We're going to have company pretty soon."

Russell Madison hesitated only for a moment. "Thanks, Nick. I know she'll be in good hands." He ducked his chin into his coat collar and hurried off down the street.

Jennie watched him disappear into the mist then turned back to Nick Edwards. She gripped her parasol in both hands and drew herself up to her full height, putting the top of her head even with his shoulder. She allowed an icy mask to settle over her features.

"You may be on your way, Mr. Edwards. I don't need to be left in anyone's charge, and certainly not yours. I can get back to the Hamilton perfectly well on my own."

His dark eyes sparkled. "I can see you are a woman of considerable spirit and more than capable of looking after yourself. However, I happen to be going that direction myself. Would you allow me to accompany you?"

Jennie opened her mouth to refuse but couldn't think of a way to do so without appearing churlish. She dipped her head in a brief nod and set off in the direction of the Hamilton.

She marched along at a quick gait, wishing the sun shone brightly enough to give her reason to unfurl her parasol and put further distance between herself and her unwelcome escort. Beside her, Nick Edwards kept pace, every one of his long, smooth strides equal to two of her own. He hummed a ditty as though he hadn't a care in the world.

He probably doesn't, Jennie fumed. The man received plum assignments without having to bother coming in to work. What did he have to worry about? They covered two blocks before Nick spoke.

"Please don't feel the need to keep up a running commentary, Miss Montgomery. I'm quite content with my own thoughts."

Jennie slanted a baleful look up at him, wishing she knew a way to wipe that smirk off his face. She lowered her chin and increased her pace. Just a few more blocks and she would be free of his loathsome company.

Then the idea struck her.

Jennie's steps slowed while she pondered the thought. She had an opportunity, and she ought to make use of it. Nick Edwards might be an insufferable, egotistical boor, but he did know a lot about the city. And if she phrased her request with skill, he might unwittingly help her write her own story.

Summoning up all her charm, Jennie slowed even more and turned on the smile that showed her dimple off to best advantage. "There is something I'd like to ask you before we part company."

"I'm neither married nor engaged, but I am free for dinner on Friday, if you're interested."

Jennie resisted the urge to slap him and kept her smile planted firmly in place. "Not exactly." She pulled her sketches from her reticule and held them out to him. "Do you recognize either of these men?"

Nick gave her a puzzled grin and bent his head over the drawings. His smile faded, and he looked back at Jennie with a solemn expression. "Where did you get these?"

"That isn't important. Just tell me, do you know them?"

Nick nodded slowly. "This man"—he tapped the sketch of the pallbearer—"is Calvin Harper, one of the owners of Pacific Mutual Investments. And this. . ." He held up the sheet bearing the likeness of the man she nicknamed Shabby. "This is Ned Mulrooney, a well-known thug from Sydney Town." He looked at Jennie thoughtfully. "Now what would you be doing with sketches of two such completely dissimilar men?"

"Pacific Mutual," Jennie repeated. "Didn't Vincent Collier have ties to the same place?"

"Harper was his partner. But what does. . ." The light of discovery quickened in his dark eyes. "That's right. You covered Collier's funeral in my place. Is that where you saw Calvin Harper?" He glanced back at Ned Mulrooney's picture then held the two up together. "And these are the two men you saw arguing at the cemetery?" He pursed his lips and gave a low whistle. "What business would Harper have with Mulrooney?"

"Precisely." Jennie retrieved the sketches and returned them to her reticule. "What business, indeed? Unfortunately, Mr. Madison does not share your feeling that the circumstances warrant investigation."

"It may not mean as much as you think," Nick cautioned.

"Now, about Friday evening. . ."

The warmth Jennie had begun to feel toward her nemesis congealed into a block of ice. "Good evening, Mr. Edwards."

Nick watched the diminutive woman stalk off, golden curls bobbing with every angry step, until she flounced up the steps of the Hamilton and disappeared inside. One corner of his mouth quirked up, and he allowed himself to release the chuckle he'd been holding in ever since she lit into Russell Madison like a terrier going after a mastiff. The chuckle grew into a low rumble of laughter. He had a strong feeling Miss Jennie Montgomery would object to the comparison.

He swung around and went on his way, feeling oddly bereft at the lack of her company. Maybe he would have to break down and stop by the *Gazette* office, after all. And try not to provoke another such outburst. He chuckled again. *How did a temper like that wind up encased in such a tiny frame?*

And what about that notion of hers that something sinister lay behind that altercation at the cemetery? Nick's instincts told him she was right: There was a story there. Odd that Russell hadn't picked up on it, but maybe he'd been too busy fending off her verbal assault to listen to his intuition.

Whatever the case, the situation bore investigation. Nick vowed to keep his eyes and ears open, and perhaps do a little probing of his own.

One thing was for certain: Even with that china doll face, Miss Montgomery had no business trying to crack a story on her own.

Chapter 5

*T*o relieve the pain of chapped hands, mix the yolk of a fresh egg and a dollop of honey with lard. Add fine oatmeal, and work the whole into a paste to be applied to the hands as required.

Jennie laid down her pen and wrinkled her nose. The concoction would probably live up to its promise more than Professor Mountjoy's Elixir ever had. But would readers of the *Gazette* hasten out to gather the necessary ingredients after reading her column? She slid her top desk drawer open and stared at the sketches resting there. For days, the image of those quarreling men had haunted her.

A story lay behind that altercation. She knew it. She could almost taste it. But here she sat doing the Miss Minerva column. And if she couldn't persuade Mr. Madison of her ability to sniff out a story, she would probably still be writing the column when she was old and gray. She slammed the drawer shut. "What's happened to your backbone?" she muttered. "It's time to show some fortitude."

Jennie gathered up the sheets containing her column and

carried them to Russell Madison's corner office. She would give it one more try. And another, and another, until she convinced that stubborn man to let her have her chance.

Even the high-and-mighty Nick Edwards had recognized the potential in what she'd seen. Remembering that, her confidence rose. When she told him that, Mr. Madison would have no choice but to listen to her.

The heavy office door stood slightly ajar. Jennie paused to draw a calming breath, then tapped on the door and stepped briskly into the office. "Mr. Madison, I—"

Jennie stared at the empty chair. Her breath left her lungs in a *whoosh*. When did he leave, and how had she missed seeing him? Tears stung her eyes. It didn't matter. He had gone, and that's all there was to it.

Jennie laid her column on the editor's desk. *Maybe tomorrow*, she thought dispiritedly. *Or the day after that.* She started to leave, then turned back, her attention snagged by the page squared neatly on the corner of the desk. An obituary in Mr. Madison's handwriting. Jennie frowned. Why had those paragraphs captured her notice?

She twirled the paper around to take a closer look. The first line sprang out at her. "Calvin Harper, prominent business leader, will be laid to rest tomorrow morning at ten o'clock."

Jennie wrapped her arms about her midsection and doubled over, feeling as though someone had driven a fist into her stomach. She fought for breath then picked up the obituary and read aloud in a low voice.

"Mr. Harper passed away early Wednesday morning as a result of injuries suffered when he was accosted by unknown assailants while walking near his home Monday night."

Jennie's voice trailed off, and she stared at the paper in her hand. Her gaze fell on a line at the end of the piece: "Investors concerned about the continued success of Pacific Mutual after the recent death of another partner may have their questions answered at the Pacific Mutual office at one o'clock this afternoon."

Jennie pressed her palm to her chest in an effort to calm her racing heart. She had to talk to Mr. Madison and get his permission to check this out.

But Mr. Madison had gone, and Jennie had no idea where he might be. In that case. . .

She set the paper back on the desk. In that case, she would just have to act on her instincts. . .as any good reporter would do.

A crowd had formed in front of the new brick building and spilled over into the street. Nick Edwards arrived in time to take a position about midway along the right side of the gathering, near enough to hear the speaker but far enough back to get a good view of the crowd and its reaction to the deaths of Pacific Mutual's owners.

He scanned the assembly, taking note of the stiff postures and tense faces. Anger crackled in the air. Nick sensed it was an anger born of the fear of investments gone bad. From the looks of those around him, they could ill afford a large financial loss. Nick shook his head, sympathy warring with irritation. Why did people who didn't have money to spare risk it on what amounted to nothing more than a gamble?

At the far edge of the crowd, a flicker of movement caught his attention. Something bobbed up above the grim faces then dropped down again. Nick stared, bemused, as it popped up again, then disappeared, this time recognizing it as the top of a blond head. There was something familiar about those golden curls. He tilted his head and waited for another glimpse.

Jennie Montgomery. Nick's lips curved upward in a grin. The woman just didn't give up. She had evidently followed the same intuition that brought him here. Too bad her small stature would prevent her from viewing the proceedings. Nick stifled a snicker at the thought of her hopping up and down, trying to see over the people in front of her.

He followed the progress of her bobbing head along the perimeter of the crowd. As she drew nearer, he caught the determination in the set of her chin and the single-minded look in those china blue eyes. If she were a man, she just might have the makings of a good reporter.

Jennie stopped at a point directly behind where Nick stood. He watched the men at the edge of the crowd turn to speak with her. It looked like she was pleading with them to let her pass. To a man, they shook their heads and took a firm stand. Even from this distance, Nick saw her eyes narrow ominously.

He chuckled. It would take more than a glare or a pretty smile to make those hard-faced men give way. A murmur began at the front of the crowd and rippled back to where Nick stood. Senses alert, he turned his attention toward the office building, where a portly, dark-haired man stepped up onto a makeshift platform.

The murmur died down, and a hush settled over the gathered investors. Nick cast a quick glance around the crowd, taking mental notes. Every eye focused on the dark-haired man, who spread his hands wide and smiled reassuringly.

"My friends, I thank you for coming. My name is Alexander Sibley. In our company charter, Vincent Collier and Calvin Harper appointed me to act in their behalf in the unlikely event they both became unable to perform their duties as directors." Sibley dipped his head for a moment. "Little did any of us dream such an eventuality would come to pass. But it has, my friends, and I stand before you today to assure you that business at Pacific Mutual goes on as usual and to address any concerns you may have. Your investments are safely at work as we continue to move forward."

Someone jostled Nick from the rear. He planted his feet to keep from being knocked off balance, intent on catching every word Sibley said. No telling what scrap of information might turn out to be the very thing that would point him in the right direction.

Nick heard the brief scuffle of feet and a mild oath behind him, then felt a tap on his arm. He turned his head and looked down into a pair of guileless blue eyes.

Jennie Montgomery smiled up at him sweetly. "Excuse me, Mr. Edwards, may I get by?"

Nick blinked. How had she managed to work her way through that tight knot of people?

"Please." Jennie fixed him with a look that would have melted his heart under other circumstances. "I have a story to write."

The bold statement proved Nick's undoing. He let out a short bark of laughter. "This story—if there is one to be found here—will require tenacity, grit, and experience. I'm afraid you, my dear Miss Montgomery, are far more a lapdog than a newshound." He watched Jennie's eyes narrow to angry slits and turned his back, congratulating himself on not being taken in by shimmering curls and wide blue eyes. Interest alone did not make a reporter. It took a degree of toughness and sometimes a bit of deviousness to—

A sudden pain stabbed at his lower ribs. Nick yelped and clutched at his side. When he doubled over, Jennie moved by him, offering a triumphant smile as she passed.

Nick massaged the tender spot on his ribs with his fingertips and watched in astonishment as she breezed past, stroking her furled parasol. Then he returned his attention to the pain that had come and gone in a flash. What could it have been? He straightened gingerly, relieved when there was no recurrence.

Jennie nudged the man in front of Nick and spoke to him briefly. The man returned her bright smile, doffed his hat, and allowed her to move ahead of him. The next man gave her the briefest of glances over his spectacles before shaking his head and turning his attention back to Sibley. *Blocked again.* Nick grinned. *You might as well give up, Miss Montgomery. You're out of your element here.* He saw the bespectacled man jump to one side and clutch his ribs much as Nick had done.

Jennie swept through the resulting space. Nick watched in disbelief as she made her way to the front of the crowd, then unfurled her parasol and held it over her head. Sunlight glinted on the parasol's ferrule.

A terrible suspicion welled up in Nick's mind. *No, it couldn't be.* Still. . .

He fingered the spot on his side, wondering if he would find a bruise when he got home—a bruise the size of the tip of a parasol ferrule.

An angry shout reclaimed his attention.

"Both of them died within a week. I think this company is cursed. I want my money back."

Sibley patted the air as though calming a nervous child. "I understand your concerns, but you have nothing to worry about. Not only is Pacific Mutual protecting your investments, but we have plans for expansion as well. Mr. Collier and Mr. Harper, God rest their souls, did such an outstanding job managing your funds that we are going to be able to do more than even they thought possible."

"Why don't you tell us about these so-called plans?" cried a whiskered man on Nick's right. "We have a right to know what you're doing with our money." The crowd murmured assent.

Sibley gave a smile that reminded Nick of a shark. "If I were free to do so, I would provide you with every detail of the proposed transaction. However, we are in the midst of negotiations even as I speak. I am sure that men of the world such as yourselves will understand the delicacy of such a situation. If even a breath of what is about to transpire leaks out—and let me assure you this is big enough to make you all wealthy men—it could be disastrous to our plans. And I know you don't want that." Sibley favored the crowd with a broad wink.

"Again, let me reassure you that your investment is safe with Pacific Mutual. A little patience on your part now, keeping your eyes on that certain goal of our mutual success, will pay off handsomely in the very near future." Sibley raised both hands in the manner of one pronouncing a benediction. "Thank you for your trust in this company. We will continue to serve you as faithfully as we have in the past." With a final wave, he turned and left the platform.

Chapter 6

Nick stood still and listened to the departing crowd.

"I'm not sure that was enough to satisfy me," a gray-haired man said to his neighbor. "What did you think of it?"

"I came here thinking to get my money back, but after listening to him, I believe I'm going to let it ride awhile. I like the idea of being rich."

Nick followed the last of the stragglers, deep in thought. He caught a glimpse of Jennie, marching off with a determined stride, no doubt heading back to the *Gazette* to file the story of the century. The thought of her resolve lifted his somber mood for a moment and brought a faint smile to his lips. *She has the desire, no doubt about that. It's a shame she's not a man. She'd make a great reporter. Then again, there are reporters aplenty, but there's only one Jennie Montgomery.*

Jennie disappeared around a corner, and Nick's thoughts sobered again. Something was wrong. Every instinct he had developed in his years as a reporter told him so. If everything was as rosy with Pacific Mutual as Sibley claimed, why the connection with Ned Mulrooney and his ilk?

Nick didn't believe in coincidence. Two deaths in quick succession raised his suspicions to a fever pitch. He no longer discounted Jennie's insistence that a story lay buried somewhere. But the questions remained: what was it and where to look?

He reviewed the faces at the meeting. He'd spotted several with ties to the shipping industry. Could there be some connection there? His mind turned up one possibility after another. What if Pacific Mutual was trying to take over the shipping yards? The thought stopped Nick in his tracks as he pondered the ramifications of such a scheme.

If one person or group could gain control of the longshoremen and the warehouses, they could name their price for unloading ships and storing goods until they could be distributed farther inland. No, surely such a grandiose plot was too farfetched to be plausible. But the more Nick tried to set the theory aside, the more it gnawed at him.

He couldn't prove or disprove the idea with the knowledge at hand. He needed information.

A thin cry reached his ears. "Papers! Get your *Golden Gate Gazette* here!"

Nick grinned and hastened to the corner where a skinny newsboy hawked his wares.

"Paper, mister?" The boy beamed up at him with a gap-toothed grin.

Nick smiled back. "It's Gabe, isn't it? I've seen you around the *Gazette* office."

The lad's eyes grew round. "Mr. Edwards! Sure, I ought to

have known you right away. I guess you won't be wanting a paper, will you?"

"Not a paper, but information if you have it. Would you like to help me out on a story I'm working on?"

The boy's freckled face split in a wide grin. "Would I? Just tell me what you want me to do."

Nick leaned over and lowered his voice. "You newsboys see and hear quite a bit around the city, don't you?"

"You bet! Sometimes even before you reporters."

Nick nodded. "I want you to keep your ears open for talk about Pacific Mutual Investments or two men, Vincent Collier and Calvin Harper. Or anything about someone trying to muscle in on the shipping yards. Can you do that?"

"Surest thing there is!" Gabe's face glowed with the light of hero worship. "I'll put the word out and let you know what we turn up."

"That's fine, Gabe. I appreciate it." Nick turned to leave, then hesitated. "And if you hear anything about Ned Mulrooney or any of his buddies, I'd like to know about that, too."

Nick tweaked the boy's hair and walked away. The first step of his plan had been set in motion.

Jennie knit her brow and mulled over Alexander Sibley's speech while she walked back to the *Gazette*. She had to admit she'd been impressed by his delivery. He managed to strike just the right balance between sorrow at the loss of the partners and hearty optimism for the future. To unsuspecting investors, he surely offered the reassurance they sought.

But she recognized the pattern all too well. His words promised a bright tomorrow in only the vaguest of terms. He offered no specifics, no guarantees, nothing tangible. Just the kind of promises her father and brothers claimed for the Elixir of Health. Something was amiss at Pacific Mutual, and she had to discover what that might be. Perhaps she could find something in the *Gazette*'s archives.

The sun hovered low in the sky by the time Jennie folded the last of the papers and added it to the towering stack on the corner of her desk. With a low moan, she rested her head on her crossed arms and closed her eyes. After hours of scanning back issues of the *Gazette*, she had found precious few mentions of Pacific Mutual, Collier, or Harper.

Jennie pushed herself back to a sitting position and leaned her head on her left hand. She cast a mournful look at the much smaller stack in front of her and retrieved the top paper from that pile.

Her brow knotted as she reread an article written several years previously. A group had been looking toward the building of a transcontinental railroad. Vincent Collier and Calvin Harper were listed as partners. Jennie stared at the article, then let out an impatient huff and pushed it aside. A minuscule reference in a piece written so long ago could have little bearing on recent events.

The only other mentions of the two men were found in more recent articles on Pacific Mutual, detailing its founding two years before, the company's interest in shipping yards, and their plans for future investments in inland shipping. According to the glowing reports, the business was thriving. From the investors' standpoint, it would seem all was right with their world.

Jennie tapped her thumb against the worn desktop and chewed her bottom lip. It all looked good on paper. She winced at the memory of one of her father's favorite lines: "People want to believe they're getting something wonderful, even if common sense tells them it's too good to be true. No one will question what you're doing, so long as it looks good on paper."

But Jennie had learned long ago that the fact of something being set down on paper by no means made it true.

She rubbed her eyes with her thumb and forefinger and bent over the articles again. The Bible told her God could work all things to the good for those who love Him. She often wondered how even He could redeem her shady past. Perhaps she had found a way. If nothing else, she had the expertise to spot a flimflam job a mile away. And this whole situation reeked of chicanery. All she had to do was figure out how the pieces fit together.

Ned Mulrooney. If it hadn't been for his presence at Vincent Collier's funeral, she never would have realized something was wrong. What was his part in all this? Jennie leaned her head against the back of her chair and pondered the reasons an underworld figure would have contact with a supposedly upright businessman.

What if hoodlums were using the company to skim money from their various building projects? Jennie shook her head impatiently. The amount involved, though sizable, would hardly make it worth taking one man's life. Or possibly two.

She pushed away from her desk in disgust. It all kept coming back to motivation. There had to be some bigger goal she had not yet discovered. Until she knew what that might be, she didn't have enough information to compose her story. The whole thing reminded her of a tangled snarl of yarn.

Wait a minute. Jennie sat upright and hitched her chair forward. She could hardly write a complete exposé. But perhaps if she tugged at the ends of those tangled pieces, it might bring something to light that would help her unravel the rest.

Spurred to action, she pulled a fresh sheet of paper toward her and reached for her pen. It was something like stirring an anthill, she thought, as she penned her opening line. The hill remained quiet at first, but if you kept stirring, eventually something would surface that could be caught and examined.

As Jennie continued with her story, she wondered how this would stir the anthill at Pacific Mutual. *Did the warehouse fire have any connection with the deaths of Collier and Harper? Was Collier's death truly an accident? Is some unknown person or group trying to destroy Pacific Mutual?* The more she thought, the more she realized what a quagmire she was trying to wade through.

Chapter 7

Nick exited his favorite restaurant, enjoying the contentment brought on by a fine meal. It would have been more pleasant had he shared it with Jennie Montgomery, but perhaps in time. . .

"Pssst!"

Nick halted in midstride and looked around. He grinned when he spotted Gabe poking his head out of a narrow passageway. The newsboy glanced furtively from side to side then beckoned to him.

Getting into the spirit of the boy's theatrics, Nick slid into the alleyway alongside him with an appropriate show of stealth. "Do you have something for me?"

"Do I ever!" Gabe puffed out his skinny chest. "Me and the boys have done some checking, just like you asked us to."

"And?" Nick leaned closer.

"This stuff is the goods, all right. You know that Mr. Collier, the one the paper said all those nice things about? Well, maybe you want to print a retraction or whatever it's called. Turns out Mr. Swell wasn't such a swell fellow at all."

Nick pulled out a sheet of paper and a pencil. "Go on."

Gabe glanced over his shoulder. "That Mr. Collier may have done all those good things the paper said, but there's another side to him." He lowered his voice to a whisper. "I bet you didn't know he spent a lot of time in Sydney Town."

Nick's eyebrows soared toward his hairline. "Are you sure?"

"Sure as can be." Gabe nodded emphatically. "We also heard tell he gambled a lot at Donovan's. You know the place, Mr. Edwards? I mean, do you know of it? It's a regular dive. And guess who the owner is? None other than Ian McDermott, who just happens to be Mulrooney's boss and one of the biggest thugs around."

Nick scribbled furiously. "How do you know all this?"

"Andy, one of the other newsboys, hawks papers on a corner over that way. He's seen Collier going in and out of Sydney Town plenty of times." Gabe hitched up his trousers. "It just so happens the bartender at Donovan's is one of Andy's regular customers. He told Andy after Collier's accident that McDermott was mad because he wouldn't be able to collect his gambling debts."

Nick whistled.

"Do you want us to keep listening? Me and the boys will be glad to help you, Mr. Edwards. All you have to do is say the word."

"Go ahead." Nick pulled a coin from his vest pocket and pressed it in the boy's hand. "But promise me you'll be careful, do you hear?"

"Don't worry. We're on the job."

Nick slipped out of the alleyway and strolled toward his

lodgings, mulling over Gabe's news. He wasn't surprised to learn Collier indulged in gambling, but he would have expected it to be done around a gentlemen's card table, not at a seedy dive like Donovan's. . .or anywhere else in Sydney Town. The reputation of that district alone should have been enough to make anyone of Vincent Collier's standing steer clear.

Nick reevaluated his position. He had more information now than he did before. Still, he had a long way to go before he could see the picture clearly. It looked like a little more digging would be in order. And the next step would be one he couldn't delegate to Gabe and his pals.

Jennie held the morning issue of the *Gazette* and read every word of her story—her very first story—aloud. Penney, Helen, and Amy listened with gratifying attention. " 'And so we ask,' " she concluded, " 'Have Pacific Mutual's investors gotten the whole story, or have they been sold a bottle—or a caseload—of snake oil?' "

"Wonderful!" Penney clapped her hands. "You've fired the first salvo for the girl reporters of the *Gazette*."

"However did you persuade Mr. Madison to let you write the story?" Amy queried.

Jennie tore her gaze away from the article with its byline— J. Montgomery—long enough to smile at her friends. "I didn't." She laughed at their startled expressions. "I did the research, wrote the story, and laid it on his desk when I turned in Miss Minerva's column. Putting pressure on him didn't work, so I let him judge the story on its own merit."

"He obviously saw its worth." Penney's grin matched Jennie's own broad smile. "And well he should. You have a true gift with words."

"You do, indeed," Amy said. "That line about snake oil was a stroke of genius. It immediately brings to mind thoughts of charlatans and fakery."

Helen's forehead puckered. "I don't know. My grandmother swears by Professor Mountjoy's Elixir of Health."

Jennie's smile froze. Not daring to look at her friends, she turned her attention back to the front page. Her gasp brought the other girls crowding around.

"What's wrong?" Penney asked.

Jennie could only point at the columns directly across the page from her own piece.

Helen took the paper from Jennie's nerveless fingers. Her eyes widened as she scanned the paragraphs. "Why, it's another story on Vincent Collier."

Jennie retrieved the paper and read snatches of the article aloud. " 'It has come to our attention that highly regarded businessman Vincent Collier may have led a secret life, a life far different than the one he carried out in public. . . . Why would an upstanding citizen like Collier frequent Sydney Town? Gambling—and subsequent heavy debts—are reasons that have come to this reporter's attention, along with activities deemed unmentionable for fear of offending the gentler sex. . . . Questions abound, and this reporter intends to find the answers. Our readers will be the first to know as further information comes to light.' " She lowered the paper. The other girls' faces mirrored her own disbelief.

"Does the story have a byline?" Amy asked.

Jennie nodded and blinked back the hot sting of tears. "Nick Edwards." She wadded the newspaper in her hands. "That scoundrel! He went after my story. And he never would have known about it if I hadn't told him in the first place. But his piece wouldn't have gotten into the paper without..." Her voice trailed off, and she directed a baleful glare at the corner office.

"Jennie." Helen's voice held a note of caution.

Heedless of the warning, Jennie lowered her head and charged down the center aisle toward the editor's office. She gave a peremptory knock on the heavy door then flung it wide. She stormed inside the small room and planted herself in front of the desk.

Russell Madison looked up with a bland expression, smoke from his cigar curling around him. "Yes?"

Jennie slapped the crumpled newspaper down on his desk. "Why did you print Nick Edwards's piece alongside mine? This is my story. I discovered it; I followed it up. I did all the ground work on it when you didn't even believe a story existed."

"And a fine story it is." Madison leaned back in his chair and folded his arms behind his head. "I have to admit I'm impressed. You have a nice style."

"Then why?" Jennie's chest heaved. "Why give it away?"

Mr. Madison blew a smoke ring toward the ceiling. "It looks like you've stumbled onto quite a story, one that requires experience as well as enthusiasm." He held up his hand to quell Jennie's outraged sputtering. "Toughness and tenacity, that's what this story needs. Neither of which are attributes of a respectable young lady."

He stubbed out his cigar and leaned forward, tenting his fingertips. "The *Gazette* has only respectable young ladies in its employ, does it not, Miss Montgomery?"

Unable to think of a suitable retort, Jennie could only nod.

"That's why I've put Nick on the job." Mr. Madison went back to editing copy.

The humidor on his desk caught Jennie's attention. She curled her fingers and held her hands tight against her skirt, resisting the urge to bash her employer over the head with the heavy wooden box. She turned on her heel and swept out of the office.

I refuse to admit defeat. She might have suffered a momentary setback, but she wouldn't give up, not by a long shot. Chin held high, Jennie strode down the center aisle to her desk and snatched up her reticule.

Penney swung round from her place at the typesetter. "Where are you going? He didn't fire you, did he?"

"Hardly." Jennie placed her hat on her head and thrust her hatpin in place. "Miss Minerva's column is done for today. I'm going out to find some real news."

Ordinarily, the damp spring air would have chilled Jennie right through her cloak, but today her blazing anger sufficed to keep her warm. Too wound up to sit still long enough for a cab ride, she walked the whole distance to the Pacific Mutual building, using the time to devise a plan.

Her story had been written from sheer instinct. Now she needed facts to back her up. . .and to warrant the *Gazette* running another article. One she—not Nick Edwards—would write.

The thought of carrying on a conversation with Alexander Sibley made her skin crawl, but she needed the company's side of things to give a balanced view. Whether she could believe anything the man said remained to be seen. Jennie's lips tightened in a thin smile. Even if he lied through his teeth, it would tell her something. She had too much experience concocting duplicitous statements to be deceived by pretty words and vague promises.

She marched up to the Pacific Mutual building and paused at the bottom of the steps to review the questions she planned to ask. Satisfied with the mental list she'd drawn up, she started up the steps just as the door opened.

Jennie glanced up at the figure emerging from the interior and stared, aghast. "You!"

Chapter 8

Nick stopped dead in his tracks at the top of the steps and stared down at Jennie. He turned, saw no one behind him, and realized he must be the cause of her horrified expression. Pulling the door shut, he strode down to meet her at the foot of the steps. Anger replaced her look of dismay.

"What are you doing here?" she demanded.

"My job," he replied evenly. Inwardly, he smiled. With her glittering eyes and general air of bristling, she reminded him of an outraged kitten.

"And does your job include taking over my story? You know I'm the one who realized something was amiss. You and that human smokestack of an editor wouldn't have given it a second thought if it hadn't been for me."

The way she spat out her words made the resemblance to an angry kitten even more pronounced. Nick held back a chuckle with an effort. What would it be like to have this little spitfire talk to him with a smile instead of a hiss? The thought made his head swim.

If he couldn't persuade her to make a truce, at least he could prolong the encounter. He offered Jennie his arm. "Let's continue this conversation elsewhere. No point in making Pacific Mutual's employees privy to our discussion." He led her away from the brick building and down the street.

Nick walked on, surprised by the mounting pleasure Jennie's nearness brought. He fancied he could feel the warmth of her small hand through his coat sleeve. He swallowed to regain control of his emotions and bent his head to speak to her.

"Russell and I are well aware of your contribution to this story, but it may require going places that wouldn't be appropriate for a young lady. It's best to let us men take over from here." Seeing the rebellious set to her jaw, he hastened to add, "I enjoyed your piece in today's paper. You did a fine job on it, very persuasive." He watched closely for her reaction and saw her chin wobble. The sight caught at his heart.

"To think of the hours I spent doing the research. All that time poring over stacks and stacks of old papers. And all for nothing."

Nick felt sorry for her. She did have the makings of a fine reporter. . .except for her gender. He could only imagine the frustration she must feel at seeing her work on the story cut short. He spotted a teahouse a short distance up the block, and a happy thought struck him. Maybe he could make it up to her in part, let her know her effort wouldn't go to waste.

"I'd like to hear more about what you found out. Would you care to tell me about it over a cup of tea?"

Jennie halted so quickly her grip on his sleeve swung him around. She snatched her hand from his arm and clasped it around the handle of her parasol. "I opened my mouth once and told you my suspicions about Harper talking to Mulrooney. What happened? You stole my story! Despite what you may think, I am not a fool, Mr. Edwards. I'm not about to feed you one more morsel of information to help you do it again."

She snapped the parasol open, and Nick took a cautious step back. "I will continue my own investigation," she said. "If there is a story—and there is—I'll be the one to write it." She turned in the direction of the *Gazette* and stalked away.

Nick stared after Jennie's retreating figure, reminded that even kittens have sharp claws. He started to follow then halted. In her present frame of mind, she'd be likely to swing that parasol at his head. And she'd probably connect. He contented himself with trailing some distance behind. Not until he saw her enter the *Gazette* building did he turn and go his own way.

Like a bloodhound following a scent, he knew he was on the right track. His interview with Sibley confirmed it. But trying to pin down anything specific was like trying to catch the wind. Recalling something Sibley said about acquiring property, his steps slowed. Maybe he hadn't reached a dead end after all.

Nick closed the last of the heavy books and slid it back across the counter to the waiting clerk with a sense of defeat. He had thought he was closing in, but it appeared he'd been wrong. The tax records listed Pacific Mutual as owning several warehouses near the wharfs—including the one that burned the day of Vincent Collier's funeral. But the company hadn't purchased additional property near the shipping yards for some time. For a firm supposedly interested in investing in that area, that seemed odd—one more thing that didn't make sense. Unless. . .

"Excuse me. Could I look through those books again?"

The clerk gave Nick a cold look over the top of his spectacles but returned the records without comment.

Nick opened the volume marked A–D and ran his finger down a column of entries: *Clemens, Coble, Collier.* He found four parcels listed under Vincent's name. The first Nick recognized as Collier's residence. The others had lower values: rental properties, perhaps.

With a feeling he'd picked up the scent again, Nick reached for the next volume, E–H, and looked for Calvin Harper's name. There it was. Nick pulled a sheet of paper from his pocket and copied the extensive listing.

Some of the properties named Harper as statutory agent for Pacific Mutual. At least half showed him as agent for another entity, Transwestern Amalgamated. In addition, Harper held a fair number of properties under his own name. According to the map pinned on a nearby wall, not one of them was near the shipping yards.

Nick pursed his lips. What had Harper been up to? Though moderately well off, owning that number of properties seemed excessive. And what about this second group?

He turned to the clerk. "I'm curious about Transwestern Amalgamated." He pointed to one of the entries. "Do you know anything about it or who else may be connected with it?"

The clerk rubbed his hand over his balding pate and stared hard at Nick before answering. "All Mr. Harper said was that he'd put together a special group of investors. No names—he kept the whole thing rather hush-hush—but I got the impression it was a high-rolling bunch."

Nick nodded his thanks. He gathered his notes and left, deep in thought. Thanks to Jennie, he had stumbled into something far bigger than a minor investment swindle. *A bunch of high rollers, eh?* Digging into the private lives of the very wealthy could be tricky. Rich people knew ways to cover their tracks and had the means to buy muscle to keep investigators at bay.

How was he going to accomplish this? He needed some way to obtain inside information on San Francisco's elite. He snapped his fingers. Of course!

~

The hired cabriolet let Nick off near a stately home on Rincon Hill. He stared up at the imposing edifice before mounting the steps to the broad front porch.

A stiff-featured butler answered his knock and sniffed at Nick's request to see the lady of the house. "I will inquire whether Madam is in," he intoned.

Behind him, a fluttery voice called, "Quit trying to sound pompous, Thomas, and let the boy in."

The butler stood aside with an aggrieved air, and a snowy-haired woman descended on Nick like a miniature whirlwind. "How's my favorite member of the press?"

Nick disengaged himself from the tangle of flounces and furbelows and laughed. "Hello, Aunt Edith."

His hostess clasped both his hands and fixed him with a delighted smile. "It's been a long time, Nicky. Far too long. Now come sit down and tell me what brings the son of my dearest friend for a visit." She led him to a parlor where she seated herself on a creamy gold sofa and patted the cushion beside her. "I'm not vain enough to think it's a desire for my company that drew you here, so dispense with the pleasantries, and tell me the real reason you came. I am all agog." She folded her hands in her lap and leaned toward him.

A sense of well-being flooded Nick's soul. Aunt Edith might have married well, but she never lost the wide-eyed wonder she'd had while growing up with Nick's mother in Philadelphia. She lived in one of grander places on Rincon Hill yet retained a down-to-earth common sense Nick found refreshing.

He got right to the point. "I need information from someone in the know. How would you like to help me play detective?"

Aunt Edith's cheeks glowed a rosy pink. "Snooping around after one of your special stories, are you? I was afraid the strike might put an end to your work at the *Gazette*."

"It has made my work difficult," he admitted. "Among other things, Madison hired several young ladies to fill in during the strike. One of them—a Miss Jennie Montgomery—fancies herself a reporter. She discovered what looks to be a rather juicy scandal, something that demands investigation, but it's far too dangerous for her to handle on her own. This is going to require some digging into the seamier side of our fair city, not a job for a golden-haired slip of a girl with a dimple in her chin and eyes the color of sapphires."

"Hmm. How very interesting."

Nick smiled. "You haven't even heard what the story is about."

"Not the story. This girl. Did you know your face turns pale pink when you mention her name?"

Nick cleared his throat and floundered for a reply. "I think you're just the person to help me learn some things that might break this story wide open."

Aunt Edith clapped her hands. "How exciting! What can I do?"

Nick breathed a prayer of thanksgiving for the success of his diversionary tactic. "I need all the information I can get on the upper crust." He grinned at the eager woman.

Aunt Edith lowered her right eyelid in a conspiratorial wink. "I glean more dirt from the meetings of my ladies' clubs than an innocent young man like you could possibly imagine. How much would you like me to dish out?"

Nick grinned. "Here's the background." He gave a quick outline of events from the warehouse fire to the deaths of Collier and Harper, the altercation with Ned Mulrooney, and the discovery of Transwestern Amalgamated. "And that's what brings me here. I need to find out who is in this group and what they're up to. Has anyone in your set been making large investments lately?"

Edith Wells leaned back against the damask cushion and hooted, bringing a disapproving Thomas to the doorway. She waved the butler away and dabbed at her eyes with a lace handkerchief. "Oh, honey, investing is the way to make money, and folks who have plenty of it never tire of making more. They're always looking for new places to invest."

"Oh." Nick took a moment to absorb this truth then voiced his thoughts aloud. "That means these people are experienced in discerning a good opportunity from a bad one. So why would any of them be pouring large amounts of money into worthless desert property?"

Aunt Edith tilted her head to one side. "Are you sure you've got your facts straight? Some of these people have been known to take a pretty risky plunge from time to time, but that just doesn't make sense."

Nick sighed. "None of it makes sense right now. That's the trouble." He gave the older woman a peck on the cheek and rose. "Let me know if you hear anything that might have some bearing on this, will you? I'll just have to keep digging and see what I can turn up."

He let himself out the front door, narrowly avoiding a collision with a dignified-looking man just raising his hand to knock. The men nodded, and Nick went on his way, wondering who the caller might be. A whimsical smile crossed his lips. Aunt Edith had been widowed for a good many years. Maybe this man was the other half of an autumn romance. Nick chuckled. If that turned out to be the case, he wished them well.

Chapter 9

To make baking powder, mix two large spoonfuls bicarbonate of soda and a smaller amount of tartaric acid with a quarter pound of ground rice. Keep the mixture in a tightly closed container. You will be delighted with the results when using this powder in cakes and other pastry.

Jennie turned from her desk and stared out the window. The overcast day looked as bleak as her current mood. How utterly frustrating to write about baking powder when real stories waited to be covered! At least it was almost quitting time. In a few more minutes she could go home to the Hamilton and forget about Miss Minerva until morning.

The outer door opened and closed. Jennie heard Helen's quiet voice ask, "May I help you?"

"I certainly hope so," a high voice fluted. "I have some information I must get to Nick Edwards." Jennie swiveled around to see a well-dressed, white-haired woman standing near the doorway. "With this horrid strike going on, I don't know how to reach him. Can you help me?"

"I—I don't know how to reach him," Helen stammered.

"I've never met the man. But I believe Jennie is acquainted with him."

Over near the typesetter, Penney cleared her throat. A dark flush suffused Helen's face. "That's Jennie." She pointed. "Over th–there."

The woman turned and swept across the office to stand in front of Jennie's desk. Jennie eyed her well-cut clothing and perfectly fitted gloves. Everything about her spoke of money and plenty of it. Jennie drew her brows together. This woman looked the type to have a multitude of servants at her beck and call to cater to her needs. Why would she be running her own errands?

The woman inclined her head. "So you know Nicky? Could you help me get this to him?" She held out an envelope with Nick's name written on the front in graceful script.

Nicky? Bile rose in Jennie's throat. The last thing she wanted to do was carry messages for the man. She squelched her reluctance long enough to dredge up a gracious reply. "I'll see what I can do."

Her visitor leaned across the desk and spoke in a confiding tone. "I'm helping him with some research. This is information regarding a story he's working on."

Jennie's gaze locked on the envelope, and she sprang to her feet. "I'll be happy to take care of it for you." Her visitor pressed the envelope into her hand. Jennie's palm tingled at its touch.

To her surprise, her visitor didn't turn to leave but studied her with bright eyes. "So you're Jennie." An approving smile lit her face.

"Uh, yes." Jennie squirmed under the frank appraisal.

"Allow me to introduce myself. I am Mrs. Joseph Wells.

Nicky's mother and I grew up together back in Philadelphia a lifetime ago." The older woman tilted her head. "After Nicky stopped by the other day, I went through some back issues of the *Gazette* and read what you've done. You're very good, my dear, very good indeed."

Somewhat appeased, Jennie allowed a smile to soften her expression.

"Nicky told me all about you," Mrs. Wells went on. "And I must say he did an admirable job of describing you. I feel foolish not to have recognized you at once. You're quite the china doll."

China doll? After their last encounter, Jennie would have expected a description more along the lines of harpy or shrew.

"May I sit down?" Mrs. Wells indicated the straight-backed chair facing Jennie's desk.

"Of course." Jennie flushed at her lack of courtesy. But who would have expected a society matron to want to spend one more moment than necessary in this place?

Mrs. Wells clasped her hands and leaned forward in the chair. "Forgive me for asking, but did I detect a lack of enthusiasm when you spoke of Nicky?"

"He's a fine writer," Jennie hedged. "Very talented." *And good-looking, rather full of himself, but with eyes that make me feel like melting into a puddle.* She pulled herself back to the moment and cleared her throat. "It's just that he feels I'm incompetent to cover a story simply because I'm a woman."

Mrs. Wells made clucking noises. "I've known Nicky since he was a baby. A lovely boy, but rather entrenched in the thinking of our day that considers the female of the species inferior." She reached across the desk and patted Jennie's arm, giving her a quick wink. "You and I, of course, know that a woman is capable of doing anything she wants."

Jennie brightened. "Of course."

"Call me Aunt Edith," her visitor invited. "I feel like I already know you."

Jennie stared, unable to stop the broad grin that spread across her face. Who would have believed Nick Edwards could know such a forward-thinking woman? "I'd be happy to."

"Tell me, are you going to continue pursuing this story? Nicky seems to think some of my friends may have inadvertently become involved in some nefarious scheme. I've listed a number of names for him to consider." She nodded to the envelope in Jennie's hand.

"Indeed?" Jennie fingered the heavy paper. "This is important information, then. I'll try to get it to him as soon as possible." She glanced at the clock atop the shelf of reference books. "As a matter of fact, we might be able to catch him at his favorite restaurant now. It's just around the corner."

"What a wonderful idea." Edith Wells rose with a delighted smile. "We can deliver it together."

"Some apple pie, Mr. Edwards?"

"After that enormous meal? I really shouldn't, Bessie. Well, maybe just a thin slice." The waitress giggled and sailed off back to the kitchen.

Nick leaned back in his chair and let his eyelids droop. Did his waistcoat feel just a bit tighter this evening? He fingered the buttons. Maybe he should have turned down the pie.

Two women threaded their way through the tables, headed in his direction. Nick watched them idly through half-closed eyes then snapped to attention.

"Aunt Edith!" He leaped to his feet and pulled out a chair, then turned to greet her companion. His jaw dropped. "Miss Montgomery?" He managed to pull out a second chair despite the fact that the world had just tilted on its axis.

"Thank you." Jennie seemed perfectly at ease, as though at a regular meeting of friends.

Nick resumed his own seat and tried to find his voice. "What an unexpected pleasure, ladies. What brings you here, Aunt Edith? This is hardly the kind of dining atmosphere you're used to."

Edith Wells shook her head and smiled. "I've never forgotten my roots, dear boy. It reminds me of the places Joseph used to take me when we were first married."

Silence settled over the table. Both women smiled at Nick. Aunt Edith wore a pleasant, motherly expression, while Jennie's resembled that of a cat about to lick cream from its whiskers.

"Here's your pie, Mr. Edwards." Bessie flickered a curious glance at the new arrivals. "Will there be anything else?"

"Coffee and pie for the ladies, please."

Bessie nodded and returned in short order. Nick's two companions ate their desserts with relish. His own pie seemed dry and caught in his throat. The silence stretched out.

Nick coughed. "To what do I owe this. . .honor?" he asked.

Jennie smiled sweetly. "Aunt Edith and I brought you something."

Nick's eyes bulged. "Aunt Edith?"

"That's right." Jennie's dimple deepened. "We've had a lovely time getting acquainted. She brought something to the office for you." Jennie pulled an envelope from her reticule.

"Yes," the older woman put in. "It's the information you asked me to get. I wrote everything down for you."

Nick's teeth snapped together with an audible *click*. He held out his hand. "May I have it, please?"

Jennie dangled the envelope just out of his reach. "Will you agree to share the information with me so I can work on the story, too?"

"Not in a million years." Nick set his lips in a firm line and kept his gaze riveted on the envelope.

"Come now, children." Edith Wells fluttered her hands like a schoolmistress calling her charges to order. "It's time to quit squabbling. Can't you see there's an obvious solution?"

Nick shifted his chair. "Such as?"

Aunt Edith beamed. "Why don't you two work together instead of competing? You both have good ideas. Why not share them? I have a feeling our Jennie is going to stay with the story, regardless of your wishes. If the matter truly is as dangerous as you implied, remember there is safety in numbers."

Nick recognized the truth of her statement. Jennie had the tenacity of a terrier going after its quarry. He looked at her across the table. "What do you think? I'll declare a truce if you will."

Jennie hesitated a moment, then held out her hand. "Done." They sealed their pact with a solemn handshake. She handed him the envelope.

Nick tore it open and pulled out the single sheet of stationery. He studied the lengthy list of names, then sighed and passed the paper to Jennie.

Aunt Edith's brow furrowed. "What is it?"

"It would take far too long to set up interviews with all these people. And that's assuming they would be willing to cooperate." He reached across the table and patted Aunt Edith's hand. "It was a good idea. Thank you for taking the time to draw this up. I'm just sorry you went to all that trouble for nothing."

Aunt Edith stared at a point past Nick's left ear. "What if I throw a party?" she asked. "None of these people would have any reason to turn down an invitation to my home. I could invite everyone on this list, and a few more besides, so it won't be obvious I have a select guest list." She clasped her hands, warming to her topic. "You two can be my guests as well. If you phrase your questions carefully, you can do your interviews while you mingle with the others. No one will suspect a thing."

Jennie gripped the edge of the table. "That's a wonderful idea. What do you think, Nick?" She unleashed the full force of her blue gaze upon him.

Seeing the unguarded excitement shining in her eyes, Nick felt something break loose inside him. At that moment, he would have agreed to anything. He nodded his head, unable to speak.

Aunt Edith tapped the table with her spoon as though calling a meeting of her ladies' group to order. "Then I suggest we take advantage of this opportunity and make plans while we're all together."

Nick tore his gaze from Jennie and tried to focus on the topic at hand.

"We'll hold the party one week from tonight," Aunt Edith continued. "That seems a bit rushed, I know, but I'll come up with some credible reason for doing it on such short notice." Her eyes widened, and her lips formed an *O*. "I have it!" She reached over and patted Jennie's arm. "How long have you been in San Francisco, dear?"

"A year."

"Close enough." A flush of pink tinged Edith's cheeks. "You'll be a dear acquaintance of mine—which you have just become—recently arrived in the city. The party will be to introduce you to the cream of San Francisco society. . . ." A look of satisfaction settled over her face. "And to announce your engagement."

"Wait a minute," Nick protested. "Just whom is she supposed to be engaged to?" Edith directed a bright smile his way. "Oh no. . ." *Well, why not?* Jennie had certainly thrown him off stride by her appearance with Aunt Edith. It was time for him to turn the tables. "It sounds like a grand plan to me. What do you say, Jennie? A small sacrifice for the good of the cause?"

Jennie's lips parted, and a haunted expression swept over her face. Then she squared her shoulders and looked him in the eye. "Of course. For the cause."

Chapter 10

J ennie pulled her cloak more snugly about her shoulders.
"Are you cold?" Nick asked. "I'll put my coat around you."
She shook her head, not trusting herself to speak. The
breeze that blew off the bay was enough to chill her to the
bone, but she would let herself freeze solid before she would
wear Nick's coat. Just having him walk beside her set her heart
to racing at a dangerous rate.

When she agreed to allow him to see her home after saying
good-bye to Edith Wells outside the restaurant, she never
thought about the potential consequences. Now she wondered
if she should have accepted Mrs. Wells's offer to have her driver
take Jennie back to the Hamilton.

Grateful that Nick didn't seem to be in a chatty mood, she
pondered the scheme they had worked out. She should be
thrilled to be working on the story again, she reminded herself.
The party had been a stroke of genius on Mrs. Wells's part, a
marvelous scheme that would allow them to converse freely
with the very people who might shed some light on the mystery.

As for being the guest of honor, Jennie could accept that

role, knowing it gave the plan credibility. Announcing her engagement to Nick, though. . .

Why had he capitulated so quickly to that part of the plan? Jennie remembered how he fairly bubbled with excitement at the thought. Perhaps he merely saw it as a clever means to achieve their mutual goal.

A sour knot formed in Jennie's stomach. She knew how to play a part well enough. Somehow, she would find the strength to act this one out. But could she look into those brown eyes, pretending to feign love, when her feelings for him became more real every time she was with him?

Once she quit the family business, she'd thought she'd left her days of playacting behind forever. According to the Bible, she was a new creature in Christ. How could she go back to living a lie, even for a worthy cause?

Nick stopped at the next street corner and drew nearer to her. Jennie felt an invisible spark leap between them. Did Nick sense it as well?

"Look." He pointed to the left.

She followed his gesture and caught her breath at the brilliant hues that splashed across the western sky. They stood in silence, watching the last of the sunset colors fade until the shadows joined together and became night.

"Tell me something." Nick spoke casually, his eyes still focused on a point in the distance. "Why is it you're so bent on sticking your lovely nose into something that only a man should be doing?"

Jennie lifted her shoulders in a tiny shrug. "It's something I have to do."

Nick turned to face her, a puzzled look wrinkling his brow. Jennie lowered her gaze. "I have a lot to make up for."

"Make up?" Nick placed his fingers under her chin and tilted her head until she looked squarely at him. The tenderness in his smile made her breath catch in her throat. "What could a sweet thing like you possibly have done that requires restitution?" A low chuckle rumbled in his chest. "As your newly appointed fiancé, I feel I have a right to know."

Jennie pulled away. Turning, she wrapped her hands around the corner lamppost and rested her head against the cold metal. "It isn't just me," she said in a dull voice. "It's my whole family."

She sensed Nick step up behind her and felt his hands cup her shoulders. He leaned closer. "What about your family?"

Jennie shivered. Because of the chill night air, or the brush of Nick's breath across the back of her neck? She couldn't be sure. She tightened her grip on the lamppost and shut her eyes tight. "Where were you born, Nick?"

"Philadelphia." His warm breath tickled her right ear. "But what does that have to do—"

"And how many places have you lived?"

"Philadelphia and San Francisco." He paused. "Why?"

Jennie sighed. "I was born in Cairo, Illinois, but I've lost track of the number of places I've lived—if you could say I stayed long enough in any place to qualify as living there." She drew a shuddering breath. "Have you ever heard of Professor Mountjoy's Elixir of Health?"

Nick's thumbs stroked her shoulders in slow circles. "I can't say that I have. It sounds like one of those patent remedies that promise a miracle cure for every ill known to man."

"That's exactly what it is." Jennie choked back a sob. "It's also my family's livelihood. My father is Professor Mountjoy, Nick. The elixir is supposed to relieve everything from bunions to vertigo. But of course, it does no such thing."

She steeled herself to go on. "My mother died when I was little. My father, brothers, and I lived out of the medicine wagon and traveled from town to town. We'd set up a show in the new location, wait until a crowd gathered, and assure the people they were getting a 'magical nostrum.' But it was nothing more than red pepper, turpentine, and a hefty helping of alcohol." She gave a bitter laugh. "I ought to know. I helped make up enough bottles of the loathsome stuff."

"Jennie." A wealth of tenderness lay in Nick's tone. Jennie fought the longing to fling herself into his arms. She had to finish the story before she lost her nerve.

"That life was all I knew, and for years I saw nothing wrong with it. It seemed like a game of wits, one we nearly always won. Then one day I heard my father and brothers talking about a man who died after dosing himself with the elixir." Tears squeezed past her eyelids. "From that moment on, I knew I could never again help peddle the elixir with a clear conscience."

"So you put your foot down and refused to be a part of it anymore?"

Jennie shook her head sadly. "I didn't have the courage to defy my father. Not until we came to San Francisco. Not until I found Jesus." The beginnings of a smile tugged at her lips. "He saved me, made me clean again." Her shoulders drooped. "But my family is still at it."

"Are they still here in the city?"

"No. They left months ago. There's no telling where they are now. All I know is that I have to make up for the years my family spent hurting people. And for what they're doing now. That's why I want so much to expose the evil behind whatever Pacific Mutual is up to. Maybe that will help tip the balance a bit. I just wonder if I can ever do enough." Unable to contain her sobs any longer, she buried her face in her hands and wept.

"Jennie." Nick's voice barely penetrated the misery that enveloped her. "Jennie," he repeated, louder this time. He took hold of her shoulders and turned her to face him. "Look at me."

She pulled her hands away from her eyes, barely able to meet his gaze.

"Don't you understand that the penalty for all your wrong-doing has already been paid? Jesus took care of that at the cross; there's nothing more you can add to it."

"But my family. . ."

He cradled her face in his hands. "That's a decision they'll have to make for themselves. You can't make their choices for them or do anything to atone for what they've done."

Jennie let the truth of his words penetrate her soul. The sense of freedom nearly lifted her off her feet. She wanted to float right up through the night sky and touch the stars overhead.

Nick seemed to sense her relief. His eyes gleamed with joy then took on a more sober sheen. His hands slid to the back of her neck, and he pulled her toward him. Jennie let her eyelids close.

The *clip-clop* of horses' hooves rang out on the street. Jennie felt Nick draw away and opened her eyes, flustered at the thought of a stranger witnessing their near kiss.

A closed carriage drew up beside them. The driver leaned down from his seat and called, "Could you give me a hand here? There's someone inside who needs assistance."

Nick stiffened and put his arm around Jennie. Behind her, she heard something scuffle and turned to see what it could be. Her eyes saw nothing unusual, but she sensed movement in the shadows just outside the street lamp's circle of light.

"Please." The driver's voice held a note of urgency. "I don't think there's any time to lose."

Nick's gaze darted from the driver to Jennie to the carriage. Nothing appeared to be wrong, but a sense of evil pervaded the night.

Jennie stepped toward the carriage, intent on helping the person within.

"Wait," he commanded.

His sharp tone brought her up short. Heavy boots rattled over the boardwalk behind them, and two roughly dressed men sprang into the lamplight. One grabbed at Nick. He swung at the ruffian and connected with his shoulder. The man staggered to the side, and Nick stepped in to throw another blow. He swung again. This time the attacker grabbed Nick's arm and pulled him into a headlock.

"I wouldn't," the thug rasped, swinging Nick around. Nick's blood ran cold at the scene before him.

The other hoodlum stood with his arm around Jennie's throat and a gun pointed at her head. "She's an awfully little thing," he said. "It wouldn't take much to break her pretty neck."

Nick forced himself to go still at the sight of Jennie, wide-eyed and pale in the lamp's glow. "What do you want?"

The driver had gotten down from his box during the scuffle. He now swung open the carriage door and gestured inside. "If you please." He bowed mockingly.

Nick endured the humiliation of being forced into the carriage. Had he been alone, he would have fought to the death, but he couldn't risk Jennie's safety. Her captor shoved her in after Nick, and she stumbled into the seat beside him. She pressed close and clasped his arm with both hands while the two hoodlums climbed in and took their places on the opposite seat, pistols trained on Nick and Jennie.

Nick felt Jennie tremble. A dark rage engulfed him. "What is this?" he demanded.

"Just sit quiet, Mr. Edwards," said the thug on the left. "You'll find out soon enough."

Nick exchanged a quick glance with Jennie and saw his own thoughts reflected in her eyes. They knew his name. That eliminated the possibility of a chance abduction or mistaken identity.

"Whatever you want me for, there's no reason for the lady to be involved. Can't we drop her off somewhere?"

The man sneered and waved his pistol casually in Jennie's direction. "I'm afraid Miss Montgomery's presence is required as well." His face hardened. "You'll do well to keep quiet if you don't want anything to happen to her."

Nick felt Jennie flinch at the mention of her name. He clasped her hands, wishing he could tell her everything would be all right. Instead, he kept his silence. It wouldn't pay to antagonize these men.

Frustrated by the blinds that masked the carriage windows, he tried to gauge their location as the carriage rattled along. But the conveyance made so many twists and turns, he lost track of their direction. From the salty tang in the air and the strong odor of fish, he judged they were nearing the waterfront. Beyond that, he could tell nothing.

The carriage slowed then jerked to a halt. Nick's pulse pounded in his temple. Whatever threat loomed outside, they were about to face it. He tightened his grip on Jennie's hands and waited for the door to open.

"Not so fast." Their abductors held up two long strips of cloth. Nick gritted his teeth and submitted to having his eyes blindfolded.

Chapter 11

A llow me to assist you." The oily voice set Jennie's nerves on edge. "We wouldn't want you to slip and twist one of those dainty ankles." Rough hands encircled her waist and lifted her to the ground.

Jennie clamped her lips together to keep from screaming and forced herself not to struggle. If the fellow dropped her, she would be even more at their mercy.

What had she and Nick gotten themselves into? These men knew their names, had been able to lie in wait for them. That argued advance preparation and the probability they had been watched.

If she only had her parasol! But it wouldn't have done much good against these men. They had the advantage in both numbers and surprise.

Steely fingers gripped her elbow and forced her to move forward. She inched her way step by cautious step across the rough ground, praying her captor wouldn't lead her to a drop-off and send her over the edge. The thought brought forth a whimper despite her best efforts.

The hand squeezed her elbow tighter. "Hush up. There'll be reason enough for you to cry later."

Jennie bit her lip and floundered through the terror of the darkness in silence.

"Step up here." The words came an instant too late to keep her from stumbling. If not for the iron grip on her arm, she would have fallen. Jennie regained her footing and continued across a wooden floor. They must have entered a building. Behind her, she heard Nick stumble over the step.

A different voice spoke. "You may remove your blindfolds now."

Jennie ripped the fold of cloth from her eyes and blinked in the glare of light from a trio of oil lamps sitting beside a pile of wooden boxes partially covered by a cloth. The pool of light they cast spread only a short way, to be swallowed up by darkness. Nick moved up beside her. She stepped close to him and linked her fingers in his.

A stately, gray-bearded man stepped out of the shadows and stood before them. He waved his hand, and a small group of men came out from the opposite side of the circle of light. Jennie gasped when she saw the shabby man from the funeral.

The bearded man gave her a grandfatherly smile. "I see you recognize Mr. Mulrooney. Are you acquainted with the rest of our little band?"

Jennie peered at the other three. "I've seen him." She pointed to a dapper man on the right. "He was with the mayor at the cemetery."

"Ah, yes. Elwood Barton, one of our esteemed city supervisors."

The dapper man smirked and bowed.

"You may not know Ian McDermott, Mr. Mulrooney's employer."

The stocky man's leer sent a cold shiver up Jennie's spine.

"But the last of our number you should be well acquainted with."

The fourth member of the group, a portly dark-haired man, stepped forward and grinned.

"Alexander Sibley," Nick said. He glared at the spokesman for Pacific Mutual Investments. "Why am I not surprised?"

Their host chuckled. "Well said, Mr. Edwards."

Nick turned his gaze to the speaker. "And I've seen you somewhere before."

"Allow me to introduce myself." The bearded man inclined his head. "Daniel Weston, at your service. I met you coming out of Mrs. Wells's house not long ago. A lovely woman, Edith, but inclined to chatter. She talks incessantly about your journalistic prowess and your ability to ferret out all kinds of facts. Once you got on to us, we knew we couldn't let you continue." He smiled at Jennie. "And it appears you've met your match in Miss Montgomery. Her article was just as troubling as yours. As a matter of fact, the two of you have caused us nothing but trouble ever since Calvin Harper's demise."

"I don't understand." Jennie faltered. "What could the five of you possibly have in common?"

Weston chuckled. "That's simple, my dear—our love of money. You see before you the members of Transwestern Amalgamated, a group formed for the express purpose of increasing our mutual wealth. I modestly admit the idea for the group originated with me, but without the proper partners, the realization of our goal would never have been reached."

Nick cut in. "What exactly is your goal? What do you hope to do with a vast expanse of desert?"

"You still haven't figured that out? I'm disappointed." Weston clucked his tongue. "The railroad, Mr. Edwards. Plans have already been laid for a transcontinental railway. Thanks to information from a source I will not name, we know the fastest route will pass through a specific area, and we control it all."

Jennie could sense the anger coursing through Nick. "So you think you can gouge the railroad when it comes time to purchase land?" he demanded.

"That's only a small part of the picture. We'll parlay money from the sale of that land into control of the goods coming in by sea as well." Weston spread his hands wide. "Between us, we'll rule the West."

Jennie tightened her grip on Nick's hand. "How did Vincent Collier and Calvin Harper figure in this?"

"Mr. Collier had a weakness for the pleasures that Mr. McDermott offered. We decided that he—or rather, his investors—could provide the seed money we needed to begin. Unfortunately, Mr. Collier developed a case of cold feet, a terminal case, one might say." Weston shook his head. "He wanted out. We could not allow that."

Jennie stared. "So the carriage accident was staged?"

"Let us say that a slingshot is capable of sending a projectile that can cause a normally calm horse to turn into an uncontrollable runaway."

She swallowed hard. "And Calvin Harper?"

Weston's face hardened. "Mr. Harper made the mistake of stealing from me, or trying to. It turns out he was skimming money off the top of the money we were skimming from his investors. The man decided he would go into business for himself, a very unwise choice as it turns out."

"Then his attack was staged as well?" Jennie couldn't keep the disgust she felt from coloring her tone.

"Hardly staged, my dear. The role of assailant was taken on by the two gentlemen who brought you here tonight, a part that happens to be their chosen profession." He smiled gently when Jennie grimaced. "And now, that brings us to you."

Jennie took courage from Nick's presence beside her. "We have enough information to hang the lot of you," she declared.

Nick turned to her, his expression grave. "I have a feeling they aren't too worried about that."

Weston stroked his beard. "Very astute, Mr. Edwards. You see, Miss Montgomery, it doesn't matter that you know, because you won't have an opportunity to tell anyone." He turned to his confederates. "Mr. Mulrooney?"

Mulrooney nodded. His two henchmen stepped out of the shadows, each carrying a length of rope. In a matter of moments, Jennie and Nick lay on the hard wooden floor, bound hand and foot. A metallic taste filled Jennie's mouth. Her heart felt like it would pound right through her chest.

Weston strolled across the floor and stood over them. "As you may have guessed, you're in one of Pacific Mutual's warehouses. You may remember the fire that took place on the day of Mr. Collier's funeral?" He went on without waiting for a response. "I'm afraid there is going to be another explosion here tonight. It ought to make quite a stir. These old wooden buildings burn so easily, you know."

Jennie couldn't see Nick, but she heard him shift position on the floor. "One fire is a surprise," he said. "Two are highly suspicious. You're bound to be caught. You can't get far enough away in time."

"On the contrary," Weston said with his gentle smile. "With little to do but find ways to make my money grow, I have a fair amount of time on my hands. I derive a great deal of relaxation from toying with different ideas. Tonight we're going to put my latest project to use."

He nodded to Mulrooney and McDermott, who pulled the cloth away from the pile of boxes. Jennie stared at the contraption thus revealed.

"Rudimentary, I'll admit," Weston said, "but it serves tonight's purpose admirably." He pointed to the candle set atop the stack. "You're quite right about our needing time to get away, and fuses can be so untrustworthy. When this candle has burned halfway, the flame will come in contact with the cord you see stretched from the rafter above. The flame will burn through the cord, releasing the brick tied at its other end onto this lamp." He indicated one of the coal oil lanterns at the base of the boxes. "The brick shatters the lamp, and the resulting fire will ignite the dynamite in these crates."

Weston smiled. "By my estimate, it should take anywhere from thirty minutes to an hour, plenty of time for us to establish alibis elsewhere. And you'll be able to watch the process and try to guess just how much time you have left."

He pointed a finger at Nick. "You strike me as the type to

indulge in a bit of heroics, Mr. Edwards. Let me assure you that any attempt to knock the candle over will only speed up the course of events. And I'm sure you will both want to prolong those last precious seconds of your lives."

Jennie heard scraping sounds from Nick's direction. "Leave me here if you must, but let her go."

Weston leaned over to pat Jennie on the shoulder. "I do apologize, Miss Montgomery. I am not in the habit of killing women. But you would force yourself into a man's world, so I must make an exception in your case."

Jennie watched in reluctant fascination as he struck a match and set the candle alight. Footsteps rumbled across the floorboards as the gang vacated the warehouse.

"I bid you farewell," Weston said from the doorway. "Or maybe more appropriately, go with God."

Jennie blinked back tears. "At least I know He will welcome me home when I stand before Him. Can you say the same?"

Weston shrugged. "I might be worried if I believed there was a God. Good-bye, my friends." He closed the door quietly.

Chapter 12

Jennie stared at the flickering candle and strained against the rope holding her wrists. Behind her, she could hear Nick making a similar effort to free himself. "How much time do you think we have?" she asked.

"I figure about twenty minutes."

"Twenty! I thought he said thirty at the least."

"You're going to trust a murderer?" Nick scooted on the floor, and Jennie felt him bump up against her. "That's better," he said. "Can you reach my wrists?"

Jennie squirmed closer to him. Her fingers fumbled at the knots. "They're too tight," she moaned. She cast another look at the candle. "How long now?"

"Don't think about it." Nick tried loosening her knots, with the same results.

Jennie rolled to one side and pulled her knees up toward her chest. With her fingertips, she started inching her skirt upward.

"What are you doing?"

"Just a minute." She felt the hem of her skirt slip up above her boot top. If only she could reach far enough! Twisting her body, she stretched her arms to their limit and managed to hook one finger in the top of her boot. "Please, Lord," she whispered.

She kept wriggling and pulled her foot closer to her hand. Now she had two fingers inside the boot. She probed frantically until she felt the tip of the knife handle in its sheath. Placing one finger on either side of the bone handle, she squeezed them together and pulled. The knife slid free.

Jennie breathed a prayer of thanks and gingerly held the knife out to Nick. "See what you can do with this."

Nick sucked in a quick breath. "You carry a knife?"

"Sometimes a parasol just isn't enough."

Nick roared with laughter. "Jennie Montgomery, you never cease to amaze me. Hold still now. I don't want to cut you." A moment later, the rope lay on the floor.

Jennie made short work of the rope around her feet then sawed at the knots holding Nick.

Scrambling to his feet, he pulled Jennie up beside him. "Come on."

"Wait. We need to put out the candle."

Nick pushed her toward the doorway. "They'll be waiting for the sound of the explosion. If they don't hear it, they'll be back to investigate."

Ducking outside, they kept to the shadows. They were several blocks away when the explosion thundered and flames lit the darkness.

Once they reached an area with light enough to illuminate the street signs, they were able to make their way back to the *Gazette* quickly.

Halfway up a hill, Nick stopped to catch his breath. "This is going to be the biggest story I've ever written," he panted.

"Just a minute." Jennie stopped beside him and planted her fists on her hips. "This has been my story from the beginning. I'm the one who's going to write it."

"I have a better idea." Nick smiled. "How about if we write it together?" Before Jennie could answer, he pulled her into the shadows, away from the streetlight.

"What are you doing?" she demanded.

Nick took her hands in his. "What do you say we form a partnership? We could write lots of stories together, maybe have a joint byline."

"A wonderful plan," Jennie said. "But we don't need to discuss it in a dark alley."

"I have something else to discuss." Nick pulled her into his arms and held her close. "It occurs to me that Aunt Edith had a brilliant idea. What if we make this more than a business partnership, say an alliance of the heart?"

Jennie squinted against the darkness, wishing she could see his face to tell whether he was serious. "Is this a proposal?" Her voice came out in a squeak.

"It is indeed, my dear Jennie. I am asking you to be my wife. Will you marry me?"

What if he's joking? "Are you sure you aren't just looking for an easier way to get your stories to Mr. Madison?" she hedged.

Nick pressed closer. His breath tickled Jennie's ear. "I have too much respect for your ability with a parasol to toy with you like that."

"But how do I know you're—" Jennie's words were cut off by a kiss that convinced her of his sincerity.

~

"It's a good thing you still have a key," Jennie said. "Otherwise I don't know how we would have gotten into the office." She carried a lighted lamp to her desk and pulled out a fresh stack of paper. "Let's get to work."

"At least in the middle of the night we shouldn't have any interruptions." Nick pulled off his coat and rolled up his shirt sleeves.

An hour later, Nick looked at their story with a pleased expression. "Finished. I'll just go over this one more time before we leave it for Russell." He leaned back against the desk while Jennie pulled out a clean sheet and continued writing.

Nick laid the paper in his lap with a satisfied grunt. "Want to come with me to put the story of the year on Russell's desk?"

Jennie dimpled. "I'd be delighted." She followed Nick to the corner office, where he centered the story on the editor's desk.

"What's that?" He pointed to the paper Jennie held in her hand.

"This? It's an item for my next—and final—column as Miss Minerva. Would you like see it?"

Nick glanced at the paper and chuckled as he read aloud:

"Recipe for a happy marriage: Take one man and one woman, equally matched in intelligence and commitment, with mutual respect for one another's abilities. Add hopes and dreams for the future, stir in a liberal dash of willingness to please each other. Blend with prayer. Store in a happy home for a lifetime. The flavor will grow sweeter with each passing year."

Jennie grinned up at him. "What do you think?"

"I think it has merit." Nick let the paper flutter to the floor. "Would your readers also be interested in a recipe for the perfect kiss?" He took a step toward Jennie and wrapped his arms about her waist.

She pressed her hands against his chest and tilted her head. "Do you happen to have that in written form?"

"No." Nick bent his head so close his breath stirred the curls at her temples. "I'd prefer to demonstrate."

And he did.

CAROL COX

Carol Cox is the award-winning author of seven novels and eleven novellas, four of which have appeared on the CBA Bestseller list. A voracious reader since an early age, she's a strong believer in the power of the written word to impact lives.

Carol and her family make their home in northern Arizona where they enjoy the slower pace of small-town life. "We are blessed with clear skies, rolling hills, and wide open spaces," she says. "We don't have to travel to experience nature. From our back porch, I can watch spectacular sunsets and catch glimpses of antelope, deer. . .and the occasional javelina."

For more information about Carol and her books, visit her website at http://www.carolcoxbooks.com. She'd love to have you stop by!

Misprint

by Kathleen Miller Y'Barbo

Thank You, Jesus, for finding me
and for helping me locate chapter two.
This one is for the cheerleaders.
You know who you are.
And for Judy, companions for lunch and life.
We made it!
Finally many, many thanks
to my dear friend Janice Thompson,
who gave more than I could ever ask of her in time
and prayers to see this book into print.

Chapter 1

Friday, June 29, 1860

Truly, Penney, I'll just m–m–make a mistake; I know it." Helen Morgan shook her head and took two steps back toward the safety of her little desk in the far corner of the newspaper office.

"If I can set type, anyone can." Penney Brice scurried back to the table holding the bits and pieces of letters that would form tomorrow's edition of the *Golden Gate Gazette*. "With both of us working together, we'll finish the changes to the front page in half the time." She paused to shrug. "Of course, I'll understand if you're too busy."

Busy.

Ever since she'd accepted employment as the sole bookkeeper at the *Gazette*, her life had been one series of busy moments after the other. Not that she looked upon her chosen profession as work, for nothing could be further from the truth.

To Helen, the process of collecting the numbers and fitting them into orderly categories and columns was an occupation that bordered on a mission. Other than in the Lord, she'd never found any greater satisfaction in all her twenty-seven years than in her recent work at the *Gazette*. Finding immense comfort in the solitude her employment offered was an added bonus.

Helen leaned against the door's ornately carved wooden frame and watched Penney bend over a tray of letters. With swift movements, Penney picked out letters and set them in place, oblivious to the stifling heat. Before her eyes, Helen watched tomorrow's headline take shape.

The process did look quite simple. Any imbecile should be able to spell sufficiently to place the correct letters in a line to form words and sentences. Surely. . .

Helen's hopeful musings ground to an abrupt halt. The words of her late father James Elliston Morgan, the honorable senator from the great state of Texas, rang through her head as her fingers grasped the doorframe. "You'll never manage it, Helen," she heard the great orator declare. "Unfortunately, you've inherited your charming mother's temperament and deficit of abilities." Always, once the pronouncement was made, a proper pause ensued, followed by the postscript of "may the Lord rest her dear departed soul."

The last time she'd heard her father's words, she chimed in with a response long held in check. "I daresay Mother has finally found her rest with the Lord, as she surely did not find it here in this life."

Of course she'd chosen the most inopportune time to assert her newfound outspokenness. One does not besmirch one's father's relationship with one's mother publicly, least of all at his inaugural dinner. Surely the dear ladies and gentlemen of the

Austin elite spoke in hushed tones about the senator's rebellious daughter for many years afterward.

For Helen the evening had produced a two-fold result. First, she'd been shipped off for "finishing back East," which meant spending the last year of her second decade with a pair of maiden great-aunts who adored her but cast as little care on her whereabouts as they did on their gray-striped tomcat. Second, she'd discovered that when the senator spoke, he stated the truth. As surely as if the Lord Himself had said the words, the edict regarding Helen's competence had hit home and stuck.

She'd not only inherited Mama's temperament and abilities; she'd taken what was in her mother an endearing inability to finish the slightest detailed task correctly and perfected it, adding a general aberration for people and public places and a horrible tendency to stutter when nervous. Outside of adding and subtracting numbers, Helen Morgan was a total, unadulterated failure at every new venture she attempted.

So why in the world did she find herself gravitating toward the typesetting table and her dear friend Penney?

She mustered a smile and listened with no small measure of concern as Penney began to instruct her on the fine art of typesetting. "Surely someone will be sorry that I've taken on this task."

"Don't be silly, Helen." Penney thrust a tray full of metal letters in her direction and smiled. "Anyone who can make sense of all those numbers will find this job terribly easy."

Half an hour later, Helen had all but given up on being any sort of serious help to dear Penney. To the contrary, it seemed as though Penney spent half the energy doing twice the work while Helen struggled to match each letter, each sentence and each paragraph to the copy Mr. Madison left them. Still, she'd managed to do a decent job of it, a fact she noted with an equal measure of pleasure and surprise.

"Honestly, Penney, I don't know how you do this day after day." Helen stretched to relieve the ache in her back. "I believe I'd go stark raving mad after the first week."

Ever cheerful, Penney smiled and tossed her curls. "Oh, it's not as terrible as that. Besides, I'm just biding my time," she said with a wink.

Penney made no secret of the fact that, while she had taken a job at the *Gazette* as a typesetter, she had no intention of staying in the position indefinitely. Beneath that pretty and youthful exterior beat the heart of a reporter of serious news.

Helen shuddered. Imagine interviewing unknown persons for a living, speaking to strangers as if they were familiar, or worse, chasing down a story from a reluctant perpetrator of crime. Why, sometimes it was all Helen could do to make small talk with one of Mr. Madison's advertisement sponsors or, worse, one of her roommates' gentleman friends. Imagine wanting to do these things on a regular basis.

Shaking off the awful thought, she went back to her work with renewed vigor. The sooner she finished this task, the sooner she could get back to her familiar world of columns and balances.

"Just as I predicted." Penney reached behind her back to untie her apron. "We're done, and in half the time."

"We are, aren't we?" Truthfully, Helen had been so immersed in her work, she'd failed to notice the passage of time.

"I knew you would be good at this," Penney said. "You're good at everything you attempt."

Helen bit back a comment and smiled. How little her dear friend knew, and yet it felt nice to think someone found her competent. Wouldn't Father have been surprised?

Monday, July 2, 1860

The first workday of July, and already the heat had him bested. Henry Hill removed his hat and stepped into the welcoming dimness of the Chandler Building's outer lobby then headed for the stairs, slouching off his formal jacket as he climbed the risers by twos.

"If it were any hotter, bullets would start firing on their own," he said with a chuckle as he touched the revolver hidden under his vest with his left hand. A man in his position had to be careful, thus the firearm, though thankfully Henry had found no reason lately to have need for the weapon.

When he reached the second floor, he paused to find his handkerchief and mop his brow. A man less inclined to his work would have removed himself to the mountains weeks ago or at least taken a holiday someplace where an egg would not fry on the roof. Many had done just that, including his law partner Asa Chambers, but Henry had business that precluded any vacation, now or in the future.

How could he be about the business of making a difference, of righting wrongs in this city, if he forsook his duties to find solace in the redwoods? Henry straightened his spine and neatly folded his handkerchief back into place in his vest pocket then pushed open his office door. No, it would not do for the future mayor of San Francisco to retreat in the face of something as minor as a little warm weather.

A trickle of perspiration teased his forehead. Henry reached for his handkerchief again. At this rate he would need another one before noon.

"I certainly hope it's not this hot on Independence Day. I'll have a time with my speech if it is."

His speech. Henry made a note to take another look at the speech he'd be delivering on Independence Day. Too bad Asa would not be there to witness the festivities. After all, he'd spent the better part of two days helping Henry craft the message that would provide the official launch of the mayoral race. Asa Chambers was a friend indeed.

Casting a glance at his friend's portrait, hanging alongside his in the foyer, Henry had to chuckle. He would have preferred the money paid to the artist to have gone to charity. Asa's father, however, insisted on footing the bill. Asa called them masterpieces. Henry just thought they were pretentious.

Shutting the door behind him, Henry hung his hat on the coat rack then carefully arranged his jacket to hang beside it. Finally he removed the key from his vest pocket and unlocked the topmost desk drawer on the left then placed his revolver beneath his Bible and slid the drawer closed. After returning the key to his pocket, he checked the time. Exactly half past nine.

"Excellent," he whispered.

He always arrived precisely half an hour before his first appointment of the day, time enough to place a sizable dent in the teetering pile of papers bordering the northernmost corner of his desk. Once upon a time, Henry would never have thought of allowing such a mess in his office. But then, once upon a time, he hadn't set his cap for the mayor's job.

Mayor Henry Hill.

The phrase gave him pause each time he considered it. He'd entered the election with much prayer and still much trepidation. Dared he actually assume that God would call him to lead a city? Some days, when life bore down on him, he doubted.

The hard-scrabble way he'd come up in the world most certainly gave Henry an edge in the election, as well as empathy for the unrepresented masses who collected in the less glamorous parts of the city. No matter how long he lived, he would never forget what it was like to go to bed hungry or to wake up to a rat the size of a small dog chewing on the bedpost—or worse, on him. If the Lord allowed his victory, Henry would do his best to see that no other child had to live in such abhorrent conditions.

San Franciscans would never know from whence Henry Hill came, his change of name and adoption at the age of seven by the wealthy and tenderhearted Anna Hill, heiress to the Hill shipping fortune, precluded any questions regarding his background. Anna's story of taking in her late sister Violet's son had been accepted without question, especially given her status as a childless unmarried woman with a love of children and a long list of charities to her credit.

What Anna failed to mention was that her late sister had died destitute and estranged from the family, who had refused to accept the man who fathered her only son. Where that man was now was anyone's guess.

"A good name is rather to be chosen than great riches, and loving favor rather than silver and gold." His favorite verse and the words by which he lived. With the Lord's help, Eli Barnes would never return to besmirch the name Henry had worked so hard to keep from tarnishing.

But what if Eli Barnes did return? What if his opponent's cronies were able to track him down? Would the voters of San Francisco still accept attorney Henry Hill as a candidate once they laid eyes on the ne'er-do-well who sired him?

"God is in control," he whispered.

Bypassing a folded note and a pair of newly delivered letters that were most likely invitations to some social event, he reached for the topmost paper on the stack and dove into the intricacies of law, both his passion and his respite from thoughts too unpleasant to bear. Every time he tackled a question of legal jurisprudence, he thanked God for choosing him to be a defender of the less fortunate. With His help, Henry would soon be in a position to provide aid and assistance on a much larger scale.

Moments later, or so it seemed, a soft knock captured his attention. Henry rose and ushered the first of several dozen clients into his office. By the time he'd finished with the last one, darkness had long since settled over the city. As he opened the desk drawer to retrieve his revolver, he saw the Bible.

"Where were You today, God?" he whispered as he shrugged into his coat, donned his hat, and stepped into the foyer. "Or rather, why didn't I find time to look for You?"

Henry made the climb down the back stairs, knowing he'd find an answer to that last question but fearing he would also make the same mistake tomorrow. Someday, when the pressures of his life were lessened a bit, maybe he would find the time to earnestly search for God's presence. In the meantime, a hasty prayer and a promise for better days to come were the best Henry could offer. After all, he had a city to lead.

"No, Lord, that's not right. You'll be doing the leading. I'll just take the orders and do my best to follow."

Chapter 2

Wednesday, July 4, 1860

W hat a nice man, that Mr. Hill," Penney said with a
sigh as she and Helen strolled away from the
Fourth of July festivities. "He really seems to care
about people."

"I suppose."

Helen linked arms with Penney as they strolled past the
darkened windows of the *Gazette* and turned toward home. In
truth, while she'd found the man's message both uplifting and
God-honoring, the man himself was much more interesting.
A strange feeling, this vague attraction to one so handsome
and unapproachable, thus she reasoned it must be ignored.

No good would come of entertaining fanciful thoughts of
romance with any fellow, much less one so far beyond her in
ambition. The Bible claimed it far better to live a quiet life,
and Helen held this in no dispute. In fact, the verse in the
fourth chapter of 1 Thessalonians was among her favorites:
"And that ye study to be quiet, and to do your own business, and

to work with your own hands."

Ah yes, *quiet*. Helen's definition of the well-lived life.

Imagine making one's livelihood from public displays, such as this evening. Helen shuddered despite the lingering warmth of the day. A worse lot in life, she could not imagine.

"Mr. Hill has such exciting plans for helping the poor," Penney said as the pair stepped gingerly across a particularly muddy spot in the street. "He seems like someone who will give a voice to people like us."

"People like us?" Helen looked down into the kind face of her friend. How little Penney knew about the life Helen led before making her way to San Francisco. While she hadn't been untruthful about her privileged past, neither had she spoken in any detail. As far as her three friends knew, Helen Morgan was an average woman with an average life, and this suited Helen just fine.

"Yes, the common folk," Penney said, punctuating the statement with a smile. "He did seem quite sincere."

"I suppose," she repeated.

No need in telling her perpetually optimistic friend that in all likelihood Henry Hill was just like all politicians, as blustery as the wind and just as difficult to find in times of need. *An opinion poorly timed and quickly given bore no good return.* Words of wisdom from Father that had served Helen well through the years.

Helen smiled. Perhaps someday when she met him in heaven, she would tell Father she'd listened to each and every speech he'd delivered, albeit discreetly and selectively. Wouldn't he be surprised?

"Oh my." Penney stopped short and gave Helen a stricken look. "My reticule. I must have left it back at the celebration."

"Are you sure?" she called to Penney's retreating form. "Maybe you just forgot to bring it."

"No, I'm sure I had it when we were sitting beside the stage, and then I. . ." Penney's voice trailed off as she turned the corner. Helen rushed to catch up, nearly bowling down a well-dressed matron and her slightly younger escort.

"Forgive me," Helen said as she rushed past the pair. "It seems as though my friend has lost her—"

"Handbag?"

The question brought her to a halt. Helen whirled about to face the speaker. There he stood, the politician himself, so close she could practically read the swirling initial on his gold signet ring and count the buttons on his expensively-tailored formal coat.

Center stage, the man—what was his name?—appeared quite dashing, but here, so near, dashing was but a pale version of his true description.

The gentleman in question thrust a dark object toward Helen. "I believe this is what your friend is seeking."

Helen nodded, thankfully rendered mute, and forced her fingers to close around the item. What was it? Something soft, made of velvet, with a fringe that tickled her palm. She stole a glance at her still-outstretched hand. Ah, yes, Penney's reticule.

Helen lifted her gaze and found the politician and the woman staring expectantly. She should speak, should say something—anything. But about what? Ah, yes, the handbag.

The moment she made the determination, her fingers rebelled and released their grip. Helen watched as Penney's handbag slipped out of her reach and landed with a thud in the muck.

"Dear," the woman said, "are you ill?"

"I–i–ill?" Helen forced her lips closed and swallowed hard, then took a deep breath and exhaled slowly. With concentration, she managed to focus on the politician's companion. "Thank you. No, I'm fine."

Dark eyes smiled back from a kind face, slightly weathered by a sum of years that seemed to have treated her most kindly. "Perhaps we could see you home then?" She gave the politician an almost imperceptible nudge in the rib with her elbow.

"Yes," he said quickly as he once again retrieved the velvet bag and thrust it into her hand. "Yes, do accompany us, Miss. . ."

"Morgan." She tightened her fingers around the reticule and tried not to jump with joy that the single word hadn't come out as a string of unintelligible gibberish.

The woman offered her gloved hand. "How do you do, Miss Morgan? I'm Anna Hill."

Helen somehow completed the exchange of pleasantries without further embarrassment then took a step backward. "Thank you, but I—I—I really must go." She tested her footing on the uneven thoroughfare and found it lacking. Her ankle turned, and a sharp pain preceded a humiliating stumble forward. The politician immediately came to her aid.

"Dear, do assist the young lady to the buggy. I shan't imagine she will be going home on her own."

Ignoring the urge to flee, Helen called upon the manners

she'd learned at her mother's knee and prayed her faulty phrasing could enunciate the words she needed to say. "Thank you, but it isn't necessary t–t–to—"

"Nonsense," argued the matron as she bustled toward a rather elegant carriage parked just ahead.

Somehow Helen felt herself moving forward, placing one foot ahead of the other and progressing toward the selfsame coach. Had she gathered any senses, she might have resisted. Rather, Helen fell into step beside the gentleman and stared at his hand on her arm, the signet ring with the swirling double H on his hand, and finally, into the eyes of her escort.

As her gaze locked with the politician's, she froze. *What's come over me?*

Helen cleared her throat and enunciated slowly. "Do unhand me, sir."

The gentleman removed his hand and frowned. "Forgive me," he said, although the apologetic sentiment did not quite match his amused expression.

When he looked away, Helen turned and fled without so much as a proper farewell.

"Helen?" Penney asked as Helen approached. "You found my reticule. I don't know what I would have done if I'd lost it."

"Actually, I didn't find it." She paused to gesture toward the politician now walking toward them. "He did."

"Why, isn't that the fellow from this afternoon?" She waved her reticule in his direction. "Mr. Hill? I'm ever so grateful for you—"

"Don't give it another thought," he said, approaching with one hand hidden beneath his coat. As he strode past, barely sparing a glance toward her and Penney, Helen noticed a glint of silver under the politician's formal coat.

A revolver.

Nothing particularly out of order about that. San Francisco could be a dangerous town, and one would assume a man of Mr. Hill's caliber would deem protection necessary. Of course, one could also assume that a man who practically raced away from his companion with his hand atop his revolver might be heading for trouble rather than protecting himself from it.

"Well, he certainly seemed to be in a rush," Penney said as she linked arms with Helen.

"Indeed he did."

Chapter 3

Thursday, July 5, 1860

Miss Morgan, there's been some late-breaking news, and I'd like very much if you would edit the copy then help the typesetter in working this article into the front page." Mr. Madison thrust a hastily scribbled paper in her direction, and she caught it just before it floated to the floor. "Facts are sketchy, so work with what we know. I'm meeting with the chief in a few minutes, but I don't expect he'll have anything new to say until the arrest is made public. In the meantime, I know it's late, but I expect you girls to get this edition in print posthaste. Can't let the other papers beat us to the story."

Helen rose and watched Mr. Madison rush toward the door. "I've left the headline to you," he called as he donned his hat. "Make it a good one."

"Yes, sir." She lowered her gaze to the paper in her hand and began to read.

"What is it?" Penney called from her spot at the typesetting table.

"Big news," Helen said, imitating Mr. Madison's distinctive voice. "We're to get the edition out as soon as possible in his absence." She shrugged and glanced around the empty newsroom. "Looks like I'm your only help."

Penney smiled. "Then let's get to it. What do we have that's so important?"

Helen laid the paper in front of Penney. "A murder. Someone named Frank Bynum was killed last night. They found his body this afternoon hidden behind the livery."

"Frank Bynum? That name sounds familiar," Penney said.

"Well, I've never heard of him, but that doesn't mean a thing." Helen paused. "Oh my. Is this the fellow who found your handbag? The one who's running for mayor?"

Penney leaned closer. "No, his name was Henry Hill. The fellow who's going to be arrested for the crime is named Henry Hall. See?"

"Well, that's a relief. He did seem like a nice fellow." *Even if he is a politician.*

Helen reached for a handful of letters and began assembling the headline while Penney deftly pieced together the body of the text. In short order, the changes had been made to the front page, the sensational news taking the place of a less important story. Helen wiped her hands on her apron and smiled. "That certainly went quickly, didn't it?"

"Yes, it did." Penney smiled. "Two heads are always better than one."

"I'm just glad I could help." Penney had no idea how very much Helen meant the sentiment. Her days of incompetence seemed destined to be over, and the successful completion of tasks such as this gave her hope that someday she might feel capable to take on larger ones.

~~~

Friday, July 6, 1860

Henry Hill pounded his fist on the table and nearly upset his adoptive mother's favorite Wedgwood coffee service. He had certainly upset her.

True to her nature, the dear woman said nothing in anticipation of the explanation she demanded with the lift of a dark brow. On another day, he might have taken heed of her warning look, might have voiced the apology she silently demanded, but not today.

Not with his career and his campaign lying in tatters. Not after having his evening ruined by a cryptic note handed to Asa during the speech and the possibility of meeting with his long lost father that thankfully had never taken place.

"Heads will roll, Mother." He pushed away from the table and tossed his napkin onto the offending tabloid, effectively hiding the headline that all of San Francisco had most certainly seen by now.

"Surely you exaggerate, dear." She reached beneath the lump of cloth to retrieve the *Gazette*. Once again her brows rose, this time as her gaze scanned the front page only to stop on the bold print of the day's headline: HENRY HILL BELIEVED RESPONSIBLE FOR JULY 4TH DEATH OF WEALTHY BUSINESSMAN FRANK BYNUM.

"Oh my." His mother carefully folded the paper in half and set it aside before lifting her gaze to meet his. Brown eyes blinked hard, and it seemed as though a tear fought for escape. "Oh my," she repeated.

"Indeed."

Henry took a deep breath and fought for composure. He forced a weak smile, then reached into his vest pocket to snap open his pocket watch. While he didn't give a fig for what time the blasted thing said, he hoped the action might make her believe he considered the morning's upset to be finished. A woman so delicate and dear need not be unduly troubled.

Nor did she need to know he planned to right this wrong posthaste.

Better for her to believe he intended to spend his morning like all the others, hard at work rather than berating some editor for a misprint that could very well have cost him the election.

Slipping the watch back into his pocket, Henry turned his attention to his mother. "If you will excuse me, I'll be off now."

Mother frowned. "Promise me you will think before you act and pray before you think."

"If only I had a vote for every time you've spoken those words, I should truly prevail as mayor." Henry gathered up the newspaper then leaned down to kiss the top of his mother's head, inhaling the soft scent of violets. "Perhaps you should do the praying for me."

"For you and for the poor soul you intend to unleash your wrath upon at the *Gazette*." Her words chased him out the door and into the dreary San Francisco morning.

"Surely she doesn't think I would—"

"To the office, sir?" The aged driver, one of Mother's many "rescue projects," turned as best as his arthritic back would allow and narrowed his dark eyes. His wrinkled face offered no expression until he lifted a bushy brow. "Or did you have business elsewhere this morning?"

He'd obviously read the *Gazette*. "Where else would I go this time of morning, James?" he asked as he climbed into the buggy.

James turned about to grasp the reins with gnarled hands, then set the horse in motion. "The office it is, then." In short order, he began whistling the first of many hymns that made up his morning concert.

Most mornings Henry either barely tolerated or completely ignored the musical stylings of his driver, but today he found both most difficult to accomplish. Was he wrong, or had James intentionally raised his volume higher than normal?

As the buggy bounced along, Henry cast a glance at the folded paper on the seat beside him. Most citizens of San Francisco were acquainted with the murder victim, if not personally, then by reputation. Bynum's money came from sources both unknown and seemingly unlimited in their nature. His style was often bold and brash, and his largesse was not limited to the tawdry taverns and bawdy houses he was reputed to own. He was known to place large sums of cash or bags of gold on the doorsteps of the local orphanage or bawdy houses or in public spots around town then laugh along with his cronies as children fought adults for a portion of the stake.

Some found this game amusing, while others offered the donations as proof of the man's soft heart and sterling character. Henry was not among either camp.

Asa once mentioned the possibility of Chambers and Hill

representing the Bynum fellow in a series of real estate deals. Henry felt it would never do for the future mayor of San Francisco's law firm to represent such a character, especially when people like Frank Bynum were the very ones Henry intended to run out of town should he be elected. Thankfully he had a friend as well as a partner in Asa Chambers. The representation was never offered, and nothing further had been spoken on the subject.

Henry tucked the offending paper under his arm and climbed out of the buggy, then gave a cursory wave to the driver and turned toward his office. When the rig clattered out of sight, Henry whirled about and headed for the newspaper office.

As he strode toward his destination, he forced out the occasional greeting to future constituents, including an elderly gentleman who grasped hold of Henry's arm and waxed poetic on the rough political waters in the States for the better part of ten minutes. After assuring the man he would look into his concerns, Henry finally wrenched free and continued on.

As he neared the *Gazette*, he straightened his shoulders and picked up his pace. No matter his mood, the campaign had to be foremost in his mind at all times. A bit of irritation at a misprint might not be remembered come election time, while a ready smile and the willingness to listen to his constituents would.

Or *was* it a misprint? Thus far, Russell Madison had kept the *Gazette* out of the political fray. Perhaps this was his subtle way of endorsing the opposition. Henry stopped short at the errant thought.

By the time he caught sight of the newspaper office, the thought had become a real concern, and he'd worked up quite a head of steam. Now to find the guilty party and unleash a bit of that steam, starting with the Madison fellow.

Despite the threat of rain, it was a beautiful morning. Helen had been at work nearly an hour, awakened well before dawn by the strangest of dreams. Someone chased her through the streets of San Francisco, some small unnamed and unseen person carrying a white object in his tiny hand and bent on an unidentified evil deed. Exhausted, she finally gave up on sleep and dressed for work, fearing her dream might end—and not happily—should she return to her slumber.

She'd arrived at the paper to find Mr. Madison bent over his desk, pen in hand. Being an absurdly early riser and generally the first on the job had its perks. Today the habit had caused her to be targeted for a special assignment: manning the front desk and attending to matters until Mr. Madison returned from yet another early morning meeting with the police chief.

Helen took to the task with trepidation. She tucked her receipts beneath her arm and reached for her stool. Perhaps she could get a bit of work done rather than standing about and merely looking foolish.

Teetering on the edge of the stool to keep from revealing her crinolines, she reached for the first of many receipts awaiting her attention. "Doesn't he realize I have a mountain of receipts that have to be—"

The doors crashed open, and an enraged man stalked

toward her. She jumped and almost fell backwards. Receipts went flying about like leaves in a strong wind.

The politician.

Straightening her skirts, Helen reached for the edge of the counter to steady herself. *Crash.* She jumped and whirled about to see the stool where she had formerly perched on its side atop the debris, a victim of her swirling crinolines. A late-falling receipt from a supplier back East fluttered past her nose and landed atop her shoe as she pressed her hands against her sides to still the movement of her skirt.

With care, she returned her attention to the red-faced man on the other side of the counter. Had she actually found him attractive upon their first meeting? Perhaps a dose of kindness would counteract his ire. When she mustered a smile, he answered with a frown.

"May I help you?" came out in a series of squeaks.

The politician slammed a folded newspaper between them, and Helen jumped yet again. "I demand to speak to Mr. Madison at once."

"He's out," Helen managed to say.

"Then I shall speak to the person in charge immediately." He leaned forward, eyes narrowed, vein pulsing on his temple. "A member of this establishment has committed a grievous error that must be corrected at once."

Something inside froze. Helen opened her mouth, but nothing came out. She tried again to no avail then attempted prayer. *Lord, please help me* was all she could manage.

The politician pounded his fist on the counter and leaned closer. Helen took a step back and collided with the leg of the overturned stool. This time her attempts to right herself were a bit more successful and no more furniture or office receipts were sacrificed. Only her pride and her shin suffered.

"Madam, have you not heard me? I insist on speaking to the person in command of this enterprise at once."

"It is I, s–s–sir." She gulped, eyes closed. "What can I do f–f–for you?"

Silence.

Helen opened her eyes to see the politician smiling. The anger that contorted his face had abated slightly, although no one short of a daft fool would mistake him for a happy man.

"No, dear," he said in a curt voice, "it's your employer to whom I wish to speak. Now run and fetch him."

Of all the nerve. "I am in charge."

A complete sentence. *Thank You, Lord.*

"Am I to understand that *you* are running this publication?"

Rather than risk further humiliation struggling with words that refused to emerge, Helen settled for a nod, then added a smile as a postscript. For a moment, the strategy seemed to work. The man's tense features relaxed, he took a less threatening stance, and he even spared her what looked to be the beginning of a smile.

"Dare I ask? Have I not met you before?"

Quite the welcome shift in topic. "Why, yes, actually." She nodded. "You see, my friend and I were attending the Fourth of July festivities, and at their conclusion, Penney left her handbag behind. You and your. . ."

"Mother," he supplied.

"Yes, well," Helen said as she reached down to right the

stool. "You and your mother were kind enough to retrieve the handbag."

The politician reached down to retrieve a pair of receipts and set them onto the counter beside the newspaper. "So you are employed by this establishment then?"

Helen settled on the stool folded her hands in her lap. "I am."

He gave her a sideways look. "In a supervisory role?"

"Well, actually, I am a bookkeeper, but Mr. Madison just asked me to—"

Without warning, his countenance changed. "Then you, madam supervisor," he said slowly, "owe me a public apology and an explanation of this." He swept his hand across the newspaper's headline. "And along with the apology and the explanation, I demand the idiot who did this be fired forthwith."

Fired?

Anger simmered then quickly hit the boiling stage. How dare this, this *politician* treat her in such a manner? Why, if she weren't a lady and the daughter of a politician herself, she would. . .

"Madam, are you daft?" His voice rose well beyond the proper tone, summoning Penney from the back.

"Well, hello, Mr. Hill." Penney smiled and wiped her hands on her apron. "Is there a problem?"

"Problem?" He held his volume in check, but his tone sounded deadly as he returned his gaze to Helen. "Do me the favor of reading this headline, please."

Helen turned the paper around and stared at the boldface type announcing a break in the investigation of the biggest murder to hit San Francisco in years. Mr. Madison had been rightly proud to have been the first in San Francisco to run the story, prouder still to have her read the copy and deliver the corrected manuscript to Penney before it went to press. She looked up to see the politician staring at her intently.

"Do you see the problem with this headline, madam supervisor?"

Once more she read the words spanning the top of the morning edition before handing it back to him. "No, actually it looks fine to me."

"I see." He nodded and studied the headline before looking up at Penney and then at Helen. "Can either of you tell me the name of the fellow the police are seeking?"

"I believe that would be Henry Hall, sir," Penney said.

"Henry Hall." The politician seemed to contemplate the name a moment before spreading the paper out on the counter. "Then pray tell me whether that is the appellation you see here?"

Penney leaned against Helen and took the paper. Her lower lip quivered as she read the name aloud. "Henry Hill." She looked up at the politician and let the paper drop onto the counter. "Oh no," she whispered.

Helen snatched up the paper. "Henry Hill." Her gaze met his. "That's you."

"Yes, madam, it is."

"Oh my."

"I'm sure there's a reasonable explanation, sir," Penney said. "This is probably one of those silly coincidences and not a mistake at all. Let me go get the copy Mr. Madison gave us, and I'll show you."

Penney's bright smile belied the tear Helen noted on the woman's cheek. How dare that *man* make her friend cry over something obviously coincidental?

As her friend scurried toward the back of the building, Helen took a deep breath and exhaled slowly—one of Mother's tricks for remaining a lady when the words you desire to speak would brand you otherwise. Feeling reasonably confident she held a measure of control, Helen leaned forward and spread this morning's copy of the *Gazette* between them. She took her time meeting his gaze and held it a bit longer than polite society might deem proper.

"Are you *sure* you're not a suspect, Mr. Hill?"

His glare precluded further argument. This time when he leaned forward, Helen took a step back even though the sturdy counter filled the space between them.

"Are you sure this is *really* a misprint?"

Her gasp of surprise must have had the desired effect, for the politician turned on his heels and strode away. "Make the necessary changes or face prosecution, madam," he called as he reached the door.

"Sir," she called to his retreating back, "to be sure, this situation must be very distressing for you but I f–f–fail to see how this sort of behavior will accomplish—"

"Here it is," Penney called as she rounded the corner and thrust the edited copy of Mr. Madison's story into Helen's hand. "I told you the headline was right. I spelled it just like it shows on Mr. Madison's notes." She stopped short and looked around. "Where did he go?"

Helen shrugged and sat the copy on the counter. "Wherever

bad-mannered politicians hide when they're not upsetting nice people." She touched Penney's sleeve. "I'm sorry he made you cry."

Penney shook her head. "I'm just glad it was all a mistake. It must be very upsetting to be running for an important political office and then learn that a murderer shares your name."

Helen watched Penney return to her work then knelt to retrieve the receipts littering the floor. Amy arrived with Jennie trailing a few steps behind. Both greeted Helen before heading toward the back of the building. Helen checked the clock. Almost nine. Mr. Madison would probably return soon as well.

As long as that awful Mr. Hill did not return.

"What an angry fellow," she said under her breath as she collected the last of the slips of paper. "He'll never be elected to anything with that attitude."

She picked up the copy to set it aside and a name caught her eye. Not the name in the headline, Henry Hill, which Helen had written at Mr. Madison's request, but the one appearing in the second sentence of Mr. Madison's story.

"Early this very evening, the citizens of San Francisco were presented with the name of the possible culprit of the murder of one of our fair fellows. Law enforcement personnel are searching for one Henry Hall. . . ."

Helen let the paper drop. "Oh no."

Chapter 4

Henry walked past the newspaper offices twice in the half hour since his confrontation with the green-eyed woman, and both times his heart told him to go in and apologize for his rude behavior. So did his conscience.

Why he'd strolled past without stopping, without doing what he knew he should, defied reason. To be certain, he owed both women an apology, for he'd surely made the little one cry, but something about his exchange with the tall one set his jaw—and his heart—on edge.

She made him want to be right.

He shook his head and went back to work on his writ. No, that wasn't it. Henry began to twirl his pen.

She made him want to be. . .

Enough foolishness.

With force, he reapplied pen to paper and attempted to continue with the writ he'd set to drafting. Instead of coherent and intelligent words filling the page, his pen stalled, and so did the eloquent phrasings.

What in the world was wrong? Even the incident with the

counterfeit note from his father hadn't caused him as much uneasiness as this.

He dropped his pen and watched a nasty splat of ink decorate a corner of the page. He'd spend another hour redrafting the document for sure, longer if he continued to let his thoughts wander.

Leaning back in his chair, Henry laced his fingers behind his head and closed his eyes. No doubt whatever ailed him, its source was the woman.

Rather bookish, that one, and well past the age of employment. To be blunt, the first time he met her she'd barely made an impression. Why until she mentioned the fact, he hadn't realized the woman at the *Gazette* was the same one whom he had met days earlier on the street.

He met so many people these days. A hazard of his chosen profession—or at least the profession he hoped would choose him. What's a politician without an office to hold?

Better off.

A strange thought. Did he really question God's plan for him to pursue the mayor's office?

Henry heard her before he actually saw her. She called his name, stiffly and formally, and with the slightest hint of a stutter.

Opening his eyes, he saw the object of his thoughts standing in the doorway. She wore yellow. Why hadn't he noticed before?

"Do come in, Miss. . ."

"Morgan." She wrung her hands together then clasped them behind her back. "M–m–may I intrude for a moment?"

He stood a bit too quickly and pushed away from the desk, then gestured to the chair nearest him. "Do sit down."

Miss Morgan waved away his invitation with a sweep of her gloved hand and fixed her attention somewhere behind him. As she exhaled, she met his gaze with a direct look. Her dark brows furrowed.

"Forgive me," she said with excruciating care. "I am. . ." She paused and closed her eyes, then opened them slowly. Henry made the absurd observation that they were green and fringed with dark lashes.

"Sir, I bear complete responsibility for the m—m—m—misprint. I assure you it was unintentional."

His heart sank, and so did he, landing in his chair with an unceremonious thud. "I assure you, Miss Morgan, that it is I who should be begging your forgiveness. My behavior was terribly and inexcusably rude."

The lady looked a bit perplexed. "I beg to differ, sir. You see I—I—I know a bit about the workings of a political campaign and a m—m—m—mistake of this magnitude that could cast aspersions on the candidate, well. . ." She paused and looked as if she'd spoken more than she intended.

The lady knows about politics? Interesting.

Henry let the silence fall thick between them, a lawyer's courtroom trick designed to cause the other party to speak rather than bear the quiet. It didn't work. Instead Miss Morgan turned on her heels and walked out without so much as a word of good-bye.

He sat for a very long time, pondering the situation and going over each word of their conversation. Somewhere his plan to apologize had gotten derailed, but he hadn't the slightest idea how to get it back on track.

The rest of the morning passed slowly with work done in fits and starts. Finally, when the clock in the anteroom rang the noon hour, he donned his coat and hat and stuffed what he could of the work on his desk into his valise. If he couldn't force his ability to concentrate into submission at his desk, perhaps he could tackle the job on the long walk home and be of some good to his clients after a proper lunch. Mother would be happy with his decision to work the afternoon away in his study rather than return to the office.

The better to drag him off to the opera or some dreadfully boring dinner all the sooner.

Henry smiled, took the back stairs two at a time, and emerged into the alley. As the door closed behind him, he realized he'd left his revolver locked in his desk drawer. He pulled on the knob. Locked tight.

Casting a glance up at the second-floor window of his office suite, Henry contemplated his choices. He could go around the block to reenter the building through the front door, or he could forget all about retrieving the revolver today. Opting for the latter, he turned to head east toward home. At Coromundel Street, he briefly considered a side trip to the *Gazette*. What would he say to her? Worse, how would he handle a casual appearance at the paper when his last visit had been anything but polite?

To be certain, apologies had been exchanged, but Henry still felt something had been left unsaid, some deed undone. If only he could ascertain just what that was.

At Baker Street, he veered to the right and began the steep climb toward its intersection with Decatur Avenue. "Thank You, Lord, for cooler temperatures today."

"You ought to be thanking the Lord that him and me don't shoot you dead right here on the street."

Henry whirled around to find himself face-to-face with two masked thugs pointing revolvers at him. The tallest of the pair, a man with more scars than teeth, lowered his weapon to wrench away the valise. The other one pressed his gun against Henry's forehead.

As Henry watched the man rifle through legal papers and court documents, he waited for his opportunity to use his own gun on the petty thieves. The gun he had left back in his office. His heart sank.

"There ain't nothin' in there worth takin'." Toothless tossed the valise at Henry's feet, and several documents slid into the street. A particularly important writ landed unceremoniously in a puddle alongside the silver pen his mother had given him when he graduated from law school.

"Just shoot him and get it over with," Shorty said.

Get it over with.

No. Not today. Squaring his shoulders, Henry prepared to use the only weapon he had left—his fists. Toothless leaned in close and narrowed his eyes. Shorty pulled back on the trigger with a loud click.

Henry refused to allow fear to cloud his thinking. If this was how God planned for him to go to heaven, then so be it. If not, then all the better. He'd take them both at once if he had to.

The tall fellow poked at Henry's chest with his free hand. "Funny, you don't look like a man who don't pay his debts." Toothless stood so near that his rancid breath blew toward him in waves. "So me and him are gonna give you a chance to pay up."

"Pay up?" Henry searched his mind for the identity of the thugs. Had he represented one of them before? Worse, had he prosecuted them? "I don't know what you're talking about."

Not the most brilliant statement but a decent stall nonetheless.

Shorty giggled. His gaze shifted from Henry to Toothless, and he giggled again. His fingers never moved, and neither did the gun.

"Look, fellows, whoever this interloper is that you seek, I assure you it is not I." Henry notched up his smile and focused on Toothless who he'd decided was the leader of the pair. "I'm not without resources." He paused a moment to let the idea sink in, all the while deciding where on the thug's body to aim his first punch. "So what do say you on this? Put those guns away, and we'll discuss this like gentlemen. Perhaps I can lead you to the person you seek."

"Gentlemen?" Toothless snorted. "That's a funny one. It truly is." His eyes narrowed. "Gentlemen don't forget when they owe somebody, though, do they?"

"My point exactly." Henry's left hand itched to connect with the criminal's jaw. "I assure you I've not forgotten any debts," he said as he waited for just the right moment.

"Maybe we oughta help him remember." Shorty's forefinger danced inches away from the trigger, which from Henry's perspective looked enormous. "You got paid for something, and you didn't deliver. Now you gotta pay that money back."

"What are you talking about?"

Toothless leaned closer. "Maybe you should ask your—"

"Hello? Mr. Hill, is that you?"

Henry tore his attention from the gun to the approaching pedestrian and groaned. The lady wore yellow and carried a folded newspaper under her arm.

"She a friend of yours?" Toothless leered at Helen, and Henry fought the urge to capture the thug's attention with his fists. With Miss Morgan so close, however, he could hardly risk the possibility of her being robbed by the hooligans as well—or worse, being shot.

"A friend?" He shook his head. "Hardly. The woman has caused me nothing but grief."

Helen slowed her pace and clutched the paper to her chest. It was warm, but the heat she felt on her face didn't come from the temperature or the steep climb up Baker Avenue.

Mr. Hill's companions whirled about and snapped to attention, hands behind their backs. An interesting pair, those two, and nothing like the fellows she expected the politician to keep company with. Perhaps they were clients.

The taller one wore a dark coat that seemed absurdly heavy for the temperate weather, while the other, a short man with a thin patch of sandy hair and what seemed to be a perpetual grin, dressed in a more conservative suit befitting a professional of some sort. Only his shoes seemed out of place, rough work boots more fit for the field than the city.

Helen returned her attention to the politician, who looked ready to bolt and run at any moment. Of course, he was a busy man, and she'd taken up far too much of his time today.

"Forgive me for intruding once again," she said, "b–b–but Mr. Madison asked that I deliver this personally."

"No intrusion at all, Miss." The short one widened his grin. "In fact, it's a right pleasure."

Henry Hill said nothing.

Her gaze landed on the overturned valise and the documents spilling into the street. The taller of the strangers must have noticed, for he stuffed something into the pocket of his coat, then quickly reached to right the briefcase and stuffed muddy papers inside. He handed the briefcase back to Mr. Hill, and the pair exchanged a terse look. "We'll be in touch," she heard the tall one say.

Perhaps these were clients with whom Mr. Hill was upset. There certainly seemed to be no camaraderie among them.

Whatever the situation, none of the three men looked particularly happy to see her. Of the three, Mr. Hill seemed to be the most bothered by her presence. Truly he looked more piqued than he had this morning at the paper. Perhaps she shouldn't have greeted the politician or interrupted what looked to be a street-side business meeting. It *was* behavior of the most daring caliber, at least for her.

Still, Mr. Madison had selected her to deliver a copy of this afternoon's special edition of the *Gazette* to Mr. Hill immediately. Considering the magnitude of her mistake, a bit more humiliation was nothing.

She took a few more halting steps and thrust the paper in

Mr. Hill's direction. He stared at her hand as if it were a foreign object. Finally he lifted his gaze to meet hers. The irritation on his face hadn't reached his eyes. No, something else lay there. Was she mistaken, or did he flash a warning with those dark eyes?

"I–i–it's this afternoon's special edition," she finally said before stabbing the newspaper toward him. "I'll not b–b–bother you further."

His curt nod served as an answer. Helen did not linger. Instead she walked back to the *Gazette* at a brisk pace, all the while praying this encounter with Henry Hill would be her last.

She cast a quick glance over her shoulder as she turned onto Freedman's Street and saw that the three gentlemen had already parted ways. The strange pair was headed south at a brisk pace, but Mr. Hill still stood where she'd left him, one hand shading his eyes from the noonday sun and the other on his hip.

He was staring in her direction.

Chapter 5

Monday, July 9, 1860

Henry spent most of Saturday and Sunday thinking about *not* thinking about Helen Morgan. It was absurd, this feeling he had that somehow he not seen the last of the timid woman. He breathed deep of the musty air and dropped his valise on his desk. "Ridiculous."

With the retraction satisfactorily printed in Friday's special edition of the *Gazette* and an update regarding the search for tavern owner Henry Hall as this morning's headline, it seemed as though Henry's tarnished image had been repaired.

"What's ridiculous?"

Henry reached for his revolver and laid aim before he could blink. When he saw Asa Chambers in his sites, he put away his gun and gave his friend a hearty slap on the back. At nearly his height, Asa wore his weight across his shoulders and in arms that belonged on a boxer rather than a lawyer.

He punched one of those beefy arms for good measure. "You scared the life out of me, Asa."

"And almost out of me." Asa took the punch with good-natured grace then leaned against the edge of Henry's desk.

"How'd the speech go?"

Henry shrugged. "Fine, I suppose. The crowd seemed to applaud in all the right places, although I did skip around a bit."

His friend leaned back in the chair and fixed his gaze on the window behind Henry. "I suppose you're wondering why I'm back in San Francisco before the end of the month."

Henry settled into his chair and steepled his hands. "The thought *had* occurred to me."

Asa plopped down in a chair across from the desk and closed his eyes. His fingers drummed a rhythm on his knees, and his foot pounded a restless accompaniment. Since childhood, or at least from the age of eight when Henry had first been introduced to his best friend, Asa Chambers had been in motion. To stop moving meant he'd fallen asleep.

"Too much to do back here," he said slowly. "And absolutely nothing worthwhile to do up there."

"Translated, my friend, that means what?"

He opened his eyes. "That means I couldn't spend another minute up there when you needed me here to help with your campaign."

"That's the sorriest excuse I've ever heard." Henry chuckled. "I can't believe your father let you go."

"Well, actually, he thinks I'm on an extended fishing trip." Asa slowed his drumming long enough to study his nails. "I figure that will buy me at least two weeks here in the city." He gave Henry a sideways look. "What? We are fishing for votes, aren't we?"

"Excuse me, sirs," a small voice called. "There be a note for you."

Henry rose to follow the voice, only to find the lobby vacant. He darted into the hall to find it empty as well. A single sheet of white paper, folded in half, crunched beneath his feet, and Henry bent to retrieve it.

"Who was that?" Asa called from his perch in Henry's office.

"Don't know," Henry said. "But he left this."

He settled into his chair and opened the note. *Pay your debt, or Miss Morgan will pay for you*, it said in an elegant script. As befitting a missive from a coward, the note bore no signature.

Interesting.

Henry threw the chair back and stormed to the door, ignoring his hat and coat. Friday he thought he'd convinced the thugs that they'd gone after the wrong man. Further, he'd convinced himself he'd been the random victim of street hoodlums and nothing more. Obviously he'd underestimated the thugs. To cast aspersions on his good name was one thing, but to threaten an innocent woman was quite another.

Asa followed him out into the hall. "Where are you going?"

"To the chief of police. This has gone far enough."

An hour later, standing outside the chief's office with Asa, Henry tried not to let his anger show. While the chief had given the impression of being appropriately disturbed by the letter, he'd all but laughed off Henry's concern for Miss Morgan's safety and ignored Asa's concerns altogether.

The chief put off the note and the message on the handkerchief to political jealousy at the least and political trickery at worst. He promised to investigate but made the statement with little enthusiasm. His parting words had been to leave the worrying to the police department.

While logic told Henry he should do as the policeman suggested and let law enforcement handle the problem, intuition told him he should at least warn Miss Morgan of the possible danger. An informed person generally took fewer risks.

A bell sounded in the distance, signaling a packet boat's arrival in the harbor. Overhead a pair of sea birds circled, their calls punctuating the dull roar of carriages and horse traffic on busy Coromundel Street.

"Well," Asa said, "what do you intend to do now?"

Henry inhaled the pungent odor of horses and the sea and shrugged. "I'm not sure."

Asa took him by the arm and darted across Coromundel Street. "Forget about the woman. You've got an office to win, and I've only got two weeks to help you win it. What say you to a meeting of the minds back at the office? I've got some ideas for winning this election that I'd like to go over with you."

Shaking off his friend's grip, Henry turned away and headed for the offices of the *Gazette* two blocks away. "Later," he called to Asa as he rounded the corner. "I've got something more important to attend to first."

Outside the newspaper building, Henry froze. His encounters with Miss Morgan, although surprisingly frequent, had not been particularly pleasant. To be blunt, the cause lay with him, and he knew it.

Perhaps he'd better take a different tack on this visit. He stared at his reflection in the window and caught himself frowning. Immediately he pasted on a smile and strode inside. He would be pleasant, state his concern for the lady, and be on his way. The less attention paid to his visit, the better, and his duty to a fellow citizen would be done.

The elderly woman behind the counter was not Miss Morgan. A setback, albeit a minor one, he decided as he upped his smile a notch and tipped his hat. "Is Miss Morgan about?" he inquired. "I'd like a moment with her, please."

With a nod, the woman scurried away in a whirl of skirts and crinolines, nearly knocking over a stool in her haste. A moment later she returned with another young woman. "Miss Morgan's been sent on an errand," the petite blond said. "Perhaps you'd prefer to wait here."

Henry cast a glance behind her and saw a gaggle of young women, three to be factual, staring at him and whispering. One smiled while the other two nodded. The blond turned and gave them a look that sent them all scampering back to their work.

"Ah, no, actually I'm wondering if perhaps you could give me an idea of where Miss Morgan's errands might take her. It might be more convenient to find her rather than to wait here." He stared pointedly at the women, who whirled about and went back to their work. "I wouldn't want to be a bother."

Moments later, Henry was heading toward the harbor where he'd been told Miss Morgan had been sent to retrieve bundles of newspapers and other parcels sent from back East. He spied the object of his concern wearing blue and making her way across the uneven boards of the sidewalk, a small army of urchins following in her wake. Each carried something—a box or a paper-wrapped package or some other container. Miss Morgan marched ahead, whistling, of all things. Her hat bobbed as she walked, and a blue ribbon bounced and fluttered in the breeze.

Rather than disturb the little parade, Henry stuck to the shadows and watched as the motley group made its way down the other side of the street. Occasionally, Miss Morgan would stop and offer a handkerchief to one or a smile to another. When the party turned the corner and disappeared, Henry picked his way across the muddy street and hugged the buildings to keep out of sight.

At Freedman's Street, he froze. Just across the way he saw a familiar face. Toothless. As Miss Morgan's group headed north, so did he. When they made an abrupt turn to the east, he did the same.

A block away from the *Gazette*, Henry saw the glint of what appeared to be a pistol in Toothless's hand. "You there," he called as he pushed past a pair of matrons and an elderly coachman to barge into the busy street. Toothless glanced in his direction, but Henry couldn't tell if he'd actually heard Henry's cry. Too much traffic and noise separated them. When Henry made his way past carriages and horses to reach the other side, Toothless was gone.

At least temporarily.

Thankfully the little parade had stopped on the steps of the *Gazette*, oblivious to the incident. Henry leaned against the side of the mercantile and watched Miss Morgan receive each urchin's package, then reward him with a coin. When all members of the group had dispersed, Miss Morgan began to stack the items to carry inside. The bundles listed dangerously toward the street, and several seemed about to burst at the seams.

Miss Morgan looked as though she could use some assistance. A perfect invitation to an accidental meeting. Henry smoothed his lapels and strolled as casually as he could toward the woman in blue. Until he could make other arrangements, he'd just have to see to Miss Morgan's safety himself.

"Well, good morning," he said with a politician's practiced smile. "Fancy meeting you again."

Helen jumped, and a paper-wrapped parcel went flying, nearly hitting a farmer square in the back of his head. Mr. Hill showed his athletic prowess by catching the bundle before it landed on the sidewalk—or the farmer. A quick flip of the politician's wrist, and the item lay in her arms once more.

"Thank you," she managed to whisper, "b–b–but I can manage, really."

"Nonsense."

He nodded to a passing citizen who called him by name, then turned his attention back to her. Helen made the silly observation that his eyes were just a shade lighter than his hair. His smile seemed just for her, as if he'd created it special and saved it just for this moment. She shook off the romantic notion and squared her thoughts and her shoulders as she watched Mr. Hill heft an inordinately large pair of boxes onto his left shoulder.

"Where do you want these, Miss Morgan?"

"No, really," she said as she scurried behind him. "You'll hurt yourself."

Ignoring her comment, he set off toward the door. "You cannot leave these packages on the street corner, and I've seen the womenfolk this paper deems suitable for employment. While they are pleasant to view, not a single one of them, yourself included, could be termed particularly muscular."

Not like you. Her face flushed with heat. *What a simpering idiot I've become.*

Before she could protest further, the politician had deposited the packages on the counter and returned to gather up an armload of items. She followed his lead, removing a box or two from the steps while he stole her breath by taking twice as much on each trip.

"What is going on?" Penney called as Helen dropped a box of newspapers atop the heap on the counter.

"I'll just put these on the floor," Mr. Hill said as he positioned a pair of small barrels against the wall and strode back outside.

Penney smiled. "Why, Helen, it looks like you've found a knight in shining armor."

The heat in her cheeks turned up a notch. "Oh, hush."

Penney giggled. "I *would* help, but then the job wouldn't take nearly as long, and your knight would have to disappear back to the castle far too soon." She said the last of the words just as Mr. Hill walked back in with another armload of items.

"Something wrong?" he asked as he straightened his hat and pressed his hand over his lapel.

"No, nothing," both women said at once.

He gave them a quizzical look then headed back to his work. Penney's giggles followed Helen as she ducked back outside.

In short order, the items were stacked inside, and Helen found herself standing on a busy sidewalk staring at one of the most public figures in San Francisco. Perspiration glistened at his temples, and his damp hair clung to his forehead beneath his hat. His starched collar hung a bit limp, and a smudge of dirt decorated his right check. As heat-wilted and mussed up as Henry Hill looked, the politician was still the handsomest man she'd seen in quite a long time.

He shifted his weight from one foot to the other, arms crossed. Helen braved eye contact only to look away. On the street, a horse nickered, a patron of the local mercantile shouted a salutation to a passerby, and a pair of nicely dressed young ladies offered Mr. Hill a giggle and greeting.

All the while he kept his gaze fixed on her.

Say something.

"I don't know how I would have m—m—managed without your help, Mr. Hill." *Wonderful, Helen. You sound like a simpering idiot. And a Morgan does not simper.*

The politician looked around as if he were trying to find someone. "My pleasure, I assure you," he mumbled.

Helen followed his gaze and saw nothing but the usual collection of San Franciscans going about their daily business. Something caught his attention, and he seemed instantly distracted by it. Only a tug at his watch chain and the checking of the time on a gold pocket watch seemed to change his focus.

Did he have an appointment elsewhere? Helen tried not to

feel disappointment. Of course her knight in shining armor had just been an ordinary man coming to her aid. No ordinary man, she corrected, but a busy attorney and possibly the next mayor.

"I've kept you from your duties far too long, s–s–sir."

He seemed surprised that she spoke. "What? No, you see. . ." He paused and cast another quick glance over his shoulder before surprising her by turning his dark gaze on her. "Forgive me," he said.

"We seem to be saying that to each other quite regularly."

Another long silence fell between them. Finally, Mr. Hill cleared his throat and placed his hand on her arm. "With your permission, I would like to change that."

She shook her head. "I don't understand. What do you mean?"

"What I mean is, I would like very much if. . ."

Another maddening pause. Helen had to remind herself to breathe.

"Forgive me," he said, then chuckled. "If only I had a vote for every time I've said that to you."

"And I to you, Mr. Hill." She took a step backward and winced when her shin collided with the steps. "So now that we have that s–s–settled, I'm afraid I really must return to work."

Chapter 6

Henry stood on the sidewalk like a fool and tried to think of something witty to say. What was it about this woman?

"Wait!" he called, but the doors had already closed behind her. He looked around and saw nothing untoward. No thugs lurking in the shadows or other oddities held him there. Why then did he follow Helen Morgan inside the offices of the *Gazette*, the very place where he'd humiliated himself venting his anger only days ago?

To keep her safe, he decided as he picked his way through the packages and barrels to reach the counter. Once the thugs had been caught, he and Helen Morgan would part ways. Until then, he had a duty to protect the innocent woman he'd unintentionally involved in a potentially dangerous situation.

"Excuse me," he called, but instead of Miss Morgan answering his call, another young lady appeared from behind the boxes. He vaguely remembered her as the woman whose handbag he'd retrieved from the Independence Day celebration. The same woman he'd upset along with Miss Morgan on his last visit to the newspaper.

"Hello, I'm Penney. May I help you?" she asked brightly.

If only he hadn't made such a fool of himself before. Where to start?

Penney leaned against the counter and gave him a sideways look. "Is there something wrong?"

"Actually, yes," he said. "I owe you an apology. I was terribly rude before, and I—"

"Don't give it another thought." The woman waved away his concerns with a sweep of her hand. "I would be upset if I were in your shoes, too."

"Yes, well, thank you." He tried to effect a casual demeanor. "Would Miss Morgan be about?"

"About what?" Penney covered her mouth with her hand and giggled. "Sorry," she said a moment later. "I couldn't help that one. Why don't I go and fetch Helen?"

She disappeared, and soon Henry heard whispers coming from somewhere behind the boxes. The whispers became a bit louder, a bit more insistent. One voice belonged to the young woman, the other, he decided, must be Miss Morgan. Unfortunately, any understanding of the words spoken escaped him.

And then Penney returned. Alone. "I'm sorry, Mr. Hill. I told her she had a visitor, but I can't seem to budge her from her desk."

So, he'd been spurned. Worse things had happened, to be sure, and yet it stung. "I see."

Penney's face brightened. "So there's nothing left to do but go to her. Follow me."

Henry followed Penney through a maze of desks and

chairs and the odd table or two until she turned abruptly. There, in the farthest corner of the building, sat a desk that looked very much like his—piled with papers organized in neat but towering stacks. Atop one stack was a thick volume of Shakespeare's tragedies, and beside another lay a battered copy of Jane Austen's *Sense and Sensibility*.

So the woman knew about politics *and* enjoyed Shakespeare. Interesting.

Behind the desk sat the object of his concern—and consternation. When she saw him, she stood.

"Penney!" Her cheeks flushed the most interesting shade of pink as she crossed her arms over her chest. "You know I don't want visitors back here."

"Mr. Hill is not a visitor, are you, Mr. Hill?"

"I know you're busy, Miss Morgan." Henry stepped forward as much to garner Miss Morgan's attention as to shield Penney from her coworker's ire. "I assure you I'll be brief."

Her countenance softened a bit, but the color remained high in her cheeks. "All right." She began to drum her fingers on the surface of her desk. "Be brief, then."

"Have dinner with me."

"Dinner?" Penney and Miss Morgan said the words at the same time.

"Yes," Penney said with a grin.

"No thank you," Miss Morgan answered a second later. "I have plans."

"Nonsense," Penney said. "What time?"

"Penney!" Helen protested. "I demand you both remove yourselves at once." She turned her wrath on poor Penney, who merely broadened her smile. "I can accept my own dates, thank you very much."

"Then you *do* accept," Henry said. "Excellent. I'll call for you at half past seven so we can dine before the opera."

"Dinner and the opera? Wait, you don't even know where I live," he heard as he stepped outside.

Helen narrowed her eyes and stared at Penney. "I cannot believe you actually made a date for me, in my presence. I am not a child. I can answer for myself."

Penney shrugged. "Oh, you answered for yourself," she said as she turned and began to walk away. "You just gave the wrong answer, so I corrected it a bit."

"Corrected it a bit?" Helen followed Penney back to the typesetting table. "I'd say that telling a man I would have dinner with him when I specifically said I would not is somewhat more than 'correcting it a bit.'"

"Oh, now don't be angry." Penney reached for the tray of letters and began to arrange them on the table. "It's just one evening, and he *does* seem to be a nice fellow." She pressed her palms to the table and looked Helen in the eye. "Besides, what did you have planned that would be more fun than having dinner with one of the most eligible bachelors in San Francisco?"

"For your information, I had planned to finish *Sense and Sensibility* this evening."

"Jane Austen again?" Penney rolled her eyes like a petulant child. "Dear, I love Miss Austen's novels as much as the next person, but I will never choose one of her books over the possibility of a lovely evening of male companionship."

"Who's spending a lovely evening with a male companion?"

The pair whirled around to see Mr. Madison standing at the door.

"Helen," Penney said quickly. "She has plans for the evening with a gentleman caller."

Helen slid Penney a warning look. Was her friend blushing? She shook her head.

With that, she began to make her way back to the solace of her little corner. Perhaps a few hours with her receipts and numbers would fade the humiliation she now felt. To her surprise, Mr. Madison appeared at her desk a moment later.

"I didn't mean to embarrass you, Miss Morgan."

She waved away his apology and picked up a pencil. "There will be no 'lovely evening,' because the man doesn't even know where I live."

"Actually," Mr. Madison said slowly, "he does now."

Helen dropped her pencil and watched it roll onto the floor. "What do you mean?"

Mr. Madison grinned and began to study his ink-stained nails. "I told him."

Somehow, Helen managed to get through the afternoon, although she knew she'd spend the next morning double-checking each column she'd added to be certain the tallies came out right. At a quarter to six, with Penney's prodding, she dropped her pencil into the drawer and reached for her reticule. Slipping *Sense and Sensibility* inside, she rose to walk past Penney and the others with as much dignity as she could manage.

She'd almost reached the door when Penney came rushing up, her shawl pulled over her shoulders and her handbag under her arm. "I'm going with you," she said as she pushed on the door and strolled outside.

"On the date?" Helen asked.

"No, silly," Penney said. "I'm going back home to help you get ready."

"I assure you I'm quite capable of dressing myself," Helen said, but a short while later, standing in the room she shared with Penney, she began to doubt the truth of that statement. It seemed as though each dress Helen pulled out of the armoire was rejected by Penney. Finally her friend sent Helen off for a perfumed bath while she picked out a "suitable outfit."

"You'd think I was headed for an audience with the queen," she muttered as she sank into lavender-scented water.

"I just want everything to be perfect," Penney called.

Helen submerged herself in the warm water up to her chin. "Why?" she called. "Are you worried I might not get another chance?"

Penney arrived with a towel and an uncharacteristic frown. "No, but I am worried that you won't *accept* another chance."

At ten minutes to seven, Helen donned a green frock that had been languishing in the back of her armoire. Leftover from her days back East, the dress was one she couldn't bear to part with and yet had never expected to have use of again.

Father had issued his only compliment of her adult years in regard to that frock. "Why, Helen," she remembered him saying, "you look stunning, simply stunning."

She also remembered waiting for the qualifying "but" that

always came after a kind word from her father. When he merely stood transfixed and smiled, she marked the moment both in her journal and in her mind. She also promised she would keep the dress forever.

Penney fussed with Helen's hair until Helen could stand it no more. "Enough, Penney," she said as she attempted to stand.

Her friend placed her hands on her shoulders and pressed her back into her chair. "A few minutes more and no longer, I promise." She struggled to tame an obstinate strand into submission then tied in a green ribbon. "There, all done." She handed Helen the mirror. "What do you think?"

Helen peered into the mirror, and her breath caught in her throat. Her hair, always hidden beneath serviceable hats or pinned out of the way, fell in curls and wound around a ribbon perfectly matched in color to her dress. A lump gathered in her throat, and tears stung her eyes.

Penney knelt beside Helen. "What's wrong?" she asked, her face stricken.

"No one's done this for me in such a long time," Helen whispered.

Her friend looked confused. "What do you mean?"

She took Penney's hand in hers. "My mother used to play with my hair for hours. She would braid it and tie it in ribbons, anything we could think of to do with it. When I tired of letting her fix my hair, I would take a turn with hers. After she died, there was no one to fix my hair. At least no one who could do it like she did." A sob caught and held just out of reach. "I miss her tonight."

"Oh, Helen," Penney whispered. "I'm so glad we're friends."

A knock at the door sent Penney scurrying. Helen followed a step behind, her heart pounding.

"Go back in there this instant, Helen Morgan," Penney said. "Don't you know the first thing about courting?"

"No," Helen said, "actually I don't." She pressed past Penney to touch the doorknob, her reticule dangling from her arm. "And furthermore, I have no desire to learn."

Penney placed her hand over Helen's and drew her back from the door. In a deft motion, she removed the reticule from Helen's arm and opened it.

"Just as I thought," she said and made little clucking sounds of disapproval. "One does not bring Miss Austen on an evening out with a gentleman." She pulled Helen's copy of *Sense and Sensibility* out of the handbag and placed it on the table nearest the door. "Now, if you insist, go ahead and open the door, but if I had things my way, I'd send you off to the other room and make Mr. Hill wait a bit. It never looks good to be too anxious, if you know what I mean."

"No, I don't know what you mean. Now if you'll excuse me." Helen opened the door and lost her breath, all in one hurried moment.

The politician wore black, and he carried the loveliest bouquet of flowers she'd ever seen. If only she could form the words to thank him.

Instead, she squeaked something that she hoped would pass for gratitude and let Penney take over. Somehow, the flowers ended up in water, and she ended up in a lovely coach with a handsome politician heading down Coromundel Street to dinner and the opera.

As Mr. Hill gave the driver, a hymn-singing fellow of lengthy years, directions, she couldn't help but think that this was a scene that even Miss Austen couldn't have written.

Chapter 7

Things were not turning out at all as Henry had planned. He cast a glance to his right. No, indeed, not at all.

First someone had shanghaied the mousy Miss Morgan and replaced her with the spectacular creature swathed in green silk and seated beside him. Second, rather than the smell of newsprint and ink as he'd half expected, she wore the most lovely fragrance of flowers, spice, and something else, a scent he couldn't put his finger on and yet knew he would always remember. And third, his normally charismatic ability to charm his constituents into lengthy conversation apparently did not apply to Helen Morgan.

Indeed, somewhere in his great scheme to protect the frail and innocent newspaperwoman, things had gone seriously awry. He had to do something fast before he became the one in need of protection.

"I'm pleased you could join me tonight, Miss Morgan."

"Thank you," he thought she mumbled.

He shifted positions to better see her. A lacy fretwork of

light and shadows teased her face, bringing softness to the angle of her chin and the tilt of her nose. Aristocratic fingers were clenched in her lap, knuckles white, and she stared straight ahead as if looking toward a destiny for which she felt no particular joy.

Silence, a politician's worst enemy, fell between them. A reminder that this was not a real date failed to soothe his bruised self-esteem. Real or not, he had to set the situation to rights. He decided to try another tack.

"I generally take my meals with a law book." He inserted an off-the-cuff chuckle to lighten the mood. "Not nearly as pleasant a companion as you, I daresay."

Inwardly, Henry groaned. *You sound like an idiot, Hill.* He forced his smile up a notch and waited for a reaction from his guest.

At first nothing. She merely clenched and unclenched her fists until he thought she might slug him. Then, slowly, she met his gaze with eyes as green as her dress.

"I'm p–p–pleased to know I'll not be asked to meet high standards, Mr. Hill."

He waited for her smile to match his, for some indication she'd made the statement in jest. It never appeared. Gradually he gave up the pretense of sociability and settled back into the seat.

James began to hum an off key rendition of "Camptown Races" as the first drops of rain hit the roof of the coach. Soon the downpour began in earnest.

Henry continued to steal covert glances at his companion, who now seemed to be oblivious to his presence. This was shaping up to be the longest night of his life.

And it had barely begun.

~⁓

He keeps staring. That's all Helen could think as she rode along in uncomfortable silence. The stillness was barely broken by small talk and inconsequential discussions of law books and the stormy weather, which bore down around them. It followed them into the restaurant, a lovely eatery on the far end of Montgomery Street famed for its seven-course meals and decadent dessert menu.

Like as not, the food would be wasted on her tonight.

Once inside and settled at a table, Helen studied her nails and contemplated the length of the torture this evening looked to become. Meanwhile, her companion greeted a seemingly endless stream of well-wishers, pausing only to whisper instructions to a waiter. Occasionally he would introduce her as his friend, once as his companion, but more often that not, she simply remained "Miss Morgan" to those who ventured forth.

As no comment seemed necessary, Helen remained quiet and listened to the men talk politics. An unhappy reminder of the first two decades of her life. *Smiling girl decorates table for politician.* A headline worthy of her life if not worthy of the newspaper.

Helen sighed. Why hadn't she returned the book to its place in her reticule, or better yet, stayed home to read in the privacy of her room? Just wait until she returned home. She would make sure that neither Penney nor the others ever coerced her into an evening out with a man again.

Her foray into the world of dating was done. At least she had the opera to look forward to.

"I noticed you read Jane Austen," the politician said in a rare moment without an audience. Her shock must have registered on her face, for he continued. "I'm sorry. Am I wrong? I just assumed as much since I saw *Sense and Sensibility* on your desk."

"Oh?"

He nodded and lifted his glass then took a sip. "Personally I prefer *Northanger Abbey*."

Finally, a topic worthy of discussion. Perhaps this evening might be saved yet.

Helen leaned forward and shook her head, warming to the topic. "I beg to differ, Mr. Hill. Why the complexity of the plot alone makes it far superior to—"

"Henry Hill, you old scalawag, is that you?"

And so it went, the moment so fleeting had absconded with her companion. Some gray-bearded gentleman had Mr. Hill's attention and would likely hold it for a while from the looks of things. Helen leaned back in her chair and crossed her arms over her chest. It seemed as though her duty tonight would be to remain awake and keep her smile propped up. Other than this, her companion seemed to have no need of her.

The waiter approached and signaled to Mr. Hill, who answered with a nod. "Forgive me, Nigel," Mr. Hill said to the elderly man, "but I'm afraid the lady and I are late for an appointment."

An appointment? We haven't had dinner yet.

Helen tamed her surprise and rose along with her companion while her heart sank. She'd made such a poor impression on the man that he'd decided to rid himself of her company before the food even arrived. In her youth she'd had a few social outings with gentlemen callers, some of which were less than memorable, but none had ended *before* dinner. Just wait until she saw Penney.

"Shall we?" The politician grasped her elbow and guided her through a maze of tables to. . .what was this? The kitchen?

Chaos greeted her, along with a wall of stifling heat. To her left, a dozen men in suits dashed about in a complicated ballet while another dozen raced about providing a symphony of sounds with their pots and pans. When taken together, the chaos fell into order, and the food went out to the guests, or so it seemed.

"Miss Morgan?" Helen turned to follow the sound of her name only to find the waiter standing there. Mr. Hill was nowhere in sight. Her heart sank, even though this was the ending she'd expected. Evidently the job of finding her a way home had fallen to the waiter. "Please follow me."

She obliged, but rather than heading out the back door, Helen found herself climbing a rather rickety set of back stairs that emerged onto a large room that seemed to be some sort of storage area. Beyond the barrels and crates, she found Mr. Hill awaiting her at a table set beside a window that afforded a view of Montgomery Street and the ocean beyond.

Or it would have had the rain not been beating a rhythm against the cracked panes of glass.

Mr. Hill pushed back a rather plain wooden kitchen chair and helped her settle into her seat before taking his place beside her. The waiter snapped his fingers, and a parade of dark-suited men, some of whom she recognized from the kitchen, paraded in, carrying trays bulging with food.

"Forgive me, Miss Morgan," Mr. Hill said as the last of the trays were placed on a pair of crates that served as a sideboard, "but this was the only way I could have an uninterrupted conversation with you."

"I see." Discomfort of another sort snaked up her spine, and the room seemed to shrink.

The politician seemed to sense her lack of enthusiasm. "Mr. Kent and his staff will be with us at all times, so I assure you there will be no impropriety." He paused and leaned back in his chair. "If you feel the least bit uncomfortable, I assure you other arrangements can be made, or I can take you home."

Warm candlelight mixed with the glow of a large whale oil lamp and bounced across the scarred wooden floorboards and danced up the walls to meet in the center of the ceiling. In lieu of a fancy tablecloth, someone had appropriated a bright red-and-white quilt. There was nothing about this room that felt uncomfortable, and strangely, neither did she.

"No," she said softly. "This will be fine."

"Excellent." He motioned for the staff to begin serving the first course. "Now I believe we were discussing the fact that *Northanger Abbey* far exceeds *Sense and Sensibility* in all aspects of the story."

Helen squared her shoulders and gave him a sideways look. "We were discussing nothing of the sort," she said with mock sternness.

Somehow the courses came and went. Helen ate little and talked almost as much as she listened. The politician, as it happened, was quite well read.

By the time dessert was served, Helen had learned that Shakespeare and James Fenimore Cooper were his favorite authors, that he was currently reading *A Tale of Two Cities*, and that he had large passages of *Last of the Mohicans* and the Bible memorized.

To her amazement, Henry Hill was actually quite a fascinating fellow. He also had an appetite. He'd partaken of all seven courses, then ordered dessert—the house specialty: apple dumpling. Each course was delivered by the dour-looking waiter, who retired between courses to the corner of the room where he had a stack of newspapers at the ready.

While they rested between courses, Mr. Hill paused in his discourse regarding his mayoral aspirations to stare into Helen's face. "You indicated once that you were familiar with the workings of a political campaign."

She froze, stricken. "D–d–did I?"

"Well, not in so many words," he said slowly. "But there was a suggestion that perhaps you'd had some experience in that arena."

Helen's mouth went dry, and she reached for her glass of water. The politician must have sensed her unease, for he placed his hand over hers. It was warm, this masculine hand, while hers felt like ice. She stared at the swirling *H*s atop the gold signet ring and slowly let out a pent-up breath.

What do I say, Lord? she found herself asking.

The truth, came the soft response.

So she told him. Speaking in fits and starts, she told the politician the whole story. About her father and her mother and the dear women who took care of her. She found that once she began to tell it, the story refused to stop until she told it all. Finally she reached the part where she attended her father's funeral and then headed West to the place her mother had once read her a story about. The first train out of Texas had brought her to San Francisco. God, however, had brought her to church and to the three friends she'd made there, friends with whom she now worked at the *Gazette*.

When she finished, she realized she'd said far too much. Covering her embarrassed frown with her napkin, she pretended to dab at the corners of her mouth. Mr. Hill removed the napkin from her hand and brought her fingers to his lips for a brief moment.

"I have a story, too, Miss Morgan, and I've never told a soul," he said softly, each breath blowing warm against her fingertips. "I believe I would like to share it with you." He met her gaze. "Would that be terribly improper?"

Her heart rose to her throat, and she found the words she wanted to say lodged there as well. "I would be honored to hear your story," she finally managed.

An eternity later, images of a young boy living in abject poverty, a youth saved by a loving aunt, and a grateful young man making a promise to the Lord filled her mind. "Thank you for sharing this," she said through a shimmering of tears. "Now I see why you feel so strongly about helping the less fortunate."

He nodded and leaned toward her. "I've never felt comfortable sharing that story with anyone. Even my best friend, Asa, hasn't heard all of it." He entwined his fingers with hers once more, and this time he held them to his chest. She could practically feel the beating of his heart as she seemed pulled toward him. "To think this all started because. . ."

"Because of what?"

"Never mind."

Her lips were inches from his when she realized she was about to kiss him.

Or rather, he was about to kiss her.

"Dessert is served!" the waiter called.

Helen jumped and nearly fell out of her chair. She cast a covert glance at Mr. Hill, who seemed just as shaken. He allowed the waiter to serve each of them, then handed her the dessert fork. "Prepare to be amazed," he said with a grin.

I already am. She tore herself away from his gaze to stab at the decadent dessert.

One taste of the melt-in-your-mouth pastry and spicy sweet apple inside, and she groaned. "Oh, this is better than reading a book," she said, then blushed when she realized she'd spoken the words aloud.

Mr. Hill laughed. "I daresay that is the best compliment I've heard in a long time. What say you, Mr. Kent?"

The waiter smiled and nodded then went back to his newspaper.

Their desserts quickly disposed of, the pair returned to a much safer and less personal topic, their debate of the merits of Shakespeare's comedies over his tragedies. While Helen favored the tragedies, the politician tended to prefer the comedies, which led to a lively discussion.

Helen never noticed the passing of time until she suppressed a yawn. "I'm terribly sorry," she said with a start as Mr. Hill checked his pocket watch then quickly rose.

She settled beside him in the coach, keeping a respectable distance. By the time the coach made its way through the drizzling rain and arrived at her doorstep, it was nearly midnight. Tomorrow she would have a difficult time making numbers add up and totals come out correctly.

No matter, she decided as she bade the politician good-bye at the door with a polite handshake and practically floated inside. What was a little exhaustion when the evening had been so perfect? As the door closed behind her, she could hear Mr. Hill's driver whistling a rather unique rendition of "Hail, Columbia."

It came as no surprise that Penney sat just inside the door, pretending to read her Bible. She might have gotten away with it had the book not been upside down. When Helen walked past without a word, Penney gave up all pretenses and followed her into the bedroom.

"So?"

She slipped out of her green dress and returned it to the back of the armoire, suppressing a smile. "So *what*?"

Penney huffed, feigning annoyance as she slipped under the covers and gave the pillow a vicious plumping. "Look, I didn't wait up half the night just to hear nothing. How did it go?"

Helen slipped into her nightdress and sank onto her bed, threading her fingers behind her head. She let a long moment pass then sighed. "It was wonderful," she said as she extinguished the lamp.

Telling Penney was like reliving the evening, and as she spoke, she tried to remember each detail. She'd nearly fallen asleep when she realized that they'd forgotten all about their tickets to the opera.

Chapter 8

Tuesday, July 10, 1860

The next morning Helen arrived at the *Gazette* with a troubled heart. What seemed impossibly romantic last night seemed more like a dream today, and in her experience, dreams never survived the light of day. Whatever insanity possessed Mr. Hill last night would most certainly be gone today.

With that thought uppermost in her mind, she tackled the day's work with a lackluster attitude. By noontime, her strength was gone, and so was her ability to add, subtract, and generally make sense of receipts and invoices. Somewhere between breakfast and midmorning tea, she'd put a name to the malady which held her in its grasp: Love.

It certainly never seemed as though the characters in Jane Austen's novels were as miserable as she; still, she recognized all the signs. Dropping her pencil, she leaned forward on her elbows and rested her chin in her hands. She'd seen the strange symptoms in Jennie and Amy, but she never expected to catch the infirmity.

"Love," she whispered. "Ridiculous."

"What's so ridiculous?"

Helen looked up to see Jennie standing beside her desk. "He's a politician, and I'm just a woman who adds numbers. I hate crowds, and he craves them. He makes these beautiful speeches, and I, well, sometimes I can't even get a word to come out properly." She lowered her head and studied the pile or receipts, already blurring from unshed tears. "It's just not what I expected."

"Do you think love is what I expected when I met Nick, or what Amy expected to find with Evan?" Jennie smiled. "Love is usually the last thing anyone who falls into it imagines will happen. That's what makes it so special."

Helen shrugged. "But I've only spent one evening with him, and we're so different. It makes no sense."

Her friend knelt beside the desk and took Helen's hand in hers. "Helen, how long do you figure it takes God to decide who we're to spend our lives with?"

"An instant, I suppose. I've never actually thought about it."

Jennie patted her hand then rose. "And maybe not thinking about it is the way the Lord wants it."

"What do you mean?"

"In Genesis, He says He will make a helper for man. Do you think God asked Eve if anything made sense when He put her in the Garden of Eden, pointed her toward Adam, and told her to go be a helper?"

Helen smiled. She couldn't argue with her friend's logic. "No, I don't suppose He did."

"Then who are we to doubt when He points us to the man

251

He's created for us?" She paused. "Even if it doesn't make sense to us sometimes, it makes perfect sense to Him."

It made absolutely no sense.

Henry carried the thought around inside his head, but it failed to drown out his need to see Helen Morgan again. He told himself he was just protecting her until the men who'd threatened her life were caught, but deep down he knew better.

One evening with the green-eyed woman had seared his heart forever.

He was in love.

It made no sense.

"What's all the groaning about?" Asa sauntered in and leaned against the doorframe.

Henry cleared his throat and reached for his pen. "Nothing," he said. "Just more work than I wanted to tackle today."

"Ah, I see." He remained there, leaning, looking past Henry to stare out the window where sunshine streamed in. Finally he shook his head. "I suppose my fishing trip's going to have to come to an end soon. Today, I think."

"Yes, I thought it might," Henry said as he reached for the topmost document in the stack. "But on the bright side, July will be over soon. Your banishment will end before you know it."

When Asa did not respond, Henry looked up to see he'd already gone.

By lunchtime, he'd wandered out intending to merely stroll past the *Gazette*. Of course he ended up inside and returned to his office with plans for another evening out with Miss

Morgan. This time they might actually attend the opera. He might actually kiss her as well.

That night the music was superb, the company delightful. Helen wore the green dress again, disguised by a lovely shawl, but he would have never let on that he noticed. Most of the time they sat in silence, holding hands and trading covert glances. At the end of the evening, with James whistling an irritating rendition of "Home Sweet Home," Henry walked Helen to the door and in a moment of stupidity, bravery, and insanity held her in his arms and kissed her.

He expected her to slap him. He certainly deserved as much. Instead, she kissed him back, then raced inside, embarrassed. The next morning he sent flowers and a lovely dress from the mercantile that he'd been unable to resist. Pale pink— it reminded him of the color in her cheeks when he kissed her.

She kept the flowers but returned the dress along with a note stating her appreciation but explaining that she was unable to keep such a personal gift. He returned the gift to her with another note, this one explaining why he chose that particular color. Not only did she keep the dress, but also she wore it that night to the symphony along with a flower from the bouquet pinned in her hair.

By the end of the second week, they had not only attended the opera, but they'd also had two picnics, visited church together, enjoyed two evenings at the symphony, endured an afternoon's sail on the choppy bay, and finally last night, had dinner with his mother.

That memory burned stronger than any of the others. Of course, Anna loved Helen immediately. There had been no doubt that she would.

Tomorrow he would see Helen again. He would ask her to become his wife.

~

Thursday, July 19, 1860

They sat at the same table in the same little room upstairs. Henry made sure every detail was perfect, even to the point of rehearsing the grand finale of the evening with the restaurant's owner. While his plan to have the ring embedded in the apple dumpling had been nixed by both the owner and the cook, Henry did manage to talk the waiter into cooperating with his alternate plan.

Anticipating Helen's surprise at finding an engagement ring slipped over the stem of her fork kept Henry on edge all day. By the time he and Helen arrived at the restaurant, she suspected something was in the offing. When she spied the ring, she burst into tears.

Henry dropped to one knee beside her and searched for the eloquent speech he'd memorized. It was gone. In its place, he found these words: "Helen Morgan, do me the honor of becoming my wife."

His beloved looked at the ring then lifted her gaze to meet his. Her eyes brimming with tears and her cheeks the color of her dress, she looked away. "It's lovely, Henry," she said softly. "I d–d–don't know what to say."

He grasped both her hands in his. "Say yes, Helen."

For a long moment, silence fell between them. Henry felt sure his heart would burst before he heard the words that would make him the happiest man in San Francisco.

Thank You, God, for giving me Helen. Now would You please make her say something?

"I can't marry you, Henry." She jumped up and ran out the door. Henry climbed to his feet and watched her go.

"That's not exactly what I had in mind, Lord."

Racing down the stairs and through the maze of tables in the main dining room, Henry ignored the calls of friends, constituents, and political allies. He had to find Helen. He pushed past the doors to emerge on the sidewalk then froze in his tracks. Helen was being hurled into a buggy, which sped away down Montgomery Street. Holding the reins was an all too familiar man: Toothless.

Henry climbed into the saddle of the first horse he could reach and set off after the buggy. The chase led him through the city's center, then east toward the water. At the edge of the bay, the buggy stopped abruptly by a stand of eucalyptus. Two dark-clad men spilled out, but Helen remained inside.

If something happens to Helen, Lord, I will die, too. So unless You want the both of us at Your door, please do something.

Dismounting, Henry reached beneath his jacket for the revolver. Before either man could take aim, Henry had fired off two shots. He strode past the two crumpled and groaning forms to lift a distraught Helen from the buggy. She nestled against his chest and let the tears flow.

"They said you owed them money," she said between deep gulps for air. "They told me you took money to guarantee a win in the election and then killed Frank Bynum so you didn't have to pay it back."

"Shhh," he whispered. "Those are lies. You didn't believe them, did you?"

Helen shook her head. "No, but—"

The clatter of horses' hooves interrupted her. A moment later, the chief of police and several of his deputies rode into sight.

"Thank the good Lord you're here, Chief," Henry said.

The chief reined in his horse and looked down at Henry. "Arrest the lot of 'em, boys," he said.

A pair of deputies dismounted and headed toward Toothless and his accomplice while a third pushed Helen away to place restraints on Henry's wrists. When Henry protested, the deputy raised his club, and the world went black.

Chapter 9

Friday, July 20, 1860

I don't care what the police say. I know Henry's not guilty." Helen tried to remain calm as she sat across the desk from the chief of police, the very man who had ordered Henry's arrest.

The chief offered a condescending smile. "I applaud your loyalty, Miss Morgan, but the facts do not lie." He leaned back in his chair. "Those two fellows he shot worked for Frank Bynum. When their boss turned up dead, they figured they would make a little money out of the deal by trying to shake down Mr. Hill for some of the gold he'd been given."

She focused on her hands rather than look directly at the chief. "That makes no sense. Henry has plenty of money."

The chief laughed. "In my line of work, I've learned that no one ever has enough money. Besides that, it wasn't just the money that made him do it. You see, Henry Hill needed votes more than he needed gold. Bynum offered him the votes, sweetened the deal with the money, and then got in the way of a bullet from Henry Hill's gun when Hill backed out of the deal."

White-hot anger boiled just beneath the surface. How dare this man accuse Henry of such things? "That's not true," she said through a clenched jaw.

"Lady, I've got a receipt made out to one Henry Hill for the sale of a diamond pin to a jeweler in Los Angeles. Cleaning lady found it when she moved the filing cabinet in the office. The jeweler has identified the pin as an identical copy of the one missing from Frank Bynum's body. To top things off, Henry Hall, the tavern owner we'd pegged as the gunman, was found dead in a shallow grave. Looks like he'd been there awhile, which means he couldn't have pulled the trigger on Bynum."

He handed her the paper, and she read it while her heart sank. A moment later, she collected her thoughts. Henry was innocent. That she knew.

"Where did you get this?"

"His partner found it in his office. Said it was behind a filing cabinet."

"It could have been planted there."

His face softened. "Look, I know you care about Henry. I like him, too. Trouble is, he's a crook."

Again her anger flared. "P–p–prove it," she said as she rose and tossed the offensive document onto the desk.

The chief pushed back from the desk and stood. "Why don't *you* prove he *isn't* a crook?"

Helen stormed out of the police station determined to do just that. Her Henry was not mixed up with thugs and hoodlums. He was a good man. But how to prove it? She smiled and turned toward Montgomery Street and Henry's office.

Perhaps a bit of sleuthing would turn up a clue to exonerate Henry. She took the back stairs up to the second floor and slipped inside the offices of Chambers and Hill as quietly as possible. Noises from downstairs floated up through the floor, but Helen soon found the offices to be empty. She stole past the portraits of Henry and his partner and hurried to Henry's office to begin her search. Something, anything had to be found to prove him innocent.

"Well, what do we have here?"

Helen nearly jumped out of her skin, and her heart raced. She whirled around to find Henry's partner, Asa Chambers, standing in the doorway. She recognized him from the portrait in the foyer.

"I'm terribly sorry. I'm Helen, Henry's fiancée." She cringed as she said it.

She should be his fiancée if it weren't for her selfishness. If only she'd told him she feared she wouldn't be the wife he needed rather than running away.

Helen pushed those thoughts aside and gave thanks that the Lord had sent help. Soon she could tell Henry everything. Soon she would ask his forgiveness and accept his offer, if it still stood. Soon perhaps she *would* be his fiancée.

"Henry told me you were away on holiday, Mr. Chambers."

His smile upped a notch, but his posture tensed. "I guess you weren't expecting me."

"Actually, no," she said, "but as long as you're here, perhaps you could help me."

She pressed past him to head for the filing cabinet in the foyer where the receipt had been found. Kneeling to open the bottom drawer, she found it stuck. She pulled hard, and the drawer flew open. An oversized book, one she recognized as an accounting ledger, slid forward with a thud. She picked it up and held it in her lap. "I'm looking for any sort of evidence that will help to prove that Henry—"

The air went out of her mid-sentence, and it took a moment to register that Asa Chambers had his hand wrapped around her throat. The ledger fell to the floor as Asa lifted her to her feet. On the opened page, she could see the names of certain prominent San Franciscans with numbers written beside them.

Contributions or bribes? She might never know, but she'd do what she could to see that Henry—and the police—found out.

"We're both on the s-s-same side, Mr. Chambers. Why don't you let go so we can talk about this?"

"You should never have seen that ledger. I honestly hoped it wouldn't come to this." Asa began to move her toward Henry's office. "Henry's my friend. I worked too hard to make sure he won the race, and look what you've done."

"What *I've* done?" Helen choked off the last of the statement when Asa's beefy arm closed around her waist.

She jabbed at him with her elbows. He only laughed.

"You weren't the right wife for him anyway."

Asa turned her around to face him, then slammed her back against the wall. Through the haze of pain, Helen could see the vein on the side of his forehead throb, could smell the sweet Macassar oil in his hair.

His lips twisted into a scowl. "He needs someone who can be an asset to him, someone who can talk and not be an embarrassment."

The truth. There it hung in the narrow space between them. For one brief moment in this horrendous conversation, Asa Chambers was right.

His eyes narrowed. The vein in his forehead pulsed faster. And then she remembered Jennie's words: "Who are we to doubt when He points us to the man He's created for us?"

"Who are we to doubt?" she whispered as she summoned all the strength, all the fight, she could muster. A well-placed kick, and he loosened his grip; another, and he crumpled to the floor, taking her with him. Helen slid from his grasp and ran as fast as her crinolines would allow, slowing only to retrieve the ledger.

She cast a glance back to see Asa climb to his feet, then fall once more. Pausing only long enough to gauge the distance to the main stairs and Montgomery Street beyond, she ducked down the back stairs. Hanging on with one hand, the ledger tucked under her arm, Helen raced down the stairs. A few steps from the bottom, she turned to see how close her captor had come to catching her.

No one was there.

She stopped and tried to catch her breath, then started to giggle. It was irrational. Ridiculous. Yet all Helen could feel was exhilaration that she'd bested Asa Chambers. With the ledger in hand, Henry would be freed and all would be well.

Click. "Give me the ledger."

Helen turned around slowly to face Asa Chambers. He held a revolver inches from her forehead.

"The ledger, Miss Morgan. I want it—"

A shot rang out, and his face registered surprise, then shock.

A second later he crumpled in a heap at Helen's feet. She looked beyond the wounded man to see Henry rushing toward her.

He gathered her in his arms and carried her out to his carriage. His driver looked frantic as he jumped up to open the carriage door. "What in the world happened back there, Mr. Hill? I done heard gunshots. Took all I had to keep the hosses from runnin' off."

Henry grasped Helen's hand, searched her face. "Did he hurt you?"

Gulping for air, she managed to say, "No. How did you get here? Why aren't you in jail?"

"When the chief explained the enormity of their crimes, the thugs who kidnapped you were only happy to oblige and tell the whole story."

"Which is?"

"Which is that Asa was behind the whole thing." Henry looked away, pained. "He sold the promise of my political influence to anyone who would pay and hired those two to make sure the payments reached him."

Helen reached for his hand and held it tight. "But why did they come after you?"

"When the Bynum fellow asked for proof of my cooperation in the scam, Asa had none to provide. Bynum had already paid up, so he asked for his gold to be returned. So did a few other people, which put Asa in quite a financial bind."

"But I thought he was fairly well-to-do."

Henry shook his head. "No, his *father* is well-to-do. Asa is still waiting for his share of the fortune."

"Oh." Helen drew closer to Henry.

"Asa sent those thugs after me and ultimately after you to try and collect money to pay his debts. Bynum got impatient, and it cost him his life." He held her against his chest, studied her for a moment, then held her tight again. "You know I love you, Helen, and I'm terribly sorry you had to be involved in this."

"I love you, too, Henry, and a *wife* should be involved in her husband's life, good or bad."

"A wife?"

When he leaned back to look at her, she nodded. "Yes, if the offer is still good."

"Oh yes, the offer's most definitely still good." He kissed her soundly, then paused and looked away. "I have to see to Asa. Regardless of what he's done, he's my friend. Do you understand?"

"Yes," she said. "But please be careful."

"I will." He turned to his driver. "See that she stays here, James, and be on the ready. Mr. Chambers may need to be transported to the hospital."

Wednesday, July 25, 1860

Helen leaned back in her chair and allowed her gaze to fall on the remains of their dinner. As in the two times before, Henry insisted they dine privately, with only the waiter, Mr. Kent, and his army of waiters as chaperones.

"Something wrong?" Henry reached for her hand and held it against his chest. "You look a bit pensive."

Helen giggled. "Pensive? Not exactly. Overfed, perhaps."

"You barely ate enough to feed a bird, my darling," he said.

"Don't tell me you're not going to have dessert."

"Apple dumpling?"

Henry winked. "Exactly what I had in mind." He motioned for the waiter, who scurried off down the stairs.

Helen leaned against Henry's shoulder and closed her eyes. The night was perfect. Almost. "How's Asa?"

"Asa?" She felt his shoulders heave. "Asa's healthy as a horse, but he'll walk with a limp for a while."

She pulled away to stare into his eyes. "You could have killed him, you know. A less understanding man might have. You did the right thing. Now it's in the hands of the judge."

Henry ducked his head. "I suppose."

"Dessert is served!"

The waiter placed two steaming apple dumplings on the table before them, then retreated to his place by the stairs. A second later he hid himself behind yesterday's copy of the *Golden Gate Gazette*.

While Henry dug into his dessert, Helen weighed the fork in her hand but did not take a bite. The last time her fork had been adorned with a beautiful ring tied up in a green ribbon. How different things might have been if she'd just said yes the first time. With time to consider the situation, Henry probably had come to the conclusion that he'd do better finding a wife who was an asset to his political career instead of a hindrance.

"Do I have to finish yours, too?"

Helen looked over at Henry's empty plate and contemplated the real threat of losing her apple dumpling to him. While he pretended to reach for her plate, she stuck her fork in and pulled out. . .a ring?

"Henry? What's this?"

He dropped the fork into the pitcher of water and fished out a beautiful—and clean—engagement ring adorned with one oversized emerald and circled in diamonds. He dropped to one knee. "Helen Morgan, will you do me the honor of becoming my wife?"

For a moment she sat stunned. Finally, she found her voice. "But Henry, I stutter, I hate crowds, and I completely disagree with your preferences in the works of Shakespeare and Jane Austen. What sort of wife would I make for the next mayor of San Francisco?"

"The only sort I want."

Epilogue

The Golden Gate Gazette
Thursday, July 26, 1860

Candidate for Mayor Henry Hill to Wed Miss Helen Morgan of the *Golden Gate Gazette*

Henry Hill, noted attorney and candidate for San Francisco mayor, wishes to announce his engagement to the lovely Helen Morgan, an employee of our own *Golden Gate Gazette*. The *Gazette* wishes to congratulate Mr. Hill on his fine choice of a wife, and the future Mrs. Hill on her decision not to continue her brief but illustrious career as a crime fighter. In response, Miss Morgan replies that being the wife of a politician will be adventurous enough for her.

APPLE DUMPLINGS SAN FRANCISCO STYLE

Ingredients:
- 8 large apples
- 2 tablespoons of butter
- 2 tablespoons of sugar
- 1 teaspoon nutmeg
- ½ teaspoon grated orange zest
- 1 cup raisins
- 2 teaspoons cinnamon
- 1 teaspoon vanilla
- 1 piecrust, unbaked
- White of one egg

Topping:
- 1–2 tablespoons sugar
- 1 teaspoon cinnamon

Mix together butter, sugar, nutmeg, vanilla, cinnamon, grated orange zest, and raisins. Core apples and stuff butter mixture inside. Cut piecrust into circles and wrap apples completely with crust. Twist dough closed on top and trim excess. The dumpling should look like a small bag. Place each apple in a custard cup (a large muffin tin is an acceptable substitute) and brush with egg white. Sprinkle with topping and bake in 350 degree oven for 30–45 minutes or until crust is brown (time will vary depending on size of apples).

KATHLEEN Y'BARBO

Kathleen Y'Barbo is an award-winning novelist and sixth-generation Texan. After completing a degree in marketing at Texas A&M University, she focused on raising four children and turned to writing. She is a member of American Christian Romance Writers, Romance Writers of America, and Writers Information Network. She also lectures on the craft of writing at the elementary and secondary levels, and conducts distance-learning classes on the university level.

Missing Pages

by DiAnn Mills

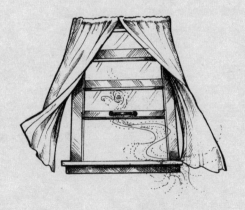

To Anita Higman,
my friend who delights in the celebration of life.

Chapter 1

Monday, October 1860

Penney Brice fought the urge to breathe. The stench of Russell Madison's cigar and the smoke billowing around his office tugged at her sensibilities. He must give her an answer soon before she fainted or fled his office for want of air.

She weighed the two alternatives, then gasped sharply, no longer able to maintain her composure. The insufferable man seated at the desk in front of her would try the patience of God with his insistence upon filling the air with his disgusting habit. The ordeal caused her to wonder if her desire to be a reporter was worth this torture.

"Miss Brice, if your intent is to cease breathing until I relent from enjoying my cigar, you are sadly mistaken." Mr. Madison took another puff, and for a moment his round face disappeared into a cloud of gray that would rival the fog rolling in off the ocean.

"But sir, I can be a good reporter. In fact, my expertise is in talking to people. That would yield the best of news." Penney managed a small intake of air and immediately broke into a fit of coughing.

"Are you ill?" Mr. Madison lifted a brow as though her lack of proper air could be attributed to something other than his intolerable cigar.

"No, I am not, but I soon will be." Penney marched to the window and struggled to open it. She stuck her head out and caught a whiff of the fisheries. Even then, the smell was a sight better than the office behind her. "Mr. Madison, there are enough fires in this city without starting one in your office."

"As your employer—"

She turned and waved the smoke away from her face. "I do apologize for my impetuous behavior, but I feared being ill. Sir, I must speak to you about a matter of utmost importance."

"I already know the topic." He stood from his chair and attempted to tower over her, except they stood eye-to-eye. Hooking his left thumb into his suspenders, Mr. Madison surveyed the object of her displeasure as though it were pure gold. "You were hired to do typesetting, not write front-page news. It's bad enough that I lost my best reporters to this strike and have to deal with the female persuasion. So don't rile my good-natured temperament."

The volume of his voice rose with each word. "I will continue to write the important events of the city until this confounded, irritating strike is over, and you, Miss Brice, will continue operating the typesetter."

"But all I want is a chance."

"Chances are gambling, and I don't believe in either one.

I rely on facts, and what I know is best." He cleared his throat. "Miss Brice, I suggest you resume your position."

She pressed her palms into his desk. The layers of dirt and dust ground into her hands. "I will cover anything. You won't be disappointed. I give you my solemn word."

"Miss Brice, you do not have the qualifications for a good reporter. That is a man's job. I admit a few of the women here have dabbled in reporting, but their success is due to a strong man assisting them."

"I'm already doing a man's job." *I should give up on this, but I can't.*

"Not because of my choosing."

Silence wafted across the room, while Mr. Madison's thunderous words rode the clouds of cigar smoke. She could taste the dry, stale air. He lifted his shoulders and slowly let them drop. He peered into her face with no trace of a smile or the mannerisms of a gentleman. "Miss Brice, every day you are in my office pleading for the same thing. Every day I give you the same answer. Not only are you interfering with my work, but you are not completing the task for which I hired you!"

She'd pushed him far enough and saw an immediate need to concede. Mr. Madison had ventured close to firing her before, and she did need the job to provide food and shelter for herself. Penney straightened and arched her back. "Yes, sir. I understand my persistence is annoying. In the future I will consider your wishes before I seek an audience."

"My wishes are for you to leave me alone and tend to the typesetter."

"Yes, sir."

He gestured toward the door. "The paper does have a deadline."

Penney turned and took two steps to the door. She needed to breathe again—and soon.

"Miss Brice."

Penney whirled around. Already she felt dizzy and took a small breath of air. "Yes, Mr. Madison." *Please, don't relieve me of this job. I need the money.*

"The other women at the paper sidestep me at every turn. You, on the other hand, don't appear to be afraid. Why is that?"

Penney tilted her head and studied the man with premature gray hair and a bushy beard—often matching the smoke circling his cigar. He could be a friend to all of them if not for his incessant barking. Jennie had referred to him as Russell Hound, of course never to his face.

"Mr. Madison." She must remain cordial no matter how unbearable his temperament. "I grew up in a mining camp. I heard men say things a proper lady dare not repeat, and I saw the worst of characters. My papa left my mama in that camp with two children to raise while he traipsed off to pan for gold. She died there. I learned early on not to be afraid of anything or anyone."

Mr. Madison eased back into his chair. For the first time, Penney viewed what some might have interpreted as a frown, but for him it was a slight upturn of his lips. "I see. And are you the oldest or is the good policeman?"

Penney folded her hands at her waist. "My brother Evan is." *Does the man find my poor mama's plight amusing? She died from consumption.*

He picked up a piece of paper from one of his stacks and appeared to focus his attention on it. Frustrated, Penney left his office.

I will never understand that man's unbearable disposition. He never goes to bed hungry, and I doubt if he cares if anyone else does either.

She closed the door behind her and headed toward the typesetter. The familiar *clickety-clack* of the press and the other noises associated with the newspaper office normally filled her with a sense of security, but not this morning. She picked up a handful of letters and let them drop with a *ping* back into the pan. This morning she felt as though if she didn't get out of that office and into the sunshine soon, she'd scream like a seagull. Mr. Madison had shattered her dreams of becoming a newspaper reporter once too often.

"Mr. Madison is still not cooperating?" Helen touched her shoulder. Compassion emitted from her hazel eyes. "From the look on your face, he must have upset you again."

Penney expelled a sigh that challenged the description of a lady. "I need to give up on this idea. After all, the strike will be over soon, and then none of us will have means of taking care of ourselves except Amy."

"I've already told Mr. Madison I intend to resign when Henry and I are married whether the strike is over or not."

Penney nodded. "I pray you, Amy, and Jennie are very happy."

"I've heard say the *Golden Gate Gazette* will have to change its name to the *Marriage Gazette*."

Penney couldn't help but smile. "Mr. Madison will need to

hire more of the female persuasion, as he calls us."

Helen laughed. "Oh my, but we are a bit of a nuisance, aren't we?"

"You would think one of us could turn him into a gentleman." Feeling her spirits lifted by the closeness of her friend, Penney leaned in closer. "As angry as he makes me, I don't mind ruffling his feathers at all."

"I'm much too afraid of him to risk reddening his face." Helen's gaze darted about. "Although I am doing much better."

"Of course you are. The truth be known, the four of us are not his favorites."

Helen covered her mouth to stifle a giggle. "I'd better get back to work."

Penney stared at the typesetter. "I am grateful for this job, but I positively despise this machine."

"Miss Brice!"

Penney recognized the voice. No doubt she had spent too much time conversing with Helen. Amy and Jennie glanced up from their work. Shaking her head to dispel any fearsome thoughts, Penney took a deep breath and headed for Mr. Madison's office. If he fired her, she could find something else. At least Evan would be appeased.

Russell Madison would rather wrestle with three rattlers than attempt to have an intelligent conversation with Miss Penney Brice. She needed to learn her place in a man's world. A newspaper reporter? That job could only be handled by a man. A woman's mind should be filled with other things like. . .tending to a home and family.

This strike had better end soon before I lose my senses. When the good Lord created a man and a woman, He didn't say a word about newspaper work.

He watched Penney walk toward him. A newspaper reporter shouldn't have those huge eyes or have golden freckles sprinkled across her nose. More importantly, a newspaper reporter didn't walk in the manner Miss Brice insisted upon. Her tiny waist and the way the bodice of her dress dropped to a *V*—well, how was a man supposed to concentrate on his work?

She wanted a column of her own? Russell laughed inwardly. He'd found a fine way to handle her impertinence. His idea would discourage her until the strike ended. In less than a day, she'd be begging for her typesetting job back again.

His cleverness amused him. Why hadn't he considered this before?

"Yes, Mr. Madison." A worried frown graced Miss Brice's usually placid features.

"I have decided to give you a column of your own."

Her gold-brown eyes widened. Tears pooled in them, and she hastily blinked. "Thank you, Mr. Madison. You will never regret this decision."

No, I won't. But you will wish you'd never approached me. "I have paramount confidence in your ability."

She leaned back on her heels. Her excitement seemed to bubble from the top of her earth-brown curly head.

"The column I'm referring to requires a good amount of time from me, especially with our growing city and its demands for a quality newspaper." The pleased look upon her face caused him to feel a twinge of guilt, but she'd imposed upon him once too often. "Are you willing to leave the typesetting machine and proceed as soon as possible with this new responsibility?"

"I am undoubtedly ready to begin this very minute."

He reached for a piece of paper on his desk. Glancing up to obtain her initial reaction, he wondered if she might quit before leaving his office. How wonderful. Then he could resume his work without this pesky woman. "I'm putting you in charge of the obituaries."

Her features appeared to be etched in stone. Not a muscle moved, ending his triumphant moment when he felt certain she'd stomp out of his office and end her employ. Suddenly his devious scheme hit him like a damp, chilly morning.

"I believe this is a challenge in which I will seek to do my very best." She punctuated her statement with a nod. "You will not be disappointed, Mr. Madison."

"I suggest you read several until you have a thorough knowledge of the manner in which an obituary is to be worded." He pointed to a stack of papers in the corner. "You can begin with those. Once you gain confidence in your abilities, then I'd like for you to compose a few for my inspection."

Miss Brice did not flinch. Her lack of irritation snatched the mirth from his little plan. Admiration took a step inside his heart, but he pushed it back. He'd see how she reacted to his assignment by the end of the day. "Do you have any questions?"

"No, sir." She turned to the corner and gathered up a tall stack of newspapers into her arms.

"If you do not have a suitable obituary written for me by the end of the day, I will need to seek another writer."

Miss Brice stiffened. "That will not be necessary."

"Very well." He opened the door of his office, leaving behind the thought of helping her carry the load. His mother would box his ears at his lack of manners, but she never had to oversee a group of women. It occurred to him that he was almost ready to pay his male workers anything to get them back to work.

Miss Brice dropped a few of the papers on the wooden floor. "Be careful. I want those back. Someday these copies will be a preserved piece of history."

Chapter 2

Obituaries? This wasn't what she'd envisioned. Good reporters didn't write death notices. Penney wanted to report on the happenings of live people, not on those who had passed on. She wanted to walk into the middle of excitement and record it for all to read. She dreamed of her writing reaching the eyes of young and old, rich and poor. San Francisco had grown from the squalor of gold camps to the mansions on Rincon Hill. Where once women and children were few, now families lived and loved. Every day, new businesses began, politicians reached out for the good of others—and sometimes themselves—and the world became more civilized. Her heart beat faster at the mere thought of it all happening. While she wrote obituaries.

Dropping the rest of the newspapers in her arms to the floor beside the typesetter, she peered around to see Amy, Jennie, and Helen studying her.

"I hope you didn't allow Mr. Madison to get the upper hand." Amy planted her hands on her hips, her shoulders squared.

"You are one to give advice. You can walk out of here today because my brother will soon marry you." Penney shrugged before she took out her frustration on her friends.

Amy pointed to the papers on the floor. "What did he ask you to do?"

Penney knew Jennie and Helen listened to every word. They offered smiles, but in a moment's notice they'd weep with her. Stiffening her back, she resolved not one of her friends would have pity on her. "I'm getting my wish. As of this moment, I have my own column. I am officially a newspaper reporter."

"Doing what?" Jennie asked. "You certainly don't look happy."

"Obituaries." She dared not look at them. One of them giggled, probably Jennie.

"We have a city that needs a newspaper," Mr. Madison said above the noise of the office.

The girls scrambled back to their assigned jobs, including Penney, who elected to sit on the floor and begin her reading. *What have I done to deserve this? Obituaries? Lord, You didn't hear my prayer. I wanted to interview people who had something worthwhile to say, some who had done great things. Now I'll have to converse with people who are grieving.*

"I'll need to take handkerchiefs so I can get a story from the family members," she mumbled. Penney didn't wear a dunce hat. The sole reason Mr. Madison had given her this column was because he didn't want to write it—and he believed she'd walk away from his precious newspaper.

A spark of anger with a flare of determination settled on her. She'd show Mr. Madison. Her column would be the most articulate and widely read obituary column in the country. Why folks would purchase the *Golden Gate Gazette* just to read her articles. And even if the newspaper strike ended, Mr. Madison would have to keep her employed. He'd lose readers if he attempted otherwise.

Penney opened the top paper and found what she needed. With stubbornness lacing her resolve, she chose to read every obituary in the entire stack.

San Francisco, Calif., on Thursday, 28 September, at the residence of his brother (James Farmer), Ebenezer Farmer, son of Jonathon Farmer, slipped to his eternal home.

"That didn't tell me a thing," Penney said. Who was this man? Did he leave a family behind? How did he pass away? Did anyone care? This notice should have held the sympathies of those who knew and loved him. From the reading of this small article, Mr. Madison certainly did not share respect for those who had gone on to their eternal reward.

I will certainly convey peace to the family and honor to the deceased in my articles. She read several more obituaries, each one cold and unfeeling.

Penney remembered her mother's passing. She and Evan had been too poor to give her the proper burial she deserved, but Evan made certain the newspaper received the notification. Penney had memorized what had been written about their mother: *Sarah Rebekah Brice, a dear mother who cherished her children. They will miss her kindly ways. She was known in life for her charity and compassion. The angels are blessed with her saintly presence as she rests at the feet of our Savior.*

Shaking her head at the next reading and the next, Penney

determined Mr. Madison's accountings of the deceased had suffered greatly during this time. Finally she reached the newspapers dated before the strike. Studying the former reporter's methods, she formed a list of what she wished to include in her column. The man had taken the time to focus on relationships, church and community work, and the families left to grieve. The ones about children brought tears to Penney's eyes. The only consolation in learning of a little one's passing was that God held them safely in His loving arms.

By early afternoon, the stack of newspapers rested in a different spot. They'd been read and notes made on what Penney deemed important. With a deep breath, she now knew how to model her work.

"How are you managing this assignment?" Mr. Madison asked.

She lifted her gaze just far enough to view his boots, layered with dust and dirt. The two peculiarities about Mr. Madison matched—raspy voice as though his throat had layers of dust and shoes coated in the same.

"Very nicely, thank you. I'm ready to compose a few of my own for you to peruse." She attempted to stand, and he reached to assist her.

"I see you've made notes." The tone of his voice reminded her of a schoolmaster ready to point out her errors and send her to the corner.

Penny refused to admit defeat and beg to operate the typesetter again or search for another job. "Yes, I have." She dragged her tongue across dry lips. "I've compiled attributes I wish to include in my obituaries."

"Commendable. I must say you are working diligently." Mr. Madison had a touch of a smirk on his face. "May I see your list?"

An air of rebellion swept over Penney, and she fought the urge to ask him to wait until she composed a few samples. Pushing the inappropriate thoughts aside, she handed him her notes.

His finger, stained dark from a combination of cigars and newspaper ink, moved down the page, leaving an unsightly smudge. "These are very good, Miss Brice. I like the inclusion of fond memories of loved ones and the various ways the deceased contributed to their family, community, and church. Discovering what gave the deceased pleasure and how others enjoyed their company is an excellent addition. The reporter who originally occupied your position resorted to poetry from time to time. I liked this addition, and I see you mentioned it as well."

Penney nearly choked. Those were the kindest words Mr. Madison had ever spoken to her. "Thank you, sir. Would you like two or three samples this afternoon?"

"Four, Miss Brice."

She swallowed a retort. "I'll have them for you."

He turned abruptly as though some villain had stuck a knife in his back. In fact, he looked rather taken aback, a bit red-faced, too. No doubt she'd foiled his plans. She resumed her position on the floor. If Harriet Beecher Stowe, her favorite author, could write by firelight after caring for seven children and enduring financial woes, then Penney could write amidst the noise and interruptions of the newspaper office.

After expelling an unbecoming sigh, she picked up her pen and dipped it into the ink well. A quote from Shakespeare would befit many. Some of his sayings danced across her mind:

Good night, good night! Parting is such sweet sorrow.
So wise so young, they say do never live long.
To sleep, perchance to dream.

That one brought tears to Penney's eyes. And then there was the quote that reminded her of Mama: *"Love looks not with the eyes but with the mind."*

She wrote the quotes most appealing to her and below them added scripture that spoke of hope and promise:

And thou shalt be secure, because there is hope.
   Job 11:18
And now, Lord, what wait I for? my hope is in thee.
   Psalm 39:7
Beloved, let us love one another: for love is of God.
   1 John 4:7

Most certainly, Penney planned to use those Bible verses and sayings which spoke to her heart. With another burst of inspiration, she thought of asking the deceased's family to share favorite scripture passages.

Two hours later, after foregoing something to eat and listening to her stomach protest, Penney had composed five obituaries, one extra in case Mr. Madison grew a little dour, as he often did in the late afternoon. She'd used Shakespeare and the

Psalms mixed with novel-like prose about supposed persons who had gone on to their heavenly home. "His family loved to hear the accountings of his childhood days in Virginia." "Her needlepoint was more treasured than feasts of the finest food." Penney gathered up the stack of newspapers and placed her notes and Mr. Madison's examples on top before heading to his office.

Hunched over his desk, reading a slip of paper, Mr. Madison did not acknowledge her entrance. Neither did she expect him to. His mustache curved into a frown, and lines etched his brow. Finally, he glanced up. "Miss Brice, I will be with you in a moment." Although his manner sounded gruff, she'd heard worse.

"I can come back later." She smoothed her skirt.

"Patience is a virtue." He nodded toward the corner, and she laid the newspapers back where they had originally rested.

Placing his reading material aside, he folded his hands atop a stack of other papers. "I'm ready to see your work."

For the next few minutes, he said nothing while he read. Penney had memorized the obituaries including the scripture and quotations used. She emulated the past reporter with a twist of her own style. She could only pray for Mr. Madison's approval.

"Some are too sweet for my taste." Not once did he lift his gaze to her face. Penney turned to face him. "But I imagine those could be used for women. The two for men are satisfactory, and the one for a child pleases me."

He picked up the same small piece of paper that he'd set

aside when she entered his office. "I just received this notification. Perhaps you could write this obituary. I know it's late in the afternoon. My driver will take you to the address." He picked up his cigar. "Catherine Wellington is an influential woman. She contributes generously to charities and is known for her work with orphans."

"She passed away?"

"No, her granddaughter." Mr. Madison handed her the paper. "The child was eleven years old, Mrs. Wellington's only heir. I can only imagine her grief." He set his jaw, and the saddened look in his eyes touched Penney. "I need this in the morning. I'll be here when you return." He expelled a sigh. "Your safety is a concern to me."

"I will go right away." Penney recognized the address as one near where Amy once lived.

"I'm sure your compassion and sympathy will help ease Mrs. Wellington's grief. God sends us His love through others."

Penney's mind raced with this revelation of Mr. Russell's Christian beliefs. "Most certainly. I'll do my best to represent the *Golden Gate Gazette* in a professional manner as well as my own faith. Do you know what happened? Had the child been ill?"

"All I know is her name—Elizabeth Wellington—and that her demise was due to an accident. I have seen her on occasion at church."

Folding the piece of paper with Catherine Wellington's information, Penney headed to the door of the office.

"Thank you, Miss Brice."

I didn't know those precious words of propriety existed in his vocabulary. "You're welcome, Mr. Madison." She smiled, and his face turned crimson.

~⁓

Russell slumped into his chair and picked up his cigar. He examined it closely and lay what he referred to secretly as "his wife" back down on the corner of his desk. A good cigar offered the same pleasantries as a spouse without the constant chatter and the expense. He could enjoy its presence and allow it to momentarily take his attention off whatever plagued him. A cigar couldn't cook, but it could be just as satisfying. The analogy no longer suited his scurrying emotions. At least not since Miss Penney Brice had been engaged in his employ.

Confound it! Penney Brice made him stutter like a schoolboy. Why, she caused him to forget his own name. Not since he was a young man of twenty had a woman affected him so.

Glancing at the cigar, he noticed the strong smell. Russell stood abruptly and opened the window. Two days ago he wouldn't have considered the amount of smoke in his office or the need for fresh air, but the woman who occupied more of his thoughts than he deemed necessary had pointed out the need.

He'd ask her to leave the newspaper if he could find a reason. Her work proved flawless, and nothing he said deterred her. Writing obituaries? What a grim task. Still she marched forward like a soldier on a mission.

I shouldn't have sent her to write the obituary for Catherine Wellington's granddaughter. One expected adults to pass from this life into the eternal, but children were such fanciful creatures. The prospect of limiting their days tore at his heart. A headline concerning his cruelty surfaced in Russell's thoughts. Miss Brice would surely end her work at the *Gazette* now. The prospect saddened him a bit, even if he'd devised the plan. He'd watched her come and go each day—work hard and involve herself in pleasantries with the other women. He'd miss her.

Nonsense! He didn't need a woman in his life. What if he sensed the need to court her? Propose marriage? What if she accepted? Hadn't he convinced himself that a good cigar had the same attributes as a wife? And his age? He must be going daft. A man fast approaching thirty-six didn't set his mind and heart on a young woman of slightly over twenty. And she surely thought he was older. His silver hair and beard gave the appearance of a man in his late forties or more—not of a much younger man whose hair had turned gray-white overnight.

Russell plopped himself into his chair and picked up the cigar; the deep, rich tobacco taste and scent was exactly what he needed. Cigars were much preferable to a wife. Whatever made him think otherwise?

Chapter 3

Penney sat stiffly on the edge of the wine-colored sofa, pen and paper in hand. She took in every inch of Mrs. Catherine Wellington's opulence—the crystal lighting; the dark, rich wood; and the flowered rugs. If not for living the past several months at the Hamilton Hotel and occasionally visiting Amy's parents' old home, she'd have felt even more uncomfortable. Growing up in a gold mining camp did not convey any luxuries to life; more so it reeked of squalor.

The Wellington mansion lived up to its reputation. Outside, the octagon-shaped home loomed larger than the Hamilton Hotel, which housed countless people. An observation tower in the center of the roof fascinated Penney. She imagined a woman staring out to sea in search of her husband's ship or watching the fog roll in from the bay. Penney wondered how people acquired such wealth—certainly not like her father, who foolishly destroyed his life in search of gold. Glancing about, she could envision the parties and gala events set here. With a wary look at the casket, she felt certain Mrs. Wellington never anticipated her granddaughter's funeral. Penney also questioned why a formal wake had not occurred, for she hadn't seen anyone but the maid. Perhaps Mrs. Wellington grieved too deeply to accept many visitors.

Harsh reality reminded Penney that her visit was not a social call. In this dark parlor where the rich draperies had been replaced with black ones in view of the solemn occasion and where windows were covered with black cloth, she shivered. Artfully displayed furnishings surrounded the still form of an eleven-year-old little girl, a child who now lived in heaven. The elaborately etched mahogany casket rested not ten feet from Penney. Quiet. Only the perpetual tick of a clock on the mantel told Penney how time marched on, ignoring the hearts and sympathies of people. She shivered. If someone didn't enter the room soon, she'd plainly be talking to the casket—not out of disrespect for the child but out of a need to simply converse with another human being.

Maybe her restlessness came in writing the column.

Perhaps once she completed the obituary today, the others would come easier. An air of melancholy overwhelmed her. The longer she waited for Mrs. Wellington to appear, the more she dreaded the interview. The task tore at her sensibilities. Mr. Madison was right; she could not write obituaries.

"Miss Brice, Mrs. Wellington wishes to know your purpose."

Penney turned her attention to the maid who had directed her to the parlor. "I am here to write the obituary for the *Gazette*. Mr. Russell Madison sent me."

"I will convey the message. Would you care for tea?" The maid's reddened eyes gave away her emotion.

"No, thank you." The thought of consuming anything

made her stomach churn. Penney waited again for nearly three-quarters of an hour before a tall, matronly woman arrived dressed in black silk with a sheer black veil covering her head and face.

The woman moved slowly to the casket. "My dear Elizabeth. How I shall miss you." She lowered her head, and Penney heard a muted sob. A moment later, she raised her head and turned to face Penney.

"Miss Brice, I am Catherine Wellington. Let us not tarry with this thing." She sat on a stuffed chair and reached out with a black, leather-gloved hand to touch the casket. "I appreciate Russell sending a woman to gather this information. It's much easier."

"In this time of grief, please accept my condolences." Mrs. Wellington nodded, and Penney continued. "Please tell me about Elizabeth."

"Elizabeth Rose Wellington was born April 11, 1849, to my son, Richard, and his wife, Lydia. We formerly lived in Pennsylvania and came to California to establish a bank. Elizabeth became my charge six years ago when Richard and Lydia drowned." She dabbed her eyes then lifted her chin. "She was a blessing, a delightful child who loved to please. When I looked at her, I saw Lydia's pale blue eyes and tiny oval face, but she shared Richard's love of people and his spirit. And just like her father, she befriended the servants and any other person she happened to meet. Elizabeth loved our Savior. I challenged her to memorize scripture, and she never refused me."

"What was her favorite passage?" Penney asked.

Mrs. Wellington smiled; her hand remained on the casket. "The accounting of Miriam and the baby Moses."

Penney returned a faint smile. She could imagine a little girl comparing her life with a biblical child.

"Elizabeth fulfilled the promise in Psalm 34. She was the desire of my heart." She took a sharp breath. "Such a terrible accident."

"What happened?"

Mrs. Wellington glanced at the casket. "She fell down the steps at school. I find this difficult to comprehend. Elizabeth always raced up and down the steps, no matter how many times I disciplined her. She never fell at home. . .never."

"What school did Elizabeth attend?"

"San Francisco Private Academy for Young Women."

Penney startled. Her pulse quickened. From the obituaries she'd read today, the San Francisco Private Academy for Young Women had been in two other reports of accidental death. She struggled to regain her composure. She must discuss this with Mr. Madison. "I'm terribly sorry about your loss."

"Thank you, Miss Brice. I so looked forward to watching her grow into a beautiful and educated young woman. I had planned her entrance into society and the joy of one day marrying a suitable young man. Ah, but more importantly I shall yearn for her sweet company. Forgive me. I am quite distraught."

"I'm sure all those who knew your granddaughter will miss her."

Mrs. Wellington stared at her oddly for a brief moment then blinked. "Please don't forget to thank Russell for sending such a kind woman to me. He's such a dear boy. I remember

Richard and Russell playing together as boys."

Russell? Mr. Madison was old enough to be Elizabeth's grandfather. In her grief-stricken state, Mrs. Wellington must be confused. Penney's heart ached for this prominent lady who apparently had slipped to such despair.

Mrs. Wellington turned her attention to the casket. "When I buried my husband, I thought I couldn't live another day, but I had my son. When Richard and Lydia were no longer with me, I clung to Jesus and Elizabeth. Now my Savior is all I have left, but I know He is all I need." She folded her hands. "Excuse me. I'm talking on about personal matters."

"Let me assure you that only the information you desire about Elizabeth will grace the pages of the *Gazette*." *I believe I would have reacted in the same manner.*

"Would you kindly deliver a missive to Russell?" Mrs. Wellington asked. "I composed it earlier."

"I would be honored."

"His Charlotte would have been but one year younger than Elizabeth." Mrs. Wellington fanned herself and continued to speak as though no one else sought an audience. "May the Lord cradle our dear loved ones in His arms."

Charlotte? Was this grief speaking? Could Mr. Madison have been married at one time and lost a child? No one had ever indicated he'd been married, and if so, his wife must have passed away, too. No wonder he could be ill-tempered. Pity consumed her for Mrs. Wellington and for all those who wept for loved ones.

"I shall pray for God to give you peace," Penney said.

"It will take Him to carry me through tomorrow's services.

Russell sent word he'd be here. Won't you please come, too?"

Mr. Madison did not accept excuses for not working, and Penney doubted if this met with any exception. "I'll inquire of Mr. Madison."

"He's a good man, Miss Brice. Perhaps you could attend with him. He's quite lonely these past six years." She shook her head. "I do wish some semblance of happiness for him, but I'm sure you have already witnessed his goodness."

The Mr. Russell Madison Penney knew did not match Mrs. Wellington's description. The poor woman was definitely disoriented.

The driver returned her to the newspaper office, but Mr. Madison only acknowledged her with a brief nod. He appeared consumed with something sorely unpleasant.

Chapter 4

The following morning, Penney's mind spun with the matters transpiring at the Wellington home. She wanted to help the older woman through her tragic loss, but how to go about this confused her. From their brief interview, Penney concluded Mrs. Wellington did not have any friends or family to help her manage the next few days. Perhaps her church would see to her needs—and help her bear the intense sorrow surrounding her loss. Then the matter came of referring to Mr. Madison as a boy, and who was the child Charlotte? The poor woman grieved more than her outward appearance noted. Penney really didn't want to attend the funeral, but she'd given Mrs. Wellington her word.

So many things perplexed Penney, and they needed to be addressed, but the matter that plagued her rested with three students' deaths at the San Francisco Private Academy for Young Women. Penney considered initiating a conversation with Evan. As a policeman, he could look into the frequency of the untimely deaths.

She remembered his latest warning. "Do not act in any

manner that would put you in harm's way. If so, I will make certain your position at the *Golden Gate Gazette* is terminated. I know you want to be a reporter, but I have seen Amy, Jennie, and Helen in dangerous situations, and I refuse to see you there, too."

Penney understood her brother didn't make idle threats. "You had a splendid position working at the mercantile before the fire." Evan's conversation ended there, and Penney knew better than to argue.

"Are you ill?" Helen asked as they made their way toward the newspaper office. The two young women walked together every morning to work. Evan normally accompanied Amy, and Jennie walked earlier with Nick. Although the newspaper strike continued, Nick often advised Jennie about how to form her articles. "Penney, you're decidedly pale, and you've barely said three words all morning. As I think about it, you didn't talk much last evening, either."

Penney refused to discuss her findings with her dear friend. After all, Helen had a wedding to plan—a reason to be happy and carefree. "The obituary took longer than I anticipated." She shrugged. "I do want it to read well for Mr. Madison."

"Of course you do, but please take care of yourself." Helen peered at her closely. "Why are you dressed in black?"

Penney hesitated. She fingered the fabric-covered button at her throat. "I guess I did."

"You're not telling me something," Helen said. "I know you pretty well by now."

Penney fought for the right words to deter the comments. "How are your wedding plans progressing?" She picked up her pace. When Helen smiled, Penney realized she'd been successful in thwarting any further questions.

"Henry is quite anxious, and we are planning it around his duties and responsibilities as an alderman. But that didn't answer my question about you."

"You two make the perfect couple. And I'm fine." Penney meant every word. At times she felt a little envious. After all, three of her dear friends were engaged. "Have you started your dress? Planned an engagement party? Where will you live?"

Helen answered each question while Penney chatted away with questions about the upcoming wedding. Soon they reached the newspaper office. Penney had successfully masked her downcast mood, but now she must set her mind on dealing with Mr. Madison. Standing before the thick wooden door, Penney breathed a prayer for wisdom and discernment. For some reason, she always frustrated Mr. Madison, and her concern about the deaths of the young girls would probably be just one more irritation—as would be the invitation to attend the morning's services for Elizabeth Wellington.

Penney dared not allow his ill temper to stop her from seeking out more information. Young girls weren't supposed to have accidents resulting in death while enrolled in school.

When at last Penney knocked on Mr. Madison's door with the obituary in hand, she trembled. Her carefully formed words escaped her mind while perspiration dotted her forehead and cheeks. As usual, he didn't appear to notice when she entered. And the smoke. . . How peculiar! The window was open.

A moment later, he leaned back in his chair and pointed his cigar in her direction. "Is that your article?"

"Yes, sir. I would have slipped it under the door." She brushed her fingers across the paper. "Except there is a rather disturbing development in the young girl's parting."

He appeared to study her face, while a slight breeze ruffled his silver hair. His visage did not carry the lines of an older man. Why hadn't she noticed before? And with his hair blown back, his face held more of an oval look. Instantly she halted her thoughts. How bold of her to scrutinize her employer's appearance.

"Is Mrs. Wellington not doing well? I can summon her physician."

A note of tenderness embraced his words. They were friends as Mrs. Wellington had indicated. "Her grief is intense, and please forgive me for saying this, but I believe she is somewhat disoriented. Although, putting the child to rest this morning will surely help."

"I plan to attend the funeral. I can visit her then. My parents are close friends with Mrs. Wellington, and I will alert them, also."

Your parents are living? They must be very old. Shaking her head to keep her thoughts in line, Penney pursued the worrisome notions. "I have two matters to discuss with you."

He had a habit of scrutinizing her for several seconds that caused her to wonder if he truly disliked her. "Tell me, Miss Brice, for I have work to do until time to leave for the funeral."

She wanted to sit, but Mr. Madison's office was bare of such luxury as an extra chair. "Mrs. Wellington asked me to attend the services this morning."

"What was your reply?"

"I told her I needed to seek your permission."

He rearranged some papers on his desk. "I suppose we could go together."

Again, as yesterday, Penney had misjudged Mr. Madison's response. "How very kind of you, sir."

"You're welcome. What is the second matter?"

"I'd like to talk to you about the child's accident. Mrs. Wellington said she fell down a flight of stairs. When you directed me to read all of the obituaries, I saw a total of three young girls who had expired at the school due to the same misfortune."

Mr. Madison leaned forward. "Did Mrs. Wellington mention this to you?"

"Not at all. I'm not sure she would even know about the other two accidents."

He scraped his chair across the floor and rose to gaze out the window. "Does your brother know about this?"

"I haven't made mention of it."

He whirled around. "Then don't say a word until I look into matters. The school has an excellent reputation, and I wouldn't want to discredit their name. On the other hand, if something is amiss, action needs to be taken."

Penney placed the obituary on his desk. Her trembling hadn't ceased. "I would like to visit the school tomorrow on the pretense of featuring it in an article." She cleared her throat. "If the headmistress allows it, I could talk to some of the teachers and possibly to the students."

Mr. Madison rubbed the back of his neck. "I'm concerned you won't know what questions to pose."

"I'm a woman, sir, and I like to talk."

"I won't deny either of those points." He chuckled—the first time ever. "But if the headmistress is involved in something scandalous, she could be suspicious."

"I understand. I've been thinking about this since yesterday."

Mr. Madison swung his attention back to the window. A puff of smoke rose above his head. He hadn't refused yet, so Penney kept her feet firmly planted onto the dirt-laden wooden floor. The pungent odor of cigars and newspaper attacked her senses.

"Your idea may have some merit," he finally said. "I would like to go over a few questions with you prior to the interview." Turning around to face her, he continued. "Would it be possible for us to have dinner tonight?"

The invitation rattled parts of her brain as though she hadn't heard him at all. Why, she would be spending most of the day with Mr. Madison. In one breath, the thought proved quite distasteful, and in the next she was suddenly very curious about her employer.

"It wouldn't be fancy, simply a quiet setting where we can talk."

The girls will never believe this. "I—I think your idea is lovely."

"We could leave from here, if that is suitable. My carriage could take you home."

She nodded, too stunned to contribute to the conversation.

"This will be a professional meeting."

"Of course," Penney replied much too quickly.

"I wouldn't want the rest of the employees to think we

were. . .uh, involved in courtship."

"Absolutely not."

Mr. Madison lifted a brow, and she grew warm. "Shall I return to my duties?"

He handed her a slip of paper with two names and addresses. "For your column." He focused his attention on the mound of papers strewn across his desk.

Once at her newly acquired desk, the floor beside the type-setter, she read through the names and addresses for her column. The woman assigned to the typesetter fumbled through the letters. *Clink. Clink.* Like rain spattering on a roof.

"Was Mr. Madison pleased with your article?" Helen asked.

Penney startled then tossed her a grin. "Yes. His approval eased my mind."

"I saw you forgot to bring something for lunch. Would you like to share my bread and cheese?"

Penney realized the truth had to be stated. "I won't be here."

"Are you visiting the families for your column?"

"Not exactly. I'm attending a funeral."

Helen touched her lips. "I'm sorry. I burdened you with senseless questioning this morning when I saw you were pre-occupied."

"No, this is not an acquaintance. The funeral is a result of my column."

"I see." Helen expelled a sigh. "We can visit tonight at dinner."

Oh no. "I have plans for dinner, Helen. I'm sorry."

Her friend's eyes widened. "What haven't you told me?

Are you having dinner with a gentleman?"

Penney grew more uncomfortable. "Tonight's dinner is about the newspaper."

"Are you having dinner with Mr. Madison?"

Penney glanced about. "Not so loud, Helen. Everyone will hear."

Helen bent to Penney's side. "Whyever did you agree to this?"

"Business. Besides, he can be kindly."

"Penney! Why, he's. . .he's old and grumpy!"

"Everyone needs a friend."

Helen crossed her arms. "I've seen him watch you work. I thought he was looking for a reason to fault you, but now I'm not so sure."

"Everyone needs a friend."

"You indicated such." Helen nodded in the direction of Mr. Madison's office. "Your friend is walking this way. Maybe he has another assignment for you."

Penney chose not to respond.

"Miss Brice, we should leave for the funeral within the hour." His gruff tone had vanished. From the smile on Helen's face, she had noticed, too.

"I'll be ready."

He turned and marched back to his office. Refusing to look at Helen, Penney feigned interest in the typesetter and the young woman operating it.

"Now I understand why you wore black. Please, don't let Mr. Madison's gruff mannerisms upset you," Helen said. "Think about all of the times he has shouted at us and let us know how much he dislikes having women working at the paper."

"I'll be careful," Penney said. "From what I've learned, tragedy has beset his life." She stopped herself short. After all, most of her conclusions were merely speculation.

"What about his standing with the Lord?"

"He spoke of his faith yesterday." Penney realized her friend meant well. "I'll be fine. I think Mr. Madison may be misunderstood."

Russell did a mental evaluation of how he'd committed his time to Miss Brice. Like a horse, he'd put blinders on when it came to this woman. She could lead him through fire, and he'd follow her like a fool. If anyone found out about his growing attraction to her, he'd be the laughingstock of the whole paper.

His mother used to say he couldn't hide the truth. His deceased wife had made the same statement. Maybe that was why the newspaper business attracted him so. Truth ruled as the source of his faith and the source of his livelihood.

And now it might be the source of laughter. Miss Brice could have her share of suitors, and at the bottom of the list was a lonely old widower who had taken a fancy to a comely, intelligent young woman.

How do I live through this, Lord? You've seen me through some hard times, and I gather You will again.

For the next hour, Russell attempted to lay out the next edition of the paper. Nothing seemed to go right. Articles were too long or too short. Ads needed to be inserted, or he couldn't find room. Frustrated and blaming it all on Miss Brice, he finally laid the work aside and moved to fetch her. The time had come to depart for the funeral service. Sweat beaded his face.

He realized his inner torment was for the present and the past. Miss Brice could heal those painful musings or cause the pain to deepen, and he didn't have the courage to discover which one.

The rhythmic *clip-clop* of the horses' hooves eased the silence between them. Miss Brice, who normally chatted quite freely, spoke little in the open-air carriage on the way to Mrs. Wellington's home, but her unusually quiet mode relieved him little when the fresh scent of roses wafted about her. He considered the option of requiring the females to take on the scent of a workingman. That would deter him from seeking an audience with them. But what about their dresses? They could not disguise their shapes, even if they elected to dress like a man.

"Thank you for allowing me to accompany you," Penney said.

The sound of her melodious voice sent a shiver up his spine. "You're welcome."

"I barely know Mrs. Wellington, yet she asked me to come today." Miss Brice shifted on the carriage seat. "She spoke quite highly of you."

He wondered exactly what the woman had said. "We have been friends for many years."

"I gathered as much. She indicated you and her late son had been friends."

Why did Mrs. Wellington reveal this information to a stranger? Did she state personal facts about my past? "Richard and I were fond companions. The Wellingtons and my parents were close friends."

Penney's gaze swung his way. Startled best described her countenance. Ah, he knew why.

"Mrs. Wellington mentioned that fact."

Past images of fishing and hunting floated before him. Those were the good days—carefree—when the future looked exciting. He and Richard had intended to pan for gold and become incredibly wealthy. They were going to buy a ship and sail the world. The two often stood on the banks of San Francisco Bay, smelled the salty air, and dreamed of clear blue skies that met the sea. Then they married the women of their dreams.

"Mr. Madison?"

Her voice shook his reverie. He wondered how long she'd been trying to secure his attention. "I'm sorry, Miss Brice. I confess my thoughts were ushered back to boyhood days."

"I thought so." A dimple deepened into her right cheek. *Very becoming, very much indeed.*

"You find that information odd, don't you?"

She blinked. A habit he'd noted on more than one occasion when words escaped her. "Merely unusual."

"Age perhaps?" Russell rather enjoyed viewing her squirm. Social etiquette with ladies proved most amusing.

"Sir, your age is not my concern." Color crept up her cheeks.

"I understand proprieties, but I believe you thought Mrs. Wellington was ill when she mentioned her son and me as companions." She said nothing, so he continued. "My hair turned the color of fog when I was twenty-five—ten years ago."

Miss Brice paled. She opened her mouth to speak, but

words escaped her. She turned her head to the carriage window then back to him. A sweet smile played upon her lips. "I'm glad to know Mrs. Wellington is of sound mind."

He nodded. He sensed a moment of regret. "I apologize for making you uncomfortable. Please promise me you will allow the other women at the *Gazette* to continue thinking I'm advanced in years." Mirth tickled from deep inside him. In the next breath, he broke into laughter. Glancing at Miss Brice, he saw her cover her mouth. Then she, too, laughed with him.

Miss Brice did suit him as friend, and it had been years since he had shared amusement with a female.

Chapter 5

Penney wondered if sharing laughter en route to a funeral was inappropriate. If she had fallen below propriety, she must ask forgiveness. Mr. Madison had assuredly surprised her, and now as she stole glances at him, he did look younger. His eyes were deep blue, a pleasing sight against his silver-white hair.

This is unbecoming of me. Mr. Madison may be younger in years than I believed, but nothing has changed about his temperament. However, the man had displayed an engaging personality for once.

At the home, Mr. Madison offered Penney his arm when she stepped down from the carriage, and he kept it. The gentlemanly gesture sent her pulse racing, and she wondered why. Had he really watched her work as Helen stated? If so, then he had seen her displays of anger when the typesetter tried her patience. And what about those times when she talked to the machine? How horrible to think her oddities had been a form of entertainment. For a moment, she saw herself kicking the typesetter and Mr. Madison watching her while he puffed on his offensive cigar.

Penney caught herself. *I'm being self-indulgent.* Later she'd mull over the new findings about Mr. Madison, but for now she chose moments of silence in view of the grievous occasion.

The parlor held a handful of people. From the grief-stricken looks on their faces, they were friends of Mrs. Wellington's. Dressed in a long black robe and a white collar, the minister spoke highly of young Elizabeth. He read the account in Genesis about Miriam and baby Moses, no doubt as a favor to Mrs. Wellington. Once the services ended, Penney and Mr. Madison rode his carriage to the graveyard.

She silently wept for a child she never met. God wanted Elizabeth for a special purpose, maybe to race up and down the mountains of heaven instead of the steps that led to her demise. She dabbed at her eyes. Sensing Mr. Madison observe her, she caught his gaze. Moistened eyes met hers. His display of emotion for young Elizabeth moved her. She had sorely misjudged this man. *Lord, forgive me for the cruel things I've thought and said about this man. These people here today are mourning the loss of a child whom You now have safely in Your arms. I pray Your peace.*

Once the services ended, Mr. Madison sought out Mrs. Wellington.

"Thank you for coming today, Russell," she said. "And thank you for bringing Miss Brice."

Penney reached for her hand, and the two embraced. Such an oddity for a woman of Mrs. Wellington's social standing. They parted, and an older couple approached them.

"James, Eunice," Mrs. Wellington said, grasping the woman's gloved hands. "How good of you to be here in my time of need."

"We are extremely sorry to hear of this misfortune," Eunice said, a thin woman with a kindly smile. "Such a beautiful child."

"Has it been so long since I have comforted you?"

Eunice dabbed a handkerchief beneath her eyes. "Oh, to understand God's ways."

An awkward silence followed as the sound of soft cries and hushed voices from the crowd reached them.

"Do excuse me," Mrs. Wellington said. "I see Miss Chambers, the headmistress at the school. I must speak with her. She's been ever so kind." She disappeared, and Penney's gaze trailed after her. She wanted to see what the headmistress looked like, but Mrs. Wellington shadowed her view.

Eunice turned to Mr. Madison. "It's good to see you, son. Time passes, and we rarely see you except in church."

"I agree," James added. "Families need to see more of each other than in dire situations like this one."

These are Mr. Madison's parents!

"I apologize, and I will visit more often." Mr. Madison touched Penney's waist. "Mother, Father, this is Miss Penney Brice."

After pleasantries were exchanged, Penney saw a close resemblance between Mr. Madison and his father; however, the younger Madison had lighter hair than the elder.

"I miss your visits," Eunice Madison said to her son. "Please say you will come to dinner soon."

"Most certainly, Mother. I apologize—spending all my time at the paper."

"And bring Miss Brice with you."

Russell Madison coughed, and Penney held her breath.

"Thank you. I will," he said.

You will? This day had been utterly confusing, and now Mr. Madison had committed her to dinner at his parents' home. If the man were not her boss, she'd let him know exactly what she thought about his presumption.

Once in the carriage, Mr. Madison appeared to sink into an austere mood, and she felt no better. Penney longed for the day to be finished, but the sun hadn't risen above their heads. As they approached the newspaper office, he cleared his throat.

"The driver will take you to the addresses for your column. We can discuss the other problem at dinner."

He had returned to his original temperament. Who was Mr. Russell Madison? Curiosity nudged her to find out. Today he'd exhibited the mannerisms of a fine gentleman. Why couldn't he always be considerate? Penney believed a kind word from him would inspire the other employees to work harder and better. She might give him her opinion on the matter, but first she needed his advice on finding out why those three young girls had died of accidents.

Snatching up his cigar, Russell wondered if his mother had taken leave of her senses. Asking him to bring Miss Brice to dinner? And he agreed! What was *he* thinking? As he had feared, people would think they were courting.

That's what happened when good men grew greedy for money and honest businessmen were forced to hire women. The time had come to give the striking men whatever they wanted. Then he'd be rid of Miss Brice and the others.

In the meantime, he had to contend with the presence of Miss Brice. Oh, he'd seen the looks of those at the funeral—matchmakers all of them, including his mother.

And now he had to deal with Miss Brice's notion that something amiss had occurred at the San Francisco Private Academy for Young Women. Furthermore, Russell had come to the same conclusions after she voiced her concern about the accidents. Miss Brice might plague him, but he refused to see her put into harm's way. In order to protect her, he'd have to guide and direct her every move.

The afternoon whittled away, and soon the time grew near for Russell to approach Penney about dinner. He'd already decided upon a modest and quiet place where they could talk. He hoped she had the sense to bring pen and paper. When he saw none of the other women were about, he approached her.

"Do you have a shawl?" he asked. "The wind appears unseasonably brisk."

She gathered up a light wrap and arranged it on her slender shoulders. He hoped she didn't become ill in the evening air.

Shortly afterward, he locked the newspaper office, and the two entered his carriage. Miss Brice had little to say, but he'd noted tired lines etched around her eyes.

Russell sliced through the beef roast on his plate, tender and juicy, just the way he liked it. The potatoes swam in brown gravy along with onions and carrots. Thick slices of bread oozing with butter rested on a separate platter. The delectable food kept his mind off the young woman sitting across from him—or so he thought. She hadn't talked as much tonight as he expected. Perhaps she was hungry, too.

When his food had vanished and as he lingered over hot black coffee, he turned his attention to the reason for their dining. "I like your idea of doing an article on the academy the young girls attended. Are you prepared to conduct a proper interview?"

She finished chewing her food and nodded slowly. "I think so. I thought of utilizing the history of the school and how it has influenced young ladies."

"Perhaps a tour would be in order," Russell said. "I'd like to see the steps where Elizabeth fell—and the site of the other two accidents—but you must be clever to find those spots."

"I understand, sir. Do you advise seeking out the kitchen staff?"

"Excellent, if you can arrange it." He marveled at her intellect. "That aspect will be difficult. I imagine they've been trained to keep their ears and mouths closed."

Penney retrieved her pen and paper from her lap. "Do you think a series of articles to give me more time might be in order?"

"I think that depends on the headmistress's willingness. If you don't find any problems, we'll have to run the story to keep her content."

Penney shook her head. "I hadn't considered the school might be blameless. How judgmental of me." She took a moment to regain her composure. "I do see how the paper might need to print a favorable story if my suspicions prove to be incorrect."

"Miss Brice, calm yourself. I, too, believe something or someone may be responsible for those girls' untimely departures." He tugged on his beard. "I want to take the risk." His lips upturned slightly. "Are you prepared to take notes?" His gentleness amazed her.

"I am." Penney pushed her plate aside and set a bottle of ink on the table beside her paper.

He suddenly noted that her black dress gave her an air of mystery. A part of him wanted to know everything about her. What had come over him? "Your thought of interviewing Miss Chambers is an excellent idea. I'm sure she will select the teachers with whom you are to confer, but see if you can talk to a few of the others in her employ—maids, kitchen staff, gardeners. Compliment her on everything. Find out what the girls are taught. Commend the teachers. Toward the end of the discussion, tell her you have a possible student for her. Ask for referrals. Inquire about church activities, mealtimes, music, and discipline. From what I remember, the girls can live at the school or merely attend classes."

Penney hurried to keep up with Mr. Madison. Her mind scurried with how she'd formulate his suggestions. "A tour also?"

"By all means. Take a look at those steps. See if the banisters are loose. We don't know how the other girls met their demise, so keep your eyes open." He stopped and took a long sip of coffee. "I may visit their parents to find out a few things on my own."

"Won't I need an introduction before paying the school a call?"

"I'll send a messenger in the morning to secure the headmistress's name and establish a proper time." In the candlelight, Mr. Madison's dark blue eyes sparkled. "I'll write a letter indicating our desire to do an article on the school and inform her that you are my best reporter."

Penney blushed. "Thank you, Mr. Madison. I appreciate your confidence in me."

"One more matter of utmost concern."

Penney dipped her pen into the ink well.

"Write these words carefully."

"Yes, sir."

"My name is Russell. When we are together outside the newspaper office, I would very much like for you to use my given name."

"Yes, sir."

He raised a brow.

"Yes, Russell, and my given name is Penney." She started to say more but thought better of it.

"Your brother will not approve of this interview with the academy."

"I don't intend to tell him. He's quite busy these days with his position as a policeman and in preparations for his wedding."

"Ah yes, he is engaged to Miss Lattimer," Russell said.

"Yes, sir—Russell."

"Your friends are good employees, even if they are women."

Penney stiffened. "We work hard."

He took a deep breath. "My point is your friends have been involved in a few precarious situations. Luckily, they weren't hurt." He leaned in closer. "Do be careful, Penney. The newspaper will go on without another big story."

A glint of emotion swept over his face, causing her to question if this evening's meeting meant more to him than a newspaper story.

Chapter 6

Stepping down from Russell's carriage, Penney surveyed the huge, stately house towering like a monument at the top of a hill. A nearly six-foot tall, deep green hedge lined the perimeter of the grounds, creating a sense of awe and a forbidding air. White railing framed the outside of the house, freshly painted and perfect.

She saw no signs of children nor heard any laughter. Thick, low vines covered both sides of the stone walkway leading up to the door. So this was the San Francisco Private Academy for Young Women. White wood trim encased the windows and doors, including two windows that extended out as though the builder entertained bringing more of the lush green inside. A round window on the second floor gave the impression of someone spying on her, or so she thought.

With a quick prayer for purpose and direction, she opened a well-oiled gate and made her way along a stone walkway to the front door.

A dried-apple-faced woman opened the door and greeted Penney. Not at all what she expected, but the stiff formality could be what the prestigious people of San Francisco expected.

"I have an appointment with Miss Chambers." Penney attempted to coax a smile from the woman. Her efforts were in vain.

"Kindly wait here in the foyer, and I will let her know of your arrival. And your name is?"

"Miss Brice from the *Golden Gate Gazette*."

Penney heard no sounds of teaching or the low hum of voices. The faint scent of roses greeted her; the only possible sign of women occupants. If she had not known better, she would have believed the school stood empty. She barely had a moment of reprieve to study the surroundings clothed in dark wood and elegant furnishings, when Miss Chambers entered the wide foyer.

"What a pleasure, Miss Brice," the woman said. "I am Miss Chambers."

Penney inwardly startled at the lovely young woman before her: coffee-colored hair, ivory skin, huge green eyes veiled in thick lashes, and a smile that could warm the coldest of nights. Miss Chambers did not possess any of the traits Penney had envisioned. "Thank you for allotting time for me this morning. I am so looking forward to writing this article about your beautiful school." She hoped her words echoed with refinement.

"On behalf of the school, I wish to thank you and Mr. Madison for the consideration." She flashed another charming smile. "Follow me to my office. After we have tea and discuss the school, I'll introduce you to my teachers, tour the classrooms, and answer all of your questions."

"That would be lovely."

Miss Chambers's small office impressed Penney with its cherry writing desk, a gold and cream settee, a small cherry table, fresh flowers, and a library that rose from the floor to the ceiling.

"Please, sit down, Miss Brice. I'll ring for tea." She took Penney's shawl and draped it across a library table.

Penney opened her leather bag and placed the bottle of ink on the desk, then pulled out paper and pen. Balancing them on her lap, she realized the interview might go quite smoothly. "I'd like to know the history of your school," she said.

"I established the school in 1850. My dream was to educate young girls not only in math, Bible, English, French, music, geography, and world history but also to instill the touches of a fine finishing school. My staff is highly qualified and eager to help mold the hearts and minds of the young women."

Penney captured every word. "Where did you receive your education?"

"Oberlin College in Ohio. My family still lives there."

The dried-apple-faced woman brought tea and served them with expertise. While Penney learned about the school's excellent educational program and esteemed contributors, she began to wonder if her original assessment of the academy had been correct. How could such a tragedy occur at this fine establishment?

Once they finished, the tour began with a French class. The girls ranging from ten to sixteen years old sat stiffly on the edge of high-backed chairs. They were dressed in identical navy blue dresses. Penney knew nothing of French, but the tall gentleman instructing the class peered down his nose at the students as though they were from the mining camps where she had once lived.

In the next class, a music conservatory of sorts, a rather large woman carried a wooden stick which she did not hesitate to use to rap the knuckles of the young women seated at three pianos.

The English teacher looked to be the same age as the older students. She read quietly to the girls, and most of them appeared interested. A good teacher, Penney surmised. She reminded Penney of the woman who had taught her how to read, write, compute math, and be familiar with geography—she had a soft voice and kindly mannerisms.

In one of the downstairs parlors, a chapel had been constructed. The teachers and students met each morning for prayers and Bible study. Penney admired two stained-glass windows that had replaced a clear pane. One window depicted Jesus holding a lamb, and the second portrayed Him praying in Gethsemane. In the dim lighting, she could envision the girls sitting in the small pews with their heads bent in prayer.

"May I see the girls' rooms?" Penney asked.

Miss Chambers folded her hands at her waist. "A few of our students live at home. The majority live here."

Penney trailed up the stairs behind her. The wide stairs wound around to the second floor. As she expected, the tidy rooms housed two to four girls each. Nothing looked amiss. After a few polite questions, Penney asked to see the kitchen and dining area. Miss Chambers introduced the servants and explained the preparation and serving of the students' meals.

"We offer the finest cuts of beef, pork, poultry, and fish,"

Miss Chambers said. "Our fruits and vegetables are selected with utmost care, and our bread is baked daily. Our cook"—she pointed to a robust woman who offered a faint smile—"trained in New York City. Our young ladies are quite happy with her culinary talents."

Penney looked for reason to fault the school, but all facets of the academy met the most rigid standards.

"Our students have gone on to marry into prominent families and serve the community with grace and knowledge," Miss Chambers said.

"I can see you are proud and pleased with the success of your school. It is indeed an excellent learning institution." Penney encouraged the headmistress in hopes that she might offer information about the deceased girls.

"Thank you, Miss Brice. Observing the girls blossom into admirable young women is all the gratitude I need."

"What are the requirements for a girl to be considered for placement?" Penney asked.

Miss Chambers walked toward her office, and Penney joined her. "Social standing of the family. Letters of recommendation. An interview with the young lady and her parents or guardian. We also have a scholastic test to see if they can follow our curriculum."

"Do you ever have problems with discipline?" Penney studied the woman's face, looking for a flash of uneasiness. "I have a friend whose daughter is high spirited. I wondered if a school of your caliber could tame her."

"Our young ladies must adhere to our behavior standards. We do not accept disciplinary problems, nor do we tolerate those students who show potential for embarrassing the school." Miss Chambers smiled between her words.

"An ill-mannered young woman would be asked to leave or denied admittance?"

Miss Chambers released a sigh. A saddened look spread over her lovely face. "We do everything within our power to train and redirect the young woman. Many times we enlist some of our mature young ladies to pray."

"Do the families and the students receive a guideline of expected behavior and the consequences?"

Miss Chambers nodded. "Yes, and those involved must sign that they have read and understand the contents. Would you like to have one?"

"Yes, thank you. I could show it to my friend for her consideration."

A moment later, the guidelines lay in Penney's lap along with several pages of notes from the tour and interview. She no longer believed Miss Chambers could have knowingly hurt anyone in her charge. Once Penney returned to the newspaper office, she'd inform Russell of her findings. The tragedies that had befallen this impeccable school must be simply that—horrible accidents.

"I believe I have plenty of material for writing my article," Penney said. "I don't know the date when it will appear in the *Gazette*, but I could send a messenger as soon as I find out."

"I am looking forward to reading it. We have room for a few more students, and the article will ensure that very thing." Miss Chambers escorted Penney to the door and graciously bid her good day.

Once Penney had settled in the carriage, the driver picked up the reins. Suddenly Penney realized she'd forgotten her shawl in Miss Chambers's office. Bidding him to wait, Penney hurried back up the stone walkway to the school. Standing outside the heavy doors, she heard voices from an upstairs window.

"How dare you not know your French lesson?" Miss Chambers said. "You stupid, stupid girl. Your father pays an exorbitant amount of money for you to live here and obtain your education. You will not disappoint him!"

Sobs met Penney's ears. Was this the same polite Miss Chambers who had spoken to her only minutes before?

"Please don't hit me," a voice said.

"Hit you?" The sound of a hand striking flesh met Penney's ears. "You will not have a midday meal or dinner, and you will spend the night in the attic. Perhaps then you will learn to study."

Deny the girl food for the rest of the day? Have her spend the night in a dark attic?

"Not there, Miss Chambers. Please not the attic."

"Enough. If this continues, you will spend two days and nights there among the rats."

Penney held her breath. The suspicions she'd earlier dismissed about Miss Chambers pelted her mind like rocks that bruised the skin.

"And don't think you can write your father about this. Remember, I read every letter before it is posted. You have no choice but to follow the rules."

"Yes, ma'am," came the crying voice. "I'll do anything, but please don't put me in the attic."

"You've given me no choice. What is this?"

The sound of the wooden frame of the window hitting the sill met Penney's ears. She clenched her fists, thinking of how she'd like to march right back into the school and tell Miss Chambers what she thought of the way she treated her students. How cruel. How deceptive.

Another thought struck her. Penney had been deceived just like the parents of those precious girls. She possessed no talent or discernment in reporting the truth. A few moments ago, she was ready to cast aside the thought of Miss Chambers being responsible for the accidental deaths. Reporting news and discerning the truth belonged to someone wiser, not to Penney Brice, and Russell needed to know as soon as possible.

Penney turned and made her way back to the carriage. Melancholy wrapped its black cloak around her, and regretful tears clung to her lashes. All her dreams and expectations in writing for the newspaper were mere ashes beneath her feet. She remembered the night the hotel burned to the ground and the heaviness in her heart for not only her loss but for the losses of others. Typesetting was the best she had to offer Russell Madison and the faithful readers of the *Golden Gate Gazette*.

Chapter 7

Russell paced the floor and pulled his pocket watch from his trousers' pocket for what seemed like the hundredth time. He'd smoked two cigars and drunk six cups of thick, black coffee, waiting for Penney to return to the newspaper. He shouldn't have sent her to the academy alone. She could have inadvertently let the headmistress know about their suspicions or worse yet be in danger. The carriage driver knew to wait for her, but the elderly man had no idea the reason for Penney's visit.

I need a beating for permitting this. Oh, Lord, why didn't I use better judgment?

He ceased his pacing long enough to stare out the open window. Strange, these days he opened the window before he lit up his cigar. Penney had a definite effect on him. . .and if he permitted his thoughts to coincide with his heart, then he'd admit he'd fallen in love with her.

How many years had passed since he'd felt a stirring of the heart for a woman? He wanted to love her, protect her, make her laugh, and share his innermost thoughts with her. Those days of his youth when he first fell in love flitted across his mind. The world had appeared brighter and more beautiful. He'd rushed into love like he now rushed into a new story for his paper. Terrible analogy, but it was true. Back then life's trials meant nothing. The future he anticipated with his new bride held all of God's blessings and promises. Then it vanished, and as much as he loved God, the idea of making a commitment again tore at his very soul. The same question knocked at the core of him: Why had God placed Penney in his life at this time? Or had Russell become so vulnerable and cynical that the evil of this world now sought another human to torment?

Yet if he considered the foolishness of losing his very mind in a whirlpool of love, Penney gave no indication of having the same regard for him. Russell smiled in spite of the gloom settling on him about her whereabouts. Learning to keep his love inside seemed a formidable task at best, but with God's help, he'd master it.

At the sound of approaching horses' hooves, he turned his attention to the street and viewed his approaching carriage. When Penney stepped down with the aid of the driver, Russell's pulse quickened. Shakespeare had penned, "This bud of love, by summer's ripening breath, may prove a beauteous flower when next we meet."

Lord, I need Your help to hide the emotions drowning me. If this is to be, please tell me so. If not, take this burden away. To love again is more than I ever dreamed possible.

Within the breath of his prayer, Penney glanced up at him. Embarrassed that she saw him watching her, he waved. Troubled best described her, for her smile lay hidden beneath something he could not claim.

Russell Madison had turned into a hopeless romantic. He thought this part of him lay buried in two graves, but instead his heart now rose from some dormant stage. *Mask it well,* he told himself. *She will not learn of this.*

Perhaps the interview had gone so badly that she'd elected to resign her employ.

He resumed his position at his desk and physically focused on pending matters before him. His cigar box enticed him, but he recognized the momentary pleasure did not touch how God could ease his pain. When he heard a light rapping at the door, he knew the center of his attention stood right outside. "Yes."

"Mr. Madison, this is Penney. May I have a word with you?" Her voice quivered, and he immediately regretted his previous thoughts. He wished her well, nothing less.

"Come in, Miss Brice." His gaze caught hers the instant she stepped into his office. Her eyes were puffy, and she trembled. "The interview went poorly?"

She swallowed hard and raised her chin. "That depends on how one views the result."

He squinted. "Kindly close the door and explain this to me." He sounded harsh, but his callous tone must rule the conversation.

She eased the door shut, and he sensed she formed her words. Although she smiled, it appeared false. What had happened at the academy? Placing her notes before him, she smoothed her brown dress and clasped her hands. "Mr. Madison, the interview went very well. Miss Chambers is a charming, gracious, and educated woman. I enjoyed touring the school. I saw teachers and students within the classroom setting, and I viewed the students' bedrooms. I even met the cook and other kitchen staff." She paused and lifted her chin. "Miss Chambers showed me letters of recommendation and spoke of past students' contributions to society. I left feeling I had no story except the article on the school's merits."

Russell frowned. "The whole idea of three tragic accidents doesn't sit well with me. Did any of the staff look or act as though they might be responsible?"

"Not really. I have more to my story." Her eyes moistened.

He turned his head. "Penney, you are obviously upset. What else happened?" He stood and pointed to his chair—behaving quite the opposite of what he had intended. "Please rest here."

She shook her head. "I'm not pleased with myself at all. After I left the school and your driver assisted me into the carriage, I realized I had forgotten my shawl. I politely excused myself and walked back to the front door of the school." Penney paused, then repeated to him the conversation she had heard from the open window. "I now believe something *is* amiss. And I was fooled by a few manners." Her shoulders lowered. "I'm obviously not a good reporter. I'm asking if I can return to my job as typesetter."

"Absolutely not."

She hastily blinked. "Has it been given to someone else?"

"Yes and no."

"I don't understand."

Russell walked to the side of his desk, placed her arm in the crook of his, and ushered her to his chair. Once she took residence in his chair, he continued. "Granted Miss Chambers displayed a different temperament to you than she did to the young lady in her charge, but you may have information that could help not only those girls but other girls whose parents are seeking application. Consider also the plight of the parents."

"I believed her!"

"Do you think you are the only reporter who has ever been misled from the truth?" The dismay in her watery eyes urged him to comfort her. Placing his hands behind his back, he stepped away from the desk.

"I thought discernment came naturally."

"If so, Eve would not have been tempted by the serpent."

She moistened her lips, the ones he longed to taste. More importantly, he needed to convey his faith in her. "You were honest with me. Not many reporters have such integrity. They would have burst into my office with this wondrous story and reaped my praises with it. But you, Penney, have the mark of a caring woman who believes her words must be steeped in truth."

She dabbed the wetness beneath her eyes with her finger. "Are you certain? You make me sound noble."

Russell smiled. He failed to stop the pleasure swelling inside him. "You are. Now are you ready to continue with what you've found?"

"I suppose so."

"Excellent. This reminds me of a quote from Shakespeare: 'Our doubts are traitors, and make us lose the good we oft might win.'"

"I adore Shakespeare."

"As do I." He caught her dear gaze again and realized he must talk professionally or else he'd drown in those gold-brown eyes. "If only you had a reason to return."

"But I do." She offered a smile. "I was so dejected that I left the school without securing my shawl."

"Do you mind returning?"

"I'll go this very instant if you like."

"Hmm. I want to think this through. Might we share dinner again tonight and discuss how to proceed?"

She appeared a bit startled, then nodded. "I'd be honored."

Warmth spread through him. "We can be thinking of ways to foil her treachery, if indeed she is guilty. We cannot discount that another individual may be responsible for the accidents." He paused. "And this warrants a discussion with your brother."

Suddenly she paled and stood from the chair. "I'm so wretched! Why didn't I pound on the door and try to help the poor girl? What was I thinking? Oh my, I'm so selfish, so concerned about myself and with no consideration for others. Russell, I must go back there. I won't be able to live with myself if another poor girl is hurt."

His insides twisted and turned. What if Charlotte had lived? He'd have done everything within his power to place her in a proper school. "Yes, you're right. Let's go there now, but first we need to talk to your brother. The police must be informed of what is going on."

"You don't think we can handle Miss Chambers alone?"

"Not without professional advice. This is dangerous, Penney. A person who resorts to murder is desperate indeed."

Penney agreed with Russell, except she remembered Evan's

words when she expressed her desire to write for the paper. *I have seen Amy, Jennie, and Helen in dangerous situations, and I refuse to see you there, too.* She released a sigh. She and Evan shared the same stubborn and impatient traits. Seeking his advice about the tragedy at the school invited an argument.

All the way to the police station, she formed this word and that in an attempt to convince Evan of her safety. She should give up and realize his reasons for her noninvolvement far exceeded her reasons to continue with the endeavor. But a child's safety was involved, and she might be the only one who could help.

"You are exceptionally quiet." Russell urged the horses down the street. He'd elected not to use a driver in view of the sensitive nature of their endeavor.

"I'm thinking." She dared not give in to the trepidation about facing her brother. Russell most likely would agree, and the two men would conjure up a new plan without her.

"I'm sure Evan will help us solve this mystery. He may even elect for us to discard our plan and allow the police to take over."

"Think about the story," Penney said.

He chuckled. "We have a story regardless of your brother's role in the matter."

And he will yank me out of it like he used to pull on my pigtails when I refused to listen to his ridiculous orders.

The two found Evan with little effort. "I'd like to discuss a situation with you," Russell said. "Is there anywhere we can talk privately?"

Evan shot Penney a menacing scowl then turned his attention to Russell. "We can take a walk."

The three fell into pace together. For the first time in a long time, Penney said nothing while Russell explained what had happened at the school and Penney's role in obtaining information by posing as a newspaper reporter.

"So you are proposing that my sister go back to the school and see if she can find anything that incriminates Miss Chambers in those girls' deaths?"

"Yes, unless you have a better idea. Of course I will be with her and assume all responsibility for any wrongdoing."

"Absolutely not!" Evan's booming voice could have been heard across the ocean and back again. "Penney, I told you before to stay out of trouble."

His demands sent a flash of heat from her stomach to her throat. "I'm getting my shawl. Russell is the one taking the tour."

"Have you forgotten I know you?"

It occurred to her that arguing with Evan only strengthened his resolve. "We could work on this together."

"And what do you know about police work?" Evan's brow lifted.

"I admit, I know very little," Russell said. "And you are right. Endangering Penney is a foolish notion."

"Excuse me, gentlemen. Hear what I have to say before you say no." When they both shook their heads at her, she continued. "I have earned Miss Chambers's confidence, and I also know that her inappropriate behavior does not mean she is guilty of the accidents. But she does have my shawl, and I intend to retrieve it. What is the harm of Russell asking for a tour while we are there? He may see or hear something you can use."

Evan tugged at his ear. "Fetching your shawl. . .I guess there is no harm in that."

Her heart pounded. Unless he agreed, Russell would take on the shawl business by himself.

"I'd like to be in the background," Evan said. "If I don't see you two leave the school within the hour, I will check on matters myself."

"Fair enough." Russell glanced at Penney. "Your brother is interested in your welfare, just as I am. Neither of us wants to see you hurt."

Penney heard a touch of something else in Russell's tone—a tenderness that he failed to disguise. "I understand. I will take all precautions to ensure my safety." *Well, I might take a few chances.*

Chapter 8

Within the quarter hour, Russell and Penney sat side by side in his carriage. Russell drove, not so fast as to attract attention but at a brisk pace.

"What will we do once I have my shawl?" Penney's heart felt as though it were in her throat. She choked back the tears and wondered if the emotion was caused by fear or guilt—or both.

"Miss Chambers will remember me. I will seize the opportunity to inform her of how pleased I am with your glowing reports of the school. Then I'll ask her to show me the school. I will act as though she is the most charming creature I have ever met."

"All right, but what about me?"

He appeared to think through her request and nodded. "Nothing more. Remember Evan's concerns?"

"Of course." *I'll find a reason to excuse myself from the tour, then see if I can find the girl.*

Penney didn't even know the child's name or the location of the door to the attic. But with God's aid, the girl would be rescued. "We make a fine pair." She caught her breath. Why did she forever say the wrong things? Warmth eased up her cheeks. "I'm. . .I apologize."

Russell said nothing for several long moments. "Your statement had a profound affect on me."

"I'm so sorry!"

"We shall talk of the familiarity when this matter is reconciled." Russell stared at the street in front of them. She could not detect irritation or embarrassment in his tone.

"Yes, sir." How else dare she respond after her inappropriate remark?

"Penney." He continued to stare at the street ahead. "I had a wife once and a little girl. They both died from fever. I—I was twenty-five."

Now she understood it all—his premature silver hair and his occasional harshness. Charlotte had been his daughter, the one Mrs. Wellington had spoken of. "I'm very sorry."

"Thank you." He faced her. Troubled lines deepened his brow. "Watching Elizabeth grow after losing them gave me a measure of comfort. Now that, too, is gone."

"The years have been hard for you," she said. "I pray for happiness to ease your pain."

"Thank you." The smile he gave her stirred a peculiar feeling—something she had never felt before.

The carriage stopped in front of the school. The late afternoon sun had begun to dip into the blue waters, and a slight chill shivered her arms. How foreboding considering the matter before them.

"Let's pray before we embark upon this," Russell said. She

bowed her head. "Heavenly Father," he began, "we believe there is danger for the young ladies inside this school. Guide and direct our ways and give us wisdom on how to proceed. Protect all who may be in harm's way. Amen."

His jaw stiffened. Wordlessly he stepped from the carriage and assisted her to the ground. His touch felt warm and strong. She'd grown to enjoy his company, but that promised to end soon.

They said nothing during the climb up the stone walkway to the school. For that consolation, she felt relieved. The dried-apple-faced maid answered the door. Her features seemed eternally etched in rock. With a nod she left them standing in the foyer for Miss Chambers.

"Miss Brice, Mr. Madison, how pleasant a surprise." She grasped Penney's hand. "You forgot your shawl. I'll get it for you."

Miss Chambers soon returned with the shawl. Penney considered what might be the best excuse to remain in the foyer or the school's office while Russell distracted her.

"Thank you. I apologize for the inconvenience," Penney said. "When I told Mr. Madison about your splendid school and my excitement over writing the article, he elected to come with me."

Russell smiled and dipped low. "My newspaper is honored to represent your fine academy. I understand this may be an imposition, but do you have time to give me a tour?"

Miss Chambers studied him, and for a second Penney saw a spark of fear.

"Of course, I could return at another time," he said.

A smile graced Miss Chambers's face. "Nonsense. Let me

take you through. After all, you are the one who initiated the article."

Penney pasted a smile on her face, one she hoped matched that of the headmistress. "If you don't mind, I should like to wait here. The day has been exhausting." She avoided Russell's stare, but she sensed his disapproval.

Compassion swept over Miss Chambers's genteel features. "You poor dear. Kindly wait in my office. Can I get you anything?"

"Not at all. And I can find my way to the settee. If you don't mind, I'll close the door and take a rest."

Miss Chambers turned her attention to Russell and began to chat away. Penney waited until the voices were muffled before she exited the door and moved toward the winding staircase leading to the bedrooms and hopefully the attic. The huge building appeared deserted. She smelled roast chicken and vegetables for dinner and once heard a faint clatter of pans. Penney's foot touched a loose board. It creaked. Holding her breath, she glanced in every direction until she felt certain no one had detected her. In the next breath, she hurried up the stairs.

She saw and heard no one. Now to find the attic. Evan told her once that many structures such as this one housed an attic above the ceiling. Some simply used an unfinished room. With her luck, the entrance would be inaccessible without a ladder. The doors to the bedrooms were closed. Defeat assaulted her.

"Who are you?" a voice asked.

Penney whirled around and nearly fell. A girl who looked to be about fourteen or so peered at her. She wore the same uniform navy blue dress as the students she'd seen earlier.

"A visitor," Penney replied.

"Why isn't Miss Chambers with you?" The girl lifted her head, not in defiance but in curiosity.

Lord, help me. "I was here earlier today touring the school."

"I remember. You observed my French class."

"When I left, I realized I'd forgotten my shawl. I returned to get it and heard something disturbing from an open window."

The girl's eyes widened. Penney ventured on. "The girl was to be placed in the attic for not knowing her French."

"I—I know whom you mean." The girl took a step back.

"Where is she?"

The girl swung her gaze up and down the hall. She wrung her hands. "I don't want to get into trouble."

"And end up like Elizabeth and the others?"

The girl covered her mouth. "How do you know?"

Penney touched the girl's arm. "I merely guessed. Please show me where the attic is, so I can help her."

"Miss Chambers will be angry. She will tie me up in there with the rats."

Penney wanted to take the girl into her arms, but the gesture might frighten her. "She will have to answer to the authorities."

The girl held her breath. "All right, follow me. The attic is locked, but Kathryn should be able to talk to us."

Penney followed her down the hallway to a far door. "This is it." The girl twisted the knob. It refused to budge.

"Kathryn." Penney leaned into the door. "Are you all right?" Silence greeted them.

"Sometimes Miss Chambers ties a cloth around a girl's

mouth during punishment. The sound of cries makes Miss Chambers more angry."

The thought churned Penney's stomach. "You've been locked up here?"

"No, ma'am. Elizabeth told me."

Penney fought the urge to weep then bit her lower lip to keep from screaming for Russell. "What is your name?"

The girl hesitated.

"You don't have to tell me. I understand you're afraid. I would be, too, but the police are ready to help." She turned to the door again. "Kathryn, I'm getting help."

Penney started down the hall to find Russell. The girl walked closely by her side. "Why haven't you told your parents?"

"She'd say we are lying. Besides, you've met Miss Chambers. She is quite convincing."

Sad but true. "I understand, but all of this is ending today. Is anyone else involved?"

"Mr. Barton, the music teacher. Please don't let them know I told you."

Penney smiled and turned back to lightly grasp the girl's shoulders. "How can I? I don't even know your name."

Footsteps sounded up the stairway.

"Hurry back to your room," Penney whispered. "Stay there until I say it's safe."

As Penney thought, Miss Chambers and Russell made their way to the second floor.

"Why are you here?" Miss Chambers voice held an icy edge to it.

"Looking for Kathryn, the girl you locked in the attic."

Miss Chambers clasped her hand over her heart. "How dare you make such an accusation?"

Penney glanced at Russell. He looked at her with what seemed to be admiration. "She's locked inside that room." Penney pointed to the door. "I understand you have the key."

Miss Chambers flushed red. "I will contact the police."

"That's not necessary. We will take you there," Russell said. He stepped in front of Miss Chambers. "I want the key, or I shall take it from you."

The woman turned and ran for the stairway, but Russell grabbed her before she made it to the first landing. "Give me the key, or I will have Miss Brice search you."

When the woman still refused, Penney rushed down the steps. She reached deep into Miss Chambers's left pocket. There rested a lone key strung on a piece of lace. In the next instant, Penney rushed up the steps, down the hall, and twisted the key inside the locked door.

The stale air assaulted her. She gasped and blinked to adjust her eyes to the darkened room. In a corner, the figure of a girl, gagged and bound, lay on the floor. "Russell, she's in here."

His boots hit hard across the wooden floor. He flew back the door as though it were paper. Penney worked with the knot gagging the girl while he released her hands and then her feet. The girl fell into Russell's arms and sobbed against his chest.

"The animal," he said. "I can't wait to talk to your brother."

Penney watched the tender sight before her. "Her name is Kathryn." Remembering the rest of the students, she left the pair alone, certain Kathryn was not the only frightened student.

Miss Chambers had disappeared, but Penney didn't care. She'd be found by Evan or one of the other policemen waiting outside.

"Girls, it's all right. You can come out of your rooms. No one is going to hurt you again." When no one emerged from the rooms, she raised her voice. "I need to contact your parents right away. They need to know what has been going on here."

First one door opened, then another. Finally twenty-five girls crept into the hallway. Late afternoon shadows bounced off the walls, silhouetting the girls in the fading light.

"You are all safe," Russell said. He held Kathryn's hand. A path of tears had dried on her dirty face. "Miss Brice is going to stay with you while I take Miss Chambers to the police. Once I return, we will notify your parents."

The girls glanced at each other as though afraid to speak.

"It's the truth," Penney said. "We are here to help."

"Why would you want to help us?" an older girl said. "My guardian did not believe me when I told him about Miss Chambers's cruelty."

Penney glanced at Russell. He stepped into the middle of the hall with his hand still firmly clasped around Kathryn's. "We have proof for the police to arrest the headmistress. In addition, we know three girls from this school have passed away."

"Who? I only know of Elizabeth," the older girl said. "Two other girls were dismissed."

Russell said nothing. Soft sobs wafted through the hallway. He bent to Kathryn. "Miss Brice will hold your hand until I return."

The girl brushed her free hand across her cheek. "Yes, sir."

Russell stood and faced Penney. His eyebrows lowered. A mixture of fury and grief met her gaze. "Will you be all right?" He placed Kathryn's hand into Penney's.

"I'll be just fine until you return." The intensity of the moment coupled with the realization of Miss Chambers's crimes caused her to appreciate once more the dearness of life.

"I should have had Evan linger closer." He inhaled deeply. "I'll find the woman and escort her to where she belongs."

"I think not."

A few girls screamed. Several shrank away. Penney pulled Kathryn into her arms. Miss Chambers stood on the top landing with a rifle aimed at Russell.

Chapter 9

Russell saw Miss Chambers tremble, although a smile spread over her face as she ascended each step. The woman had killed before and could do so again. He understood each time she took a life made the next incident easier. Shooting a man to protect herself might look justified, even a self-defense measure in the eyes of many.

"Are you sure you want to shoot a man in front of these witnesses?" he asked.

"With you and your friend out of the way, I don't have any witnesses."

"And these girls?" Russell took a step forward, but she raised the rifle. He refused to risk the lives of the girls or Penney.

"They know better than to disobey me. Get inside your rooms."

Doors slammed all around him, not that Russell blamed any of the girls.

"I see you have command of your students." He searched his mind for anything to divert her attention while all of the girls found refuge.

"That's the secret to making money—power. Power and command. Add a little charm and a flair for human nature, and one can become quite wealthy." Noise from downstairs caused her to take a momentary glance to the first floor. Two women stared in disbelief. "Get back to your duties."

"What are you doing?" one asked. "Is there someone threatening the young ladies?"

"Yes, now leave me alone," Miss Chambers nearly shouted.

"I'll go after the police," another said.

"No! I am capable of handling this without any assistance." A hint of hysteria laced Miss Chambers's voice.

"Let me tell you the truth." Russell stared into Miss Chambers's face while he talked. "Your headmistress has caused the deaths of three students. Miss Brice and I just learned the truth. She threatened to kill us when you walked in."

The women downstairs gasped.

"Call for Mr. Barton this instant," Miss Chambers said.

"Why don't you hand me the rifle?" Russell offered a faint smile. "You are only getting yourself into deeper trouble."

She shook her head. "I'm leaving San Francisco tonight. It doesn't matter what I do."

Boots thudded across the downstairs floor. "Cynthia, what is going on?" a male voice called from the first floor.

"We've been found out." Cynthia Chambers laughed. "We need to leave right away."

"Look around you. What do you see?" the man asked.

"Dead bodies, as many as we need to leave San Francisco behind us."

Russell heard a struggle below him—enough scuffling feet

and frightened cries to realize Mr. Barton had seized the two women on the first floor.

"I'll bind and gag these two and lock them in your office." Miss Chambers smirked. "You're first, newspaper boy. Come tomorrow, you and your lady reporter will be nothing but missing pages."

Russell watched her mount the remaining stairs from the landing to about twenty feet in front him. Meeting God did not shake him, and the rifle at this close range had a clear target straight through his body, but the lives of those around him weighed heavily.

"Russell," Penney said behind him. Kathryn still clung to her.

He turned, much against his better judgment, and met her tender gaze. Without a single utterance of love, he understood the depth in her eyes. "I'm sorry. I'm so sorry." Penney's lips quivered—the ones he'd waited too long to kiss.

"Turn around, Madison," Cynthia said. "I want to see your face when I do this."

Someone pounded hard on the door with so much force that the windows rattled.

"The police are here," he said. "Whether you shoot me or not, you're caught."

Shouts to open the door met his ears. She didn't blink or change her stance but squeezed her finger against the trigger. A window shattered. He heard a bedroom door squeak open. Cynthia whipped her attention toward it long enough for Russell to dive into her just as the rifle fired. A thud hit the floor. Several more thuds followed in a rumble of what sounded like muffled cracks of fire.

The rifle crashed with Cynthia Chambers sprawling beside t. Around Russell lay several shoes. Behind the shoes stood wenty-five girls armed with more.

Russell snatched up the rifle and sent it across the floor oward a bedroom door. He swung his gaze to the rear then to he ceiling where a hole revealed where the rifle bullet had found its mark. The girls huddled together unhurt, but Penney ay face down on the floor. In the ever-decreasing light, he thought he saw blood.

~~~

"Penney, Madison, are you all right? Is anyone hurt up there?" Evan's voice bellowed with the rush of heavy footsteps mounting the stairs.

"I think so," Russell said. "You can have Miss Chambers. Penney, are you hit?" He touched her shoulder. "Please tell me you're all right."

"Fine," she said. She rolled over and felt warm blood flow over her lips. Swiping at her nose, embarrassment crept over her. "I must have hit my nose when I fell. I was afraid for Kathryn."

Russell yanked a handkerchief from his pocket and wiped at her face, then pressed the linen to her fingers. "I couldn't bear the thought of your getting hurt."

She lifted her head. "What about the girls?"

He glanced about as the group crept from their rooms. He offered Penney a half smile, and his gaze radiated with compassion. "Frightened, but now it is over. Their quick action saved me from a bullet."

In the next breath, she realized how much Russell Madison meant to her. "The shoes?"

He nodded. "Their aim is pretty good—they knocked Miss Chambers off balance, and then another flight of shoes assured that she would stay on the floor."

"We have our story," Penney said.

"The story was never my concern." His words warmed her spirit. "I thought I'd lost you to this insane woman."

"I'm much too stubborn," Penney said. Kathryn stood, and another girl called to her. She left Penney and Russell alone. "Now these girls won't have to live like this again." She held the handkerchief against her nose. "Do you mind helping me up?"

His strong hands righted her to her feet.

"Is Penney hurt?" Evan's anxious voice broke through the tenderness growing in the moment.

"No, Evan, just a nosebleed," she said.

His eyes narrowed. "Didn't I tell you not to go looking for danger?"

"Yes, you did." She faced him squarely. "But I had no intentions of letting these girls face any more fearful days."

He heaved a labored breath. "But did you have to get involved?"

"I take full responsibility," Russell said. "I promise your sister will never worry you again."

"That's a promise you can't keep."

Penney silently agreed.

"Not if she agrees to be my wife."

Startled, Penney felt a strange sensation in the pit of her stomach. Evan's eyes widened. "You don't have to marry me to protect me." Her words came more as a question than a stubborn stance.

"I wouldn't dream of it. I intend to love you into docility."

Evan motioned for one of his policemen to take Cynthia downstairs. "Good luck. She's never been one to listen."

Russell peered into her face. "If you will have me and if your brother agrees, I'll spend the rest of my life proving how much I do love you."

Penney shivered with the revelation before her. "I think I'd like that very much."

Russell shrugged, and a grin tugged his silver mustache to the far corners of his face. "I've even thought of giving up my cigars."

"Now that's love." Evan glanced at the girls watching the tender scene. "What do you young ladies think? Should I let this man marry my sister?"

A burst of giggles replaced the former frightened sighs.

"I think I have my answer," Evan said. He turned to Penney. "What about you? Are you ready to give up the newspaper life for the role of a wife?"

Penney rocked back and forth on her heels. "I'm ready to share the newspaper life with Russell, knowing he comes first."

Four months later

"I believe the rumors are right," Penney said to Helen while her friend arranged her hair in loose curls that fell from the top of her head.

"And what are they?" Helen asked.

"My dear fiancé will have to change the name of the paper to the *Marriage Gazette*. Every single woman who worked for him during the strike has gotten married."

Jennie laughed and patted her stomach. "Some of us have little ones on the way to prove it was a great matchmaking venture."

"I agree," Amy said. "Who would ever have thought those months ago that the Lord would lead us into adventure and romance by way of a newspaper?"

"And Russell Madison," Penney added. She took a peek around the corner of the door to the church sanctuary where Russell waited. Soon she'd make her entrance and forever be Mrs. Russell Madison. "I don't know about the rest of you, but I got the best job promotion of all."

"You must have done something to the poor man," Jennie said. "I haven't seen him with a cigar in weeks."

Penney smiled and took a deep breath. "I had to promise not to write anything more daring than births and weddings."

Helen leaned over and whispered in her ear. "Isn't a yearning for newspaper reporting what got you into the mess with Miss Chambers?"

"Absolutely. Russell and I plan to have a long, exciting life together."

"The piano music has begun," Amy said. "And here comes Evan to escort you down the aisle."

Thank You, Lord, for Your many blessings and for Your gift of love. Keep me steadfast in Your ways and with a heart eager to please You and Russell. Draw my dear friends to Your side, and help us to cherish the lives You've given us.

DIANN MILLS

DiAnn believes her readers should "Expect an Adventure" when they read her books. She is the author of fourteen books, nine novellas, as well as nonfiction, numerous short stories, articles, devotions, and the contributor to several nonfiction compilations. Five additional books will be released in the next year.

She wrote from the time she could hold a pencil, but not seriously until God made it clear that she should write for Him. Five of her anthologies have appeared on the CBA Best Seller List. Two of her books have won the distinction of best historical of the year by **Heartsong Presents**, and she is also a favorite author by **Heartsong Presents'** readers.

She is a founding board member for American Christian Romance Writers and a member of Inspirational Writers Alive and Advanced Speakers and Writers Association.

DiAnn and her husband are active members of Metropolitan Baptist Church, Houston, Texas.

Web site: www.diannmills.com

A Letter to Our Readers

Dear Readers:

In order that we might better contribute to your reading enjoyment, we would appreciate your taking a few minutes to respond to the following questions. When completed, please return to the following: Fiction Editor, Barbour Publishing, Inc., P.O. Box 719, Uhrichsville, OH 44683.

1. Did you enjoy reading *The Golden Gate Gazette*?
   ❑ Very much—I would like to see more books like this.
   ❑ Moderately—I would have enjoyed it more if _____

   _____

   _____

2. What influenced your decision to purchase this book?
   (Check those that apply.)
   ❑ Cover   ❑ Back cover copy   ❑ Title   ❑ Price
   ❑ Friends   ❑ Publicity   ❑ Other

3. Which story was your favorite?
   ❑ *Beyond the Flames*   ❑ *Misprint*
   ❑ *Web of Deceit*   ❑ *Missing Pages*

4. Please check your age range:
   ❑ Under 18   ❑ 18–24   ❑ 25–34
   ❑ 35–45   ❑ 46–55   ❑ Over 55

5. How many hours per week do you read? _____

Name _____

Occupation _____

Address _____

City _____ State _____ Zip _____

E-mail _____

HEARTSONG ❤ PRESENTS

Love Stories
Are Rated G!

That's for godly, gratifying, and of course, great! If you love a thrilling love story but don't appreciate the sordidness of some popular paperback romances, **Heartsong Presents** is for you. In fact, **Heartsong Presents** is the premiere inspirational romance book club featuring love stories where Christian faith is the primary ingredient in a marriage relationship.

Sign up today to receive your first set of four, never-before-published Christian romances. Send no money now; you will receive a bill with the first shipment. You may cancel at any time without obligation, and if you aren't completely satisfied with any selection, you may return the books for an immediate refund!

Imagine. . .four new romances every four weeks—two historical, two contemporary—with men and women like you who long to meet the one God has chosen as the love of their lives. . .all for the low price of $10.99 postpaid.

To join, simply complete the coupon below and mail to the address provided. **Heartsong Presents** romances are rated G for another reason: They'll arrive Godspeed!